To
CATCH
A SPY

A MYSTERY

THE ESTATE-APPROVED SEQUEL TO
TO CATCH A THIEF BY DAVID DODGE

TO CATCH A SPY

THE ESTATE-APPROVED SEQUEL TO
TO CATCH A THIEF BY DAVID DODGE

MARK ONEILL

Poisoned Pen
PRESS

Published by Poisoned Pen Press, an imprint of Sourcebooks
P.O. Box 4410, Naperville, Illinois 60567-4410
(630) 961-3900
sourcebooks.com

Cataloging-in-Publication Data is on file with the Library of Congress.

Printed and bound in the United States of America.
VP 10 9 8 7 6 5 4 3 2 1

To Victoria, John, and Alicia:
You've given me everything!

CHAPTER 1

John Robie glanced over his shoulder, seeing the wind-whipped peaks of the Mediterranean glimmer like a thousand diamonds as the sun peacefully set. He then looked sixty feet straight down at the sidewalk in front of the Hotel Carlton in Cannes. Nothing between him and the concrete. A long way to fall.

He took a deep breath and steadied himself, checking his grip on the drainpipe. It ran the full height of the hotel, from the ground to the roof. It was cast iron and secured to the left side of the building. A minute ago, he'd slid his hands in behind the pipe, set one foot on each side, and marched up.

He almost smiled. This was familiar ground. He knew every bit of the hotel from his days as a cat burglar. He'd studied the building for months and knew every floor, every room, and every inch of the roof. In fact, John had climbed this same pipe before, and more than once. The last time was years ago; only then, he'd been going down with a leather pouch filled with jewels, not climbing up as a favor for a friend.

The balcony to the first room on the top floor was a few feet away. John stretched out his right leg and probed for a foothold. He found it, as he knew he would.

He shook his head in disbelief. This wasn't what he'd planned on doing. He'd reached out to his friend Paul Du Pre for help connecting with Francie Stevens. They'd had something special; at least John thought so until he got her letter calling things off. Whatever her reason, John knew if he could just speak with her, he'd get things back on track. But they never got to his favor. As luck would have it, Paul needed help and suggested they meet for drinks at the Hotel Carlton.

The pipe jerked, pulling half an inch away from the building. John raised his eyebrows. It was time to move. With his new foothold secure, he released his right hand from the pipe and quickly shot it over to the balcony railing.

He wrapped his thick hand around the lowest bar of the railing and squeezed like a python. With his grip secure, he let go of the drainpipe, his body swinging under the balcony. He grabbed the same rail with his free hand, then muscled himself onto the terrace. His dinner jacket was tight across his back, restricting his range of motion, so he took it off.

Paul's request had surprised him. They'd met in the lobby; Paul explained his ask after some small talk over two Pépas, notoriously potent Parisian cocktails of cognac and vodka. In his new role as director in the SDECE, the *Service de Documentation Extérieure et de Contre-Espionnage*, Paul followed a mysterious man from Paris to the French Riviera. His colleagues were due to arrive in a few days, and he simply needed another set of eyes on the man for a few hours, nothing more.

As Paul walked John out to the front of the hotel and pointed to the mystery man's room on the top story, the man walked out of the hotel entrance and looked directly at them. They instinctively looked back. John saw the man trace Paul's pointed finger; he knew something was wrong. John watched the man's head dart around like a bird as it all registered before he bolted back inside.

Paul shouted, "I need to talk to him," and gave chase.

John knew the man was headed up to his room. He did some quick arithmetic and knew he could climb the drainpipe at about ten feet every ten seconds. So about one minute to the top floor, then another thirty seconds to get over to the man's room. A minute and a half and he would be on the man's balcony. That decided it. He had leaped onto the pipe, dashed up, and now here he was on the sixth story.

He felt a rush of excitement as he moved from balcony to balcony. All his senses were on high alert, and his mind was focused. He hadn't done something like this in a long time, and it was thrilling. Finally, he reached the mystery man' s room. He swung both legs over the rail and headed inside when the hotel room door flew open, the man surging in, a flurry of angled, desperate limbs and disheveled clothes. He saw the man's eyes search the floor of his hotel room, stopping on the handle of a bag peeking out from under the bed. Just then, the man looked up and saw him. John pushed through the balcony doors and into the room. The man lunged forward and grabbed the handle of his duffel bag, then pulled it out from under the bed.

John picked up speed, closing the space between them. The

man stayed at the foot of the bed and spun like a discus thrower. He heaved the bag in John's direction. He raised an arm to block it. The bag twisted around his arm, and then one end, heavy and very hard, caught John square in the face. It knocked him back a few steps. He shook it off and regained his balance to see the man run back into the hallway and turn right. John kneaded the bag with one hand, finding what felt like stacks of bound cash and another familiar shape. A long barrel, a square magazine sitting in front of the trigger, and the round broom-handle grip: a vintage Mauser pistol. The man had gone back for his gun. He hadn't had time to pull it out, so he used it as a club instead. John brushed his hand on his pants as if to remove the memory of the pistol. He didn't like weapons of any sort.

He started after the man, then stopped. The man had turned right when he ran out of the room. Not the direction he had come from, and John remembered why. The staircase to the roof was on the right side of the hallway. And the roof had a few touch-points with neighboring buildings. He was impressed. The man had scouted his escape routes like a highly skilled thief.

He knew if the man made it to one of those touchpoints, catching him would be difficult. John preferred strength, not speed. That didn't seem to be the case for the man. He had to beat him to the roof, which meant going up the hotel's facade.

He walked onto the balcony, then tossed the duffel bag over to the first terrace, the one closest to the pipe. Better there than in the man's room.

John perched himself on the railing, then exploded skyward. He grabbed hold of the rooftop, and his one hand slipped a bit, causing his heart to thump. He was rusty, and he knew it. He secured his hold, then pulled himself up and onto the roof. John wiped his palms on his pants, then blinked hard. That was close, even for him. He hurried to the stairway door.

The door swung open, and the mystery man spilled out. John stood his ground, blocking the man.

A look of exasperation flooded the man's face. He turned his palms up as if to ask, "Really? You're up here now?" He turned to go back down the stairway, then tilted his head to listen. He stopped. John heard it too—Paul bounding up the stairs.

John saw the man panic. He was doing some internal calculations, and he didn't like the result. A few seconds passed. The man's eyes dropped to the ground in front of his feet. John exhaled, relieved. The first step in giving up.

Then the man took off running, not for the other buildings but toward the front of the hotel. John froze for a moment. There was nothing there, no escape line, no bridge to another building.

"Wait!" yelled John. "Where are you going?"

He took off after him, but the man had a good start. John adjusted his approach, angling toward the roof's edge, hoping to save in distance what he couldn't in time. Ten feet from the edge of the roof, John dove at him, his right hand catching the collar of the man's jacket. They tumbled and slid, and the man's lower body crept over the roofline. Then the rest of the man followed.

He felt the man's weight suspended in his jacket, wriggling like a worm on a hook, swatting at John's hand. That created a problem, and it wasn't his one-handed grip. He guessed the man to be around one hundred fifty pounds, and John knew he could hold that weight with either hand. No, the problem was momentum. The man's movement was inching John toward the edge. He extended his left arm, looking for something to grab, and caught hold of a spire.

They both stopped moving. The man hung in the air, supported only by John's hand. He heard Paul rush through the stairway door and pause.

"Over here! I've got him." John was well-positioned. They weren't going anywhere. He looked down at the man, thinking about how to get him back onto the roof. The man looked up, his eyes locked onto John's, and he let loose a deep growl of anger. John watched as the man looked down to the street. Through his right arm, John could feel the man's body relax. Then the man raised both arms and slid out of his jacket.

And just like that, he fell to his death.

CHAPTER 2

Francie Stevens flipped the hair out of her eyes and aimed her Delahaye 235 Chapron sports car at the narrow opening between the two stone buildings, standing like pillars at the entrance to the village of Tourrettes-sur-Loup.

"We'll cut through here and take that winding road to Antibes," she said. "We'll be back at the hotel in no time."

"If we make it back alive, that would be wonderful," said Maude Stevens. "I might even celebrate with a cocktail."

"That was in the cards anyway," Francie said, smiling. "You're the one who wanted a drive in the country. And I'm happy to take you. Just thought I'd add a little excitement." She reached forward and patted the car's dashboard, feeling the engine's rumble through her lambskin glove. "Easy, girl. Mother isn't used to so much speed."

Francie adored her Delahaye and had insisted on the cabriolet model so she could drive in the open air. Like today, a picturesque drive through the countryside. Perfect weather, perfect scenery, and now a perfect Riviera sunset. The heat of the sun warmed her shoulders, and the balmy air curled around her windshield and tousled loose strands of hair that had broken free of her chiffon scarf, failing terribly at holding it all in place.

The car barreled forward. She glanced at the villagers, their mouths open like the oval grille of her vehicle. She waved at them, acknowledging her good fortune. Francie believed her Delahaye to be a mirror of herself. The bright-blue color matched her eyes, just as the fiery-red interior matched her heart. Even the steering wheel on the right reflected how she viewed herself—American in personality, European in spirit.

Ahead she saw open road. She accelerated forward, catching a brief view of the sea in the distance, the swells flickering like candles as the sun called it a day. She sat back and relaxed her shoulders. Easy country driving from here on.

"This is more like it," said Mother. "Nice and peaceful. And slower, if you don't mind. You've got a big week coming up. Let's not make it more difficult."

Francie nodded. The week ahead was going to be challenging. She had agreed to participate in the first-ever Riviera Fashion Week, an event honoring Paris as the couture capital of the world by celebrating the lifestyle of the French Riviera, the most glamorous destination in the world. Marcel Julien, Paris' leading fashion designer, was ecstatic that she had agreed to represent his line. And from her perspective, it would be a rare opportunity to get a peek inside an industry she found fascinating. Riviera Fashion Week kicked off in two days with a cocktail reception Saturday night, followed by three separate shows on Monday, Wednesday, and Friday. It would be a hectic week, with leading French designers putting forward their best summer lines. Media, diplomats, and celebrities from around the world would attend. And as if that wasn't enough to fray one's nerves...

"You see that, don't you?" asked Mother, pointing. "Ahead on the right. Francie? Stop!"

That got her attention. Francie saw the bushes rustle up ahead. In a flash, a pair of deer bounded out. Her heart jumped. She shifted into neutral, then pushed down hard on the brake, lifting herself out of the seat. They came to a dead stop. The deers' hooves touched the ground once before they leaped into the brush on the other side, so synchronized that it looked athletic.

"Something on your mind, dear?" Mother tilted back, giving Francie a sideways glance. "Certainly not driving."

"No, Mother." She pulled back onto the road. Of course there was something on her mind, and her mother knew it. She was back at the Riviera for the first time in a year and almost sure to run into John Robie, despite her warnings to him. John, who had been the cause of last summer's whirlwind of mystery, adventure, and romance. By far the most exciting time of her life.

And completely unexpected. Francie had arrived at the Riviera in the middle of a police hunt for Le Chat, a legendary cat burglar separating wealthy women of the Côte d'Azur from their jewels. She'd figured out John was Le Chat, then discovered he hadn't been committing the crimes. Instead, he worked to clear his name and avoid prison by capturing the copycat thief himself.

And he had uncovered the burglar, a young woman named Danielle, who was now surprisingly married to John's friend, Paul Du Pre. John caught Danielle, then helped her elude the police, giving Francie her first glimpse of his principle of loyalty among thieves.

"He's on your mind, I know," said Mother. "He wasn't all that bad, as men go."

He wasn't bad at all. That was part of the problem. Her heart beat faster. She'd gotten to know John, and while she didn't condone his criminal past, she understood why he'd done it. She'd even empathized with him once she learned of his background. Francie was attracted to his smooth charm, brown-blond hair, chiseled features, and muscular build. And he was drawn to her, too. Very much so. It all happened so fast. They had parted ways on a road to Italy, where he hid for a while as the case wound down. She and her mother then traveled back to New York, and for several months she and John corresponded.

"Francie, I never quite understood—" said Mother.

"I don't understand!" she interrupted. "It's nothing I can point to, not a single thing. It's a feeling. Small comments, things he did, none of which mean anything on their own. But add them all up, and I know."

Francie did know. She shifted gears and pressed forward, picking up speed. Once back in New York, she'd had time to reflect, to gain perspective. Little things she'd missed kept surfacing. She had learned the police were after John and his criminal friends, men he had spent time with in prison and later in the French Resistance. They all would have been sent back to prison had the copycat burglaries not been solved. Yet John had focused on clearing his name and told her if his plan didn't work, he'd leave the country and let those men "fend for themselves." Not what she'd expected from the man who espoused "loyalty among thieves." And just before

they parted ways, a friend of his told her that John "was a thief...
and takes what he wants." Those words still rung in her ears. He
had wanted her, and she asked herself why. Did he want *her*, or
was she just another jewel to be had, one that could ensure a different life? There were other instances, too, in which he put himself first. People like that could be tolerated and even enjoyed for a
while. But in the long run, they made unsuitable partners.

"Well, I have no idea what he's done," said Mother. "I do know
you, however. And you can be very demanding. Are you sure this
isn't one of those times? Are you sure you're not looking for perfection when you should be looking for happiness?"

Francie saw a farmer's cart approaching the road. She accelerated past the cart and then thought about her mother's words. She
had considered that possibility. But she'd never imagined any man
as a husband until she met John. So, no, she wasn't holding out
for perfection. She was thinking about how happy she'd be. And
that's when doubt surfaced.

"Let's say he did something," said Mother. "Something to upset
you, betray your trust. You only knew him a little while. You can't
expect a man to break from his past so soon. It takes time, dear.
People change with time."

Francie grimaced. People don't change. At some point, they
became—and would always be—precisely who they were. That
was John. He admitted as much, telling her that he was a retired
thief, not reformed. He wasn't ashamed of what he'd done. And
he'd thought only of himself when trying to clear his name. There
was no other way to say it. John was selfish, always looking to take
what he wanted. John Robie might not be a jewel thief now, but
he was a thief of hearts.

"If nothing else..." said Mother, "be prepared. You may not want to see him, but he'll find you."

Francie nodded in agreement. She wasn't looking forward to that conversation. How would he react? Whatever might happen, Francie knew it would be worse once John saw her with Alex.

CHAPTER 3

John sprinted down the hotel hallway, his sleeves rolled up, jacket in hand, and collar unbuttoned. Paul was a step behind.

"What was all that about?" asked Paul.

"I would have pulled him up, but..."

"Not that. You said you went up that pipe. How?"

John stopped at the elevators and pressed the button. "I was an acrobat. I think you knew."

Paul bent over, hands on knees. "An acrobat and a—"

"Yes," he said, cutting him off. "I was that, too. But I learned *that* as an acrobat." John straightened his collar. "I was good." He had a lot to cover with Paul, mostly what had just happened. And he also had to figure out the best time to ask for his favor. It might seem parochial now, given the evening's events, but it was important to him.

The elevator rang, announcing its arrival. The doors parted, and they stepped into an empty car.

"You never told me you could climb a building," Paul said.

"And you never told me this little favor of yours was a full-on hunt for a dangerous man. He had a gun, you know."

Paul shook his head. "I wasn't aware. How do you know?"

"I was in his room."

Paul looked puzzled. "How did you get...?" He paused, then said, "Never mind. Look, this is a setback, John. A big one. I needed him alive. I have no idea why he came here, what he was doing, or where he was going."

"Who was he?"

Paul glanced at his watch. "In Paris, I was watching a foreign agent, and this man just appeared one day. I saw the agent passing a newspaper to him with a brown envelope inside the fold. He and the agent talked. Very tense. So I followed this man. I found no record of his entry into our country. His passport, on file at his hotel, was a forgery. Not good signs. The next day, he was walking near the College de France, just across from the Sorbonne. Do you know these universities?"

John knew them both. "They do a lot of research for the government, don't they? Everything from crops to astronomy, as I recall."

Paul nodded.

"What was he doing there?"

"No idea. And I never got the chance to find out. He spotted me, and after he thought he lost me, he came to the Riviera." Paul paused. "Why here? Politics, international issues, all of that is back in Paris."

"I see the problem," said John. *Both yours and mine.* John knew his friend very well; he would focus on this man, and nothing else, until he got answers. The window to ask for his favor had closed.

A shame, too. All he'd wanted was for Paul to get him into Fashion Week so he could see Francie. Those events were invitation-only, and Paul could quickly secure them with his connections. Not now. John needed a new approach.

The elevator doors opened in the lobby. They rushed out, heading to the front of the hotel. John sensed the frantic atmosphere as they dodged hotel workers, who were staying calm while moving at a visibly faster clip, stern looks replacing smiles.

He needed to see Francie, and this week might be his last chance. Something had happened, and he had to find out what. They had stayed in touch, writing and even speaking on the phone, then she went quiet. No letters, no calls. Until last week, when he'd received her letter stating their relationship was over. She was coming to Cannes for Fashion Week but didn't want to see him. Not even a quick hello, and she gave no reason. Whatever it was, John was sure he could work it out. But he had to see her. Right now, Paul was his only hope. Every other attempt to attend Fashion Week had failed, in no small part because of his reputation. He knew Paul was attending; he considered it his duty to participate in cultural events. And he was going to ask Paul to bring him along as his guest. That was John's favor. Now, if he asked, Paul would deny the request. But he had an idea. Maybe Paul would bring him not as a guest, but in another capacity.

They exited through the lobby doors and onto the sidewalk, turning toward the body. A crowd was gathering.

He grabbed Paul's arm, then stopped. Up ahead, hovering over the man's body, was Lepic, commissaire divisionnaire, the highest-ranking policeman east of Marseille, and the last man John wanted to see.

Lepic straightened his tie as he marched toward the police officers, standing like bookends next to the body on the ground. Lepic wiped his mustache with his fingers, ensuring no vestiges of dinner clung to his face. "Crime occurs at the most inopportune times," he thought. He cleared his throat, then shouted, "Everyone back! This is a police investigation." The officers snapped into action, moving the crowd away from the body.

As he neared the scene, he scanned the crowd for local dignitaries, knowing he could change his style based on whoever might be watching. Then he stopped and looked hard at one man in particular. There he was, standing over by the hotel entrance—John Robie himself. Lepic's lips curled. John Robie was the source of his greatest triumph and most humiliating failure. He'd worked hard to forget the shame that man had caused him, and yet there he stood, talking with Paul le Comte Du Pre de la Tour. Lepic shook his head. Count Paul Du Pre, a descendant of French royalty. Tall, broad-shouldered, handsome, and wealthy beyond comparison, Paul was a man of the highest integrity and the noblest bloodline. The exact opposite of John Robie. It amazed him that those two could be friends.

Lepic turned back to the body and noticed a shoe between himself and the dead man. Looking further, he saw it belonged to the deceased. He kicked it toward the body and seethed, "Clean this up now! I want this crowd gone, and I want this body removed. Am I being clear?"

He looked back at John and Paul. He hadn't seen John in a long time. Not since he'd coasted around like he was immune to the law, supposedly helping solve the string of robberies. He wasn't so sure, and neither were his colleagues at the regional office.

The headlines read that the jewels had been recovered, and a young gypsy was to blame, but Lepic knew better. The resolution was too coincidental, something upon which his fellow officers pounced. If it seems too good to be true, it is, they told him. But he had been dealt an impossible hand. His superiors had pressured him to close the case, then reprimanded him for the glaring holes. He gritted his teeth. Incidents like that derailed careers. And the person responsible was standing over there, in shirtsleeves, sweating like a farmhand. Just a few feet away from a dead man.

Wait a minute. Lepic put his hands on his hips, then stared. Perhaps it wasn't a wasted night after all. From where he stood, John Robie's presence was more than questionable. He nodded, agreeing with himself.

Lepic bit his lip to hold back his elation. John Robie was back in play!

"I'll wait here," said John. Paul tipped his head in agreement, then headed toward the cluster of police. John looked over at the group encircling the body, and staring right back at him was Lepic. He turned away, casually and slowly, and began drifting through the crowd. Last summer's explanation to the inspector had been a stretch. John knew as much, so he'd spent four months in Italy.

John smelled him before he saw him. That pungent, rotten stench of onions, garlic, and sour wine. From behind a wall of watchers stepped Coco, a man he knew from his days in prison and with the French Resistance. He stopped a good five feet away and eyed Coco's hands and pockets. The man was a master with a *casse-tête*, a rudimentary, compact skull cracker, which he had used to great effect during midnight assaults on German outposts. How the Germans hadn't smelled Coco, he never knew.

"Ahhh, my friend John Robie," said Coco, pronouncing it using the French "Jean" and dragging it out for effect. "Is funny, I find you over here"—he then nodded toward the police—"and a dead man over there. Are you in trouble? Has the legendary Boche-strangler come back, or is it Le Chat again? You wear many hats, as they say."

John eyed his former colleague. The man's voice hadn't changed. It still sounded like a rusty saw pulling across a limestone wall.

He put his hands out, palms up. He'd always liked Coco, and they'd worked well together in the Resistance. But there was something about him now. Something behind that grin. It came to him in a single word: *Menace.*

John cocked his head. Something was off with Coco; he was never this friendly nor was he this talkative. Why was he acting this way?

"Nice to see you, Coco. And that over there is no trouble of mine."

"Good to know. I wouldn't want to...what is the phrase...yes, bail you out again, like last August. You remember?"

"Yes, I do." John looked him straight in the eyes. Coco had helped him last summer. Nothing too risky, just staking out villas for potential robberies, hoping to catch the imitator. "And I was grateful. Still am."

"That's good. I'm glad to hear it." He put a hand on John's shoulder and steered him farther away from the crowd. "This is what we do; we help our friends. We no ask the questions. We just do."

He saw where this was going. He and Coco and several others were currently not in jail, due to the good graces of the local authorities. The German occupying forces had freed them all from a French prison, insisting they go to the unoccupied zone. In return, they joined the Resistance, choosing to fight for France. Patriotism over liberation for those men. And in return for that patriotism, the authorities looked the other way. If they all kept their noses clean, they would remain free men. If they didn't, the authorities would revoke their informal parole.

"Look, if you need some money, I'll help. I always have."

He shook his head. "I don't need your money. I need you."

"What do you mean?" asked John.

"I have had my challenges, and now the bill is due. But it is more than one man can pay. More than a dozen men. I need a wheelbarrow full of money, and the only way I know to get that is to acquire some jewels. That is where you come in." He gestured toward the hotel. "Look around, all these wealthy people. Just one night, and my problems go away."

John shook his head. "You know the deal we have with the police. Any of us breaks it, and it's back behind bars."

Coco bristled. "Last August, you needed my help. I no ask why; I no ask if we are breaking their deal. I ask nothing. I show up, I help, and I go home. And now it's reversed. I need help, and you speak of this deal." He paused, then continued. "So I help you. But you don't help me?"

"You're not asking for help. You're asking me to commit a crime. And they'll know it's me." There was also Francie to think about. He'd suspected she pulled back because of his criminal past. To wade back in might be the final straw.

Coco stared for a moment, then shook his head. "All we have, in prison and the Resistance, is based on fraternity, loyalty." He grabbed John's hand, a friendly shake, then pulled him in close and squeezed hard. "If you aren't loyal to me, what makes you think I'll be loyal to you?"

There it was. A blatant threat from an old friend. Either John helps him out, and the police suspect Le Chat, or he doesn't help, and then what? Does Coco frame him? Both were bad, but which was worse?

Out of the corner of his eye, he saw Paul approaching, shaking his head in disappointment. Paul knew his former associates by sight and had lobbied John to keep his distance. He turned to Coco. "Okay, let me think. Give me a few days."

Coco grinned, the friendliness back. "Yes, you think. Think about helping me, and think about not. Easy choice, John Robie."

Now it was Paul's turn to steer John, putting his arm around his shoulders and moving him toward the street. Away from the hotel, away from the police, away from Coco.

"Associating with men like that..." said Paul. "It doesn't help."

He knew Paul was right. But it wasn't straightforward. They'd been through prison together. They'd fought in the Resistance. He'd risked his life with men like Coco; he'd killed to protect them. Situations like that build iron bonds. A man would rather die than give up a friend. Yet here was Coco, breaking that bond, and it bothered John. After all he'd done for him, the man was an ingrate.

"What did he want?" asked Paul.

"A little help. Nothing, really."

Back to business for Paul. "So here's what's happening. Lepic's men will search his hotel room. I'll see if there are any known agents in the area. Problem is, I've no idea where to start."

The two men approached Paul's car, a Citroën 15-six cabriolet, cream-colored with a black interior. "I'll drop you off," he said. "After all this, it's the least I can do."

John walked around the car but didn't get in. He stood. Now was the time. "There's something you need to know. That wasn't an accident."

"What do you mean?"

"He didn't slip over the side. That man chose to fall. I had him. I was right there. He thought about it, then raised his arms. He knew what he was doing."

"And why is this important?"

"Because that tells us something. He had to know who you were. He'd seen you in Paris and then here. And you know what he just did. That means he feared whoever he was working for more than he feared French authorities. He'd rather die than fail them."

"I see."

"Do you? Do you see? Because from where I stand, this is the tip of the iceberg. You've got a dead man who was working for some terrifying people. You don't know who they are, you don't know who he was, you don't know what he was doing, and you don't know where he was going."

"What are you getting at?"

"You need my help, at least until your colleagues arrive."

Paul shook his head. "No, I cannot allow that. If what you say is true, and I believe it is, this situation is dangerous." He thought some more. "No, it is too risky."

"I know the risk," said John. "That man had a gun. He was going to kill us if he got the chance. And someone gave him that gun. Probably someone here, the people he worked for. Those are not nice people. Once they find out he's dead, they'll want answers."

Paul shook his head. Too much to ask, too much danger. He opened his car door.

"Like it or not, I'm already involved," said John. "People saw me up there. Besides, I know what he was up to."

Paul stopped. "What are you talking about?"

"I know where he was going."

"You can't know."

"Here," said John, tossing him the jacket in his hand.

"I don't need your jacket."

"It's not mine. It's his." John motioned toward the dead man. "Inside pocket, upper left side."

Paul reached in and pulled out a wrinkled brown envelope. Inside was an invitation to a cocktail reception Saturday night. The opening event of Riviera Fashion Week.

Paul looked up, amazed.

"What do you say?" asked John.

CHAPTER 4

Francie checked herself in the bedroom mirror, then adjusted her bikini bottom. The top was fine. She moved into the main room, pushed back the drapes, and opened the floor-to-ceiling doors, letting in the toasty sea breeze. She dropped to all fours. Time to exercise. She stuck a leg straight out behind her, lifted her heel high, and then squeezed the muscles. She held it for a thirty-count, then repeated it with her other leg.

"Good morning, dear." Maude Stevens entered her room, wearing a silk robe and carrying an impossibly small coffee cup. In her other hand was a brochure. She dropped onto a couch. "What are you doing down there?"

"I'm exercising, Mother. You know—a half hour in the room, then a half-hour swim." Francie had learned several remarkably effective moves from a young woman named Debbie Drake, an exercise enthusiast she'd met in New York.

"In that bathing suit?"

Francie rolled her eyes. "Do you know how hard it is to find exercise clothes? It's all baggy shorts and boys' shirts. And always that depressing gray." She ran her hand over her bathing suit. "This is so much better. No heavy cotton, no one sees me, and when I'm done, I head down to the beach." Francie looked up. "What are you reading?"

"The history of this hotel. Did you know the Hôtel Belle Rives was formerly the Villa Saint-Louis? It was F. Scott Fitzgerald's place. He wrote the beginnings of *Tender Is the Night* right here. The brochure says the legendary parties he threw inspired the memorable bacchanals in *The Great Gatsby*. Can you imagine?"

"I can. It's a very inspiring place." Francie rolled over. She propped herself up on her elbows and lifted a straight leg, aiming her toes at the ceiling while keeping her other leg flat on the floor.

"Where's Alex this morning?"

"He's trying to get details. I have no idea where to be or when to be there. Do I try on the outfits? Do they make alterations? I haven't a clue. It all happened so fast. One minute I'm telling Alex how I'm drawn to the world of fashion, and the next minute he's got me modeling for Marcel Julien."

"Being a cultural attaché has its privileges."

"Now, Mother. You know better than that." Francie frowned. "The diplomatic corps isn't just fashion shows for pretty girls. It's quite serious."

"I'm not saying he isn't wonderful. But you ended it with John before it got going. You never gave him a second chance."

"Did he deserve one?"

"You deserve one," said Mother. She took a deep breath and stood up. "This is the last I'll say of it. Alex is very nice. He's thoughtful and handsome, and he's got a nice career ahead of him. You'll travel. You'll be pleased. But John is special. There's something about a man like that."

"You've no argument from me," said Francie. "There's a lot to like about John Robie, especially on a short summer vacation." She rolled her eyes playfully. "But there's a lot to like about Alex, too. I've never met anyone so giving. Emphasis on that last word, Mother. Giving. Not taking."

There was a knock on the door, and they both looked over. "Come in," said Francie.

Alex Dandridge walked in, all smiles, with one hand behind his back. Francie popped up and headed right for him, planting a kiss on his cheek.

"I've got information to share. But first..." He pulled a dozen roses from behind his back and handed them to Francie. "I know it's rushed, and we don't have all the details, but I wanted you to know how much I admire you for doing this."

"Sweet of you to say so." She shot a quick look at her mother. *See what I'm talking about?* "They're beautiful."

"Not as beautiful as you." He clapped his hands together, looking as if he'd remembered something. He sat in a chair, then said, "I brought more than flowers this morning."

"What have you learned?"

"Fashion Week is focusing on holiday wear. I believe that's the first use of that phrase."

Maude smiled. "It sounds so wonderful."

"What does it mean?" asked Francie.

"It's meant to reflect what women wear here at the Riviera, on holiday," he said. "So a mix of casual and formal. And since we're at the Riviera, casual means anything but. The clothes may look relaxed, but the attention to detail, the presentation, the price... well, we can expect all of that to be fairly intense. Now, Monday's show will feature casual day attire. I believe Marcel—Mr. Julien—will introduce his new line of Capri pants. That's what they're calling them."

Mother was more excited than Francie. "Do explain, dear."

"I've been told they're three-quarter-length pants."

"Yes," said Francie. Her excitement was growing. "They fall between the knee and the ankle. Very popular in Italy. Hence the name."

"I've limited information on blouses for Monday," said Alex. "They'll be brightly colored, perhaps tropical prints, very breezy in design. But nothing on the fabric. And I've nothing on shoes or jewelry." He looked at Francie and her mother to ensure they were following along. "Okay, moving on to Wednesday, we have beachwear as a theme."

Francie was excited now, eager for more. She put her hands together in front of her chest as if she were praying. "I was hoping as much."

"You got your wish. Every designer will be introducing limited-edition bikinis, made just for this event." He looked at Maude. "Sorry, Mrs. Stevens."

"Don't be silly," said Maude. "We both agree that this particular swimsuit favors Francie."

He smiled. "Yes, we agree." Again, he made sure he had Francie and her mother's attention. "And Friday, the last day, we have formal dresses. Dresses meant for a big night out."

"You did wonderfully, dear."

"I don't want to add to the pressure," he said, "but this week is crucial to the designers and the nation of France. Expect lots of media, lots of attention."

Francie stood tall. "I'll be ready. As you can see, I'm not missing my exercises. I need to look my best, and I will."

"For whom, exactly?" asked Mother under her breath.

She shot her mother a stern stare. It had crossed her mind that John might see her. And that wouldn't be the worst thing. She half hoped he would see her, to realize what he was missing. Francie dropped her gaze. That thought made her feel vindictive, but she didn't mean it that way. She didn't know how she meant it.

"Alex, what about the clothes? I haven't tried any on. I have no idea if they'll fit properly."

He raised a finger. "And that brings us to my last gift of the day, Miss Stevens. If you pardon me for a moment, I must go to my room."

A moment later, he returned with an older gentleman. Francie liked the man immediately. He was in his seventies and radiated an old European warmth. His large eyes, magnified by his over-sized glasses, gave him the look of an owl.

"Francie, Mrs. Stevens, this is Karl. He's a tailor. He lives a few blocks in." The man bowed. "Knowing that the festivities are in Cannes, and we're staying here in Antibes, I thought it might be helpful if you had a tailor on call. Someone who could pop in, take measurements, that sort of thing."

Karl beamed, his smile twice as wide as Francie expected. "I've worked with Mr. Julien many times, Miss Stevens. I know all his tailors, I know his fabrics, his patterns, and mostly I know his intent. What he wants a woman to be, that I know."

"Well, that's wonderful, Karl. I'm delighted," she said, shaking his hand.

"Perhaps you can talk to Mr. Julien," said Karl. "I can take the measures. I can alter the clothes. Or his tailors can do the alterations if he wants the clothes near him for last-minute changes." He raised his eyebrows and nodded. "Something he is fond of, Mr. Julien. Last-minute changes." He chuckled. "Whatever is his preference, I can do. Either way, it will save you and him a lot of time."

"We'll see him tomorrow night," said Alex. "He'll be at the cocktail party."

"About that," said Karl. "Mr. Dandridge tells me you must wear a dress tomorrow night."

"That's right. Mr. Julien selected one for me back in Paris."

"If you need alterations, I can do them now. Or I can come back. As Mr. Dandridge said, I'm just a few streets away."

"How nice of you," said Francie. "I had it fitted a few days ago, and I've had limited opportunities to gain weight, so I should be fine."

"I understand. If you need me, Alex...Mr. Dandridge here...can contact me. Or the concierge downstairs. He is a neighbor."

Alex led Karl out of the room. Francie had butterflies in her stomach. Modeling was real, and it was now, and she was excited. She made eye contact with her mother. Alex had secured this opportunity for her and proven himself more thoughtful in a single morning than John had since they'd met. Maybe now Mother would understand Francie's concerns. And if she ran into John, so be it. Let him try to convince her. Francie trusted her judgment. And for the first time in a while, she trusted her heart.

CHAPTER 5

Odette Julien looked over the side of their one-hundred-fifty-foot yacht and saw her husband, Marcel, take charge. He was holding court on the quay with a French Customs official, apparently his new best friend. *Nothing to be concerned about tonight*, thought Odette. They'd docked in Livorno while Marcel had fabric brought over from Florence. Then they came straight to Cannes. Nothing of interest on the dock below.

Marcel peeled himself away from the Customs official, all laughs and shoulder claps, then headed straight for the crew, who had begun off-loading the fabric and other cargo. He jumped right into the middle of the line, easy to spot with his black pants, white blazer, and black bow tie. *A handsome man*, thought Odette. Tall and distinguished, and built like an older athlete. She could hear him directing the crew's every step as they loaded up a small troupe of cars. It struck her as odd that a man as public and powerful as her husband still had trouble handling the stress of such an important week. Named the world's most influential and creative designer for the second year in a row, the man would still sweat every moment. He was a bundle of nervous tics on the dock. Odette smiled. Not the case with her, but she didn't have his level of pressure.

She headed down to the main deck, ready for the trip to their villa nearby. "Is there anything I can do for you?" she asked.

Marcel turned to his wife. He stopped pulling on his cuffs and put his hand on her waist. "Thank you, but I'm fine. Just a bit longer," he said. "I want to make sure all the clothes get to the villa today. Such a big week ahead. But you already know that."

She nodded in agreement. "Yes." She patted his back. "And we're up to it. We're a good team."

Marcel straightened his lapels. "Everything must be perfect this week. We have a lot at stake."

"It will be fine, darling. We've had high stakes before, and you always come through. And now you have that American woman on board. Miss Stevens was the one who made such an impression as a debutante last season. People saw how stunning she was, and keeping company with that thief added an element of intrigue. People will come just to see her."

"On board but not proven," said Marcel, massaging his chin. "Tremendous potential, though."

"And you are the one who got her started. You gave her an opportunity. I think she'll be grateful."

"Grateful would be nice. Effective would be marvelous."

"I have a good feeling about her, Marcel. She's a natural. She's instinctive. She will open doors to financiers, business leaders, politicians, and media."

Odette took her husband by the hand and pulled him toward their car. She smiled, calm and confident. "Miss Stevens is going to do wonderful things for us. You'll see."

CHAPTER 6

John left his villa and headed down the gravel path to his modest vineyard. Two tall posts stood in the middle, barely visible over the vines, with a connecting beam running between them. From that beam hung a trapeze he had installed. It was time to train, and he never missed a session.

His gaze leveled as he walked, staring straight ahead yet focused on nothing. He did that when he was lost in thought, and the events of last night were fresh in his mind.

Fresh and confusing. Paul was speechless about what John had done, but not impressed enough to bring him as a guest tomorrow night. Why was he being so firm? John wasn't sure. He had to think it through. And training was always good for reflection.

He leaped up and grabbed the trapeze bar. He started swinging, gradually increasing the distance and picking up speed. His head rhythmically topped the surrounding vines, giving him a broader view of his property.

John was proud of his vineyard, and he was proud of his home, which he'd named Villa des Bijoux, the Villa of Jewels. He'd found the name amusing back when no one knew his true identity. It wasn't so clever now, not after the events of last summer. The local *flics* saw it as gloating, and his criminal friends saw it as arrogance. He had to admit, there was truth to both perspectives.

Still, it amazed him that he was the owner of anything. If people knew his story, they would be astonished.

Just then, John sensed them coming. His skin tightened, and shudders ran through his body like cigar smoke through a screen door. He shook his head, but it was no use. The memories were upon him.

As a child, he had traveled throughout New England with his mother and father as part of a carnival troupe. His parents, and later he, were accomplished trapeze artists and acrobats.

John grew up in the carnival with all of its proud, eccentric performers, and his mother made sure he knew them all. Everyone has something to teach you, she would tell him. The men who ran the joints were of particular interest to him, as they took pride in pulling small, subtle cons on unsuspecting patrons. A penny here, a nickel there. They would brag about their takes at the end of each day. Those men needed the extra money to survive. No carnie judged them for it, either.

John stopped swinging and stared up at the sky as a wave of empty wistfulness passed over him. He remembered those days fondly, although they'd had their challenges. If attendance was down, his father would go into town, find its Main Street, then string a tightrope across two buildings. From a rooftop, he'd announce the carnival. As a crowd formed, John's father would invite the townspeople to attend. He would point out his wife and son standing down among the audience. And then came the hook.

His father would take a few steps down the tightrope, then appear to nearly lose his balance. There would be chorused gasps from the crowd, which grew louder as his father repeated the drama. As he neared the end, he would slip off the rope, catch it with both hands on his way down, and slingshot himself back up and onto his feet. People would scream, none louder than John's mother, palms plastered to her cheeks.

But John had known better. They'd rehearsed it hundreds of times as a family, right down to his mother's distress. He could still see his father feigning concern, rolling his eyes and wiping his brow as he finished the walk, then announcing that his wife and son were accepting donations for a thicker rope. That always drew a collective laugh.

And it drew money. John was surprised at how much they collected. His father would say, "Put your pride aside; do what you gotta do." His parents would then get serious, for acrobatics was the one thing they never joked about. His mother would tell him it was all in the preparation. "What we practice thousands of times," she'd say, "they only see once. To them, it looks death-defying. To us, it's just another well-rehearsed theatric." And his father would tap his temple and tell him that success was in the mind, not the muscles. "Concentration is everything," he'd say.

John closed his eyes and tilted his head as a feeling of melancholy weighed him down. His parents were the best acrobats on the East Coast, the uncontested masters at defying death. Until that one moment when his father had lost his concentration.

Like a grainy, skipping newsreel, the last seconds of his mother's life played out in his memory. Two trapeze bars high in the air, synchronizing to come together; John holding, then releasing, his mother from one bar, his father catching her on another.

He'd made the perfect throw, but his father's timing was off by a single beat, and his mother fell awkwardly. She knew it was over, and her eyes caught John's for less than a second. That single look communicated everything—how much she loved her son, her belief in him, even asking John to forgive his father.

And he did, although the man couldn't forgive himself. He died shortly thereafter, leaving John alone and terrified.

He shuddered again, as he always did when those memories forced themselves forward. The devastation of that series of events was thorough. His whole world had changed. The only two people he'd ever loved, and who had loved him, were gone. His parents had no savings, no insurance, and no relatives. The other carnies had taken him in, rotating his care. They eventually found him a position with a French circus. John said his emotional goodbyes and left for the French Riviera, only to find the circus had disbanded just before his arrival.

For the second time in a few short months, he was alone and barely twenty-one years old. His situation was desperate. He didn't know a soul, didn't speak the language, and wasn't familiar with the Riviera and its curious class system—the wealthy and those who waited on the wealthy.

He had some money, but not enough to get back to the States, and he had some big decisions to make. He'd made his way to the Promenade des Anglais—the boardwalk in Old Town, Nice— and sat on a bench as dusk gently pushed the day aside. For a couple of hours, he watched the people of the Riviera walk by.

Cooks, waiters, and chambermaids of every nationality, bartenders, beachgoers and baby strollers, tourists with incredible wealth, the men with their perfectly tailored clothes, and the women with jewelry that defied description.

John had considered returning to the States but knew he'd had no one to return to, and no home. Staying in France posed problems, too. Who would hire him? Either way, if he stayed or went back, he needed money.

What could he do? He'd gone through different scenarios in his mind, everything from joining another circus to busing tables at a restaurant. After a while, the idea came to him. He'd understood the skills that made him an acrobat also made him well-suited for climbing walls, and the quiet removal of jewels.

He rolled his shoulders at the memory, then spat into the dirt. At first, the idea had repulsed him. This wouldn't be a nickel-and-dime carnie scam perpetrated on small-town drunks. This was flat-out thievery. It would be purposeful and wrong. On the other hand, John was confident he could do it well. Physically, he could climb anything, and the rest he could learn.

He dismissed the idea, but it kept coming back until, from repetition, it seemed a viable option. He rationalized. What if it was done from a place of need, not greed? How would it go? He had told himself he'd only take jewels, no cash, and only from the very wealthy. If someone could afford to buy expensive jewelry, they could also afford to lose it. And even then, stolen jewelry was reimbursed by insurance companies. If he stuck to jewels, there were no real victims.

He slipped the premise on to see how it felt. It was tolerable, which surprised him. To get more comfortable, he had set principles. He would never bring a weapon, never hurt anyone, and never damage property. And he'd set milestones, predetermined amounts of money that would allow him to return to the States or live humbly in France. Once reached, he would stop and dedicate himself to a legitimate purpose.

He had started small but soon progressed. The money came quickly, and without him consciously knowing it, his milestones changed. John kept going, with the singular objective of creating security for himself. Something he'd never truly known.

He did a slow, deliberate exhale to clear the memories, paused for a moment, and then launched into a perfect backflip. He repeated this for several minutes until his landings became sloppy. Then he headed over to an enormous European beech tree, standing peacefully among the vines like a lion guarding over her cubs. Tree-climbing was perfect practice for scaling buildings. John climbed up and across a few branches, then stopped. The cocktail party was tomorrow, and Paul wasn't budging, even after John had proven himself invaluable.

But was he, really? Paul didn't think so. What was John not seeing?

He scouted out some branches and began climbing. After a few minutes, he was overcome with exhaustion; he dropped to the ground, arms out to steady his landing.

He was near a bench with a big aluminum bucket. John sat and placed the pail between his ankles. Sand and coarse gravel filled the bucket. He plunged his hands in and began kneading the mixture. It was rough going. Within seconds he could feel his forearms heating up, then he couldn't move a finger. He took a quick break, then bent back over the bucket and punched his right fist down into the mixture. The sand and gravel gave, but not much. He did the same with his left fist, then alternated punches.

Back to Paul. His objective at the cocktail party would be to identify suspicious characters and their associates. That was different from tailing a man...

That was it. Paul would value a different type of support. Support that was better demonstrated than discussed. He rose from the bench and headed to his villa. He had a few ideas, and they all started with a single phone call.

CHAPTER 7

Francie and Alex, arm in arm, passed through the stone archway on the bay side of the Hôtel Belle Rives, walked through the sunbathers geometrically arranged on the sundeck, and approached the beach. The warm breeze puffed past her face like feathers. She tilted her floppy hat for added protection from the sun sitting just above the horizon.

She took off her shoes, stepped onto the beach, and smiled at the feel of radiant sand between her toes. She would always associate the beach with vacationing—sunshine, bright-blue water, and relaxation most of all. Francie knew herself, and a few hours of peace was what she needed before Fashion Week. Time to collect her thoughts, remind herself why she belonged, and think through possible conversations with designers. What were they likely to ask, and how should she answer? Also, what questions to ask, and what comments might impress? She sighed. So much to plan.

She saw Alex catch the eye of a beach boy, then hold up two

fingers. The beach boy grabbed two towels and placed them on a couple of recliners, half in the sun and half in the shade of three tightly clustered palm trees.

Francie paused in front of the recliners. She eyed both choices, checked her wristwatch, looked to the sky to gauge the sun's path and, therefore, the shade, then set her bag down on the chair to the right.

"You were saying..." reminded Alex.

"Oh, yes," she said. "I need to consider a career, and I remembered my father. He was a farmer, and he loved it. He told me the key to happiness is to do what you like. That way, it's not a job."

"Very astute."

"I agree. So when I began thinking about careers, I thought of fashion. I've always loved it since I was a child. It influences so much of life." She set about unpacking her bag. "The right outfit can boost your confidence, and heaven knows we need that. Women, we're our own worst critics. On the inside, we rarely feel good about ourselves. There's always something. But put the right dress on, and we balance out."

Alex nodded. "Very interesting."

She took her seat. "Fashion mirrors emotion, too. Black for funerals, white for weddings, we all get that..." She paused, then said, "It's like music, in a way. If I put on a sleek pencil skirt, I feel like I'm in charge. I get the same feeling when I listen to 'Come on-a My House' by Rosemary Clooney. Have you heard of it?"

"Yes, I have. Great song."

"Then you know what I mean." She relaxed into the recliner. "Say you're feeling romantic. Maybe you wear a dress with a sweetheart neckline, something flowing to reveal some leg." She turned toward Alex. "Try this. Listen to 'Kiss of Fire' by Georgia Gibbs, and imagine I'm with you. Then imagine what I'm wearing."

He gave it thought, then said, "I get your point."

Francie looked around, gauging their privacy from the other beachgoers. Then she whispered, "I do that sometimes."

"Do what, exactly?"

"I listen to a song, and I try to imagine a perfect outfit, one that captures the mood of that song. It's quite fun."

Alex pivoted so he could hold her gaze, then smiled and said, "You do love fashion."

"I do, and I want you to know I'm taking this seriously. In New York, I met Sunny Harnett." She checked to see if Alex recognized the name. He didn't, so Francie continued. "World-famous model, been in all the magazines. Anyway, Sunny taught me how to present clothing. How to walk, position my arms to flare a blouse, and move my hips to accentuate slacks. Most of all, to love what I'm wearing. If I love it, so will the audience."

"With your enthusiasm, they'll love everything about you. You'll be the best in the show."

She started to say something, then caught her words. She rested her hand on his forearm. "Thank you so much for making this happen."

"Of course," said Alex.

She lay back. With her eyes closed, she said, "So that's what I've wanted to share. And this"—she opened her palms to the sun—"is just what I need."

Francie stretched her legs. She sensed a shadow moving up her body. Francie heard shuffling and the dull rub of heavy fabrics moving against one another. She opened her eyes to see Karl the tailor standing before her.

Karl was looking down at his utilitarian shoes. "Leather," he said, gasping, "has no right being on a beach. Same for wheezy tailors." He rolled his eyes, then coughed. "In a bistro, perhaps, with a nice roast chicken, some fried potatoes. There, I belong. Not here."

"Karl," said Francie. "What a surprise!"

Karl held up a "wait-a-minute" finger. "Surprise is me, a tailor, wearing horse blankets to a beach," he said, tugging on his jacket. "This you wear in a St. Petersburg snowstorm. Not here."

Alex rose from his recliner. "Is everything okay?"

"Yes and no," said Karl. "Yes, for me; I found you." He pulled a handkerchief and wiped his brow, then smiled. "And no for you because I found you."

Francie swung her legs off the recliner. "Why don't you take a seat?" she said.

"I must be going," said Karl. "We must be going. You, me, and I think Alex. All of us."

"Going where?" she asked.

He puffed out his cheeks and glanced toward the sun as if noticing it for the first time. "I heard from one of Mr. Julien's tailors. I need to take the measures for the mannequin."

"What do you mean?"

He gathered himself, then said, "The cut of the clothing changes, by the hour and minute. Higher here, lower there, tighter here, looser there. Agghh! They make themselves crazy. They want perfection. So they have a mannequin for each model, like a big doll. They wrap it in different places until it is an exact match of your body. It will even have your name on it. They throw the clothing onto this doll, make their changes, and do it repeatedly, until a tailor loses his temper, gets fired, and ends up on a beach, wearing wool."

Francie chuckled. "And this all means?"

"This means you must come with me." Karl looked over at Alex. "I would feel better if you accompanied us."

She slumped back into the recliner. "Right now?"

"Yes, right now," said Karl. "I'm sorry to ruin this nice day, where you bake yourself in this oven by the sea, but they need the measures." Karl looked at his watch, then at Alex. "Might I ask if we can use your room?"

"Certainly," said Alex.

Francie nodded to herself several times. "I understand," she said. "Business comes first." She began to collect her things and haphazardly toss them into her bag. She then squared her shoulders. "Let's do this right," she said, lacing her right hand around Karl's left arm. "Alex and I shall march you to the hotel, and we'll get started."

Karl beamed. "Miss Stevens..."

"Call me Francie, please."

"Francie," Karl whispered as his eyes scanned for eavesdroppers, "I have some secret information about the bathing suit Mr. Julien has planned for you."

"Do tell," she said as they all made their way toward the hotel.

"Mr. Julien is competing with Louis Réard, a designer from Paris. You know him?"

Francie shook her head. "I don't."

"Réard is famous for his bikinis," said Karl. "This man designs them with seventy-five centimeters of fabric."

She thought about that, then looked over at Karl.

"It's nothing," he said, shaking his head in disbelief. "Maybe thirty square inches for Americans. That's less than a cocktail napkin." He wiped his brow again with his handkerchief. "Réard says, 'It's not a bikini unless it can pass through a wedding ring.' He leaned in and said, "First, never connect a bikini and a wedding. Not a good idea. Second, it should never be about size. Never. That is not fashion. That is something else. The competition should be for the best bathing suit, which makes a woman feel joy in who she is. So our Mr. Julien will compete on design, fabric, and pattern. Not size. We know he can design. Regarding fabric and pattern, I'm pleased to say he has both."

Francie caught Alex's eye and smiled. "Really? What do you know?"

Karl continued. "Mr. Julien had nylon made just for him by the Dupont Company. This material, it stretches."

Her eyes widened. "So no gaps," she said.

He stopped and faced Francie, then placed his hands on her shoulders and said, "You are exactly right, Miss—Francie. No gaps. And the pattern, I will not tell. A nice surprise for you."

The three of them approached the hotel. Karl tapped his shoes against one another, knocking sand off the bottoms. "We will have some challenges," he said. "This nylon is..." He struggled for the word, then said, "...shiny, so problems with reflection, with light. You understand?"

Francie nodded.

"But I make sure they cut the fabric right. So not a problem."

Alex was all attention. "Well done." He placed a hand on Karl's shoulder. "We're delighted you're looking out for Francie."

Alex stood aside as they approached the entrance to the hotel, allowing Francie and Karl to enter first. Just inside, Karl slapped a meaty palm to his forehead, then looked around the lobby.

"Is something the matter?" she asked.

"A small thing," he said. "I need the bus schedules."

"I can drop you off later today," said Alex. "I've got a car."

"Thank you," he said, "but it won't be today. Today we do the measures. I'll write them up tonight. Tomorrow I will take some buses to Mr. Julien's villa. So I need the schedules."

"When does Mr. Julien need the measurements?"

Francie locked eyes with Alex. She knew where he was going with his question. "Can Mr. Julien wait until tomorrow night?" she asked. "We'll see him then."

Karl thought about her question. "I suppose, but I wouldn't want to bother you."

"Nonsense," she said. "That settles it. I'll give them to Mr. Julien myself when I see him at the party. And you won't have to spend the day riding a hot bus."

CHAPTER 8

FRIDAY AFTERNOON

John's Villa, Saint-Jeannet

John stood at the base of his driveway, hands in his pockets, with a sweater draped over his shoulders, the arms loosely knotted at his chest. He looked around, taking in the rustic countryside—the mix of lavender, cypress, and pine trees; the broken stone walls that lined the street, held together by red and purple bougainvillea. He saw Paul's Citroën appear just up the road, powering forward with the top down. John waved, then Paul pulled into the driveway.

"Thanks for the call," said Paul. "I'm glad you could come. As I said, I have to meet someone at the club. But we can talk on the ride."

"No worries, my friend. You have business." He opened the passenger door, then heard a voice calling him.

"Signore Robie."

John looked back. Leaning out of the door was an attractive, petite woman, dark-complexioned, with muscular arms. She wore a loose-fitting housedress, and a warm smile.

"Yes, Vittoria?"

"Cosa ti piacerebbe per cena?" What would he like for dinner?

"Tu decidi," he said. You decide.

He got in, then Paul pulled away. John looked around the car, surveyed the road ahead, and checked the rearview mirrors. An old habit.

"What happened to Germaine?" asked Paul.

"Retired. She was getting on in years; it became too much. She's happy, living with her daughter."

"Vittoria looks quite capable," said Paul through a slow smile.

"Now, now. It's not like that."

"She's not capable?"

John started to speak, then stopped. He thought for a moment. He started again and stopped again.

"Perhaps we are discussing different things," said Paul.

John held up both hands, an unconditional surrender. "She's a friend, nothing more. Last year in Italy, she helped me out with a problem. Vittoria and her pack of brothers, that is. Must be a dozen of them. Anyway, she's in France and needed a place to stay. I wouldn't take rent, and she wouldn't stay for free. So she offered to help around the house."

Paul started to speak, but John cut him off. "Before you ask, she lives in the cottage behind the villa." He saw Paul frown. "Spoiled your fun? I'm sorry. By the way, don't wander by the cottage unannounced. She's tougher than she looks."

"Noted. I'll watch my step around your 'good friend.' But tell me this—does she laugh at your jokes?"

"She doesn't find me funny at all."

Paul chuckled under his breath. "That qualifies her to be your wife."

"Speaking of wives, how is Danielle getting on?"

"Marvelous. She's in Paris, continuing her studies. That was her priority, to attend college. Never thought she'd have the opportunity."

They drove on. After a while, Paul said, "I'm sorry we can't golf today. You're improving."

"Yes, but not enough to beat you. Not yet." Paul had introduced him to golf. They played at the Cannes-Mougins Golf Country Club, where both were members.

The road took a sharp left turn, revealing a stunning view of the coast on their right. "This meeting," said John. "Can you share details?"

"This is speculation, not intelligence. So, yes. But between us, okay?" He waited for agreement.

"Absolutely."

"The French Intelligence service, or rather those in possession of French Intelligence, have been the target of blackmail."

"Go on."

"The method is conventional," Paul continued. "The black-mailers identify their target, then they uncover something compromising. If they can't find anything, they create something, then use that information."

"Use how?"

"Here's a hypothetical. Say a coworker of mine meets a woman. One thing leads to another, they become involved. After a while, she mentions a cousin who wants to apply for a job, so she needs a contact—just the name and address of a department head, to send a letter. So our man helps. Then a few more small favors, a secretary's name here, a phone number there."

"Sounds innocent enough."

"It does," said Paul. "But it's not innocent at all. Any information about our agency is classified. Employees know this; we tell them when they're hired. A name or address in the wrong hands puts our enemies a step closer to sensitive intelligence."

Paul continued, his eyes focused on the winding road ahead. "The blackmailers, like the hypothetical woman, then demand intelligence reports. If our man refuses, she threatens to reveal him as a traitor."

"Because he's already provided sensitive information, like names?"

"Exactly."

John considered that. Very clever; a subtle lure, followed by a hard threat. "Which nations want intelligence?"

"Eastern bloc. Bulgaria is a big offender, so is Russia." He glanced over at John. "Even your United States."

"That's surprising, being allies and all."

"Allies, yes," said Paul. "Allies who verify, then trust."

"And your meeting today at the golf club?"

"Ah, yes, and this is the speculation. You know Hugo Rousseau?"

John nodded. "You've pointed him out. Distinguished, very wealthy, perfect tan."

"That's him. And wealthy is an understatement. His family's businesses span the globe, and their public service goes back a hundred years. He's a real patriot." Paul glanced at his wristwatch. "He'll be finishing his round of golf when we arrive."

"Why him?"

"These blackmailers, they target anyone with access to intelligence, and that includes Hugo."

"How so?"

"He's a member of Parliament. He sits on the Intelligence Committee, which oversees my agency, so he knows what we know. He's also on the committee that oversees the former colonies, which are now called territories, and one that funds Arts & Culture, which is why he's in town. For Fashion Week."

John rubbed his hands together. Paul's meeting would set the perfect stage for what John had planned. The pieces were falling into place. "You believe Hugo could be a victim of blackmail?"

"I've gone through the invitation list," said Paul, "and he's the only one with access to intelligence."

"But can he be compromised?"

Paul nodded. "Last year, Hugo was involved with a Parisian actress, a beautiful woman, although I'm not sure Mrs. Rousseau would think so."

"Ahhh," said John. "Now I see. Hugo has a wandering eye." He smirked. "More than an eye, is my guess. Do you suspect his mistress?"

"No, she's an actress, nothing more. We've looked. And their affair has been very discreet, but blackmail might change that."

John understood. "So you're warning him."

"It's my duty. What got me concerned was the invitation in that man's jacket." He pointed to a weathered leather attaché case on the seat.

John spotted the invitation. He pulled it from the case and reread it.

"Perhaps the dead man intended to approach Hugo at the party," said Paul. "They might have proof of his infidelity, or maybe they planned on creating a new trap for him."

"Either way, a possible target?"

"Maybe," said Paul. "We know the man who died was going to Fashion Week. We also know politicians are being blackmailed for intelligence, so..."

John followed along, listening to Paul's theories. They made sense. He started to put the invitation back when something caught his eye. There were indentations on it, as if someone had written on another paper lying on top. John tilted the invitation so the sun could highlight the markings, and there they were. Several letter impressions were visible, and a backward N was right in the middle of the string. Just a small detail, but one that might come in handy should he need to barter with, or impress, his friend. No need to share it now. John smiled to himself, said nothing, and placed the invitation back into the case.

CHAPTER 9

nspector Lepic waited a few moments, then steered his car onto the main road. He hung back so the passengers in the Citroën couldn't see him. That was critical.

Just to be safe, he slumped in his seat, decreasing his profile. He donned a casual cap with a long, low brim. He pawed about the front seat, trying to find his sunglasses. Once on, he looked up. Their car was far ahead. He could barely see the passengers. They wouldn't spot him.

His mission to catch John Robie breaking the law was officially underway. Just minutes before, Lepic had parked down the street from Robie's villa, squeezing into a space barely large enough for his car. Perfectly hidden. Not a moment later, he had seen Robie exit his villa and stand roadside, dawdling while he waited for a ride.

And, like a white knight in his cream-colored Citroën, up pulled Paul le Comte du Pre de la Tour. A man Lepic respected greatly and envied more. Descended from royalty, owner of a legendary French estate, the sole supporter of a dozen charities and cultural centers, and in possession of more money than generations of men could spend. Paul had it all. To make matters worse, he was tall, broad-shouldered, handsome, and like many "old money" Frenchmen, Paul was well-mannered. Lepic would have been content with one of those attributes.

He kept Paul's car in sight. He was an expert at following a suspect; he'd perfected his skills through twenty years of police work.

Lepic considered John Robie. The man had a "taking mind." And that "taking mind" gave Lepic confidence he would catch Robie. Thieves were driven by appetites, making them careless. Not stupid, but willing to ignore risk when eyeing a reward. John Robie had been jailed once and nearly arrested a second time. It would happen again. The odds always caught you.

Up ahead he saw the Citroën slow down. Paul was pulling into the Cannes-Mougins Golf Country Club. Lepic snorted like a bull. He'd been denied when he tried to join that club. "Appreciate your interest, not at this time, no member has sponsored you." Always some veiled excuse. Paul Du Pre as a member made sense. But John Robie? Not at all. That was an insult.

Lepic had seen Paul pull into the parking lot and turn right. He slowed down, keeping a safe distance between his car and theirs. He raised his right arm to shield his face as an extra measure, then headed in the opposite direction. Lepic checked his rearview mirror and saw them deep in conversation as they walked to the clubhouse. Good job. They hadn't seen him.

He parked and sat for several minutes as he approached the situation from a different angle, something he'd found valuable in police work. Why was John Robie spending so much time in the company of a man like Paul? He could be a charmer when he wanted; Lepic had seen it. That casual confidence, that smooth voice, those eyes that locked on and seemed to smile. Paul Du Pre could easily have fallen under Robie's spell. Was he using Paul to meet members of French society? Was he scouting new targets? If so, the club was overflowing with potential.

He lifted the corner of his lip, pulling his mouth into a mean smirk. He knew there had to be something Robie wanted. A man like that was always out for himself.

Lepic exited his car and headed toward the clubhouse. Maybe today would be the day the odds would catch up with John Robie.

CHAPTER 10

Paul held open the door to the bar and motioned to John: *After you.*

John entered and received a series of rowdy hellos from the golfers, who were all smiles upon seeing him. Several got to their feet to greet him.

"Bad news, gents," he said, a wide grin across his face. "I'm here and I'm thirsty. Who owes me a drink?" He and Paul continued through the bar, with John doling out handshakes and good-humored taunts to many of the men.

They approached Hugo Rousseau, seated in the back with a large glass of wine, his scorecard, a pocket notebook, and a couple of keys littering the table. Paul greeted Hugo, then introduced John.

"Nice to see you again," said John. "I trust the course was kind."

Hugo smiled. "It's been kinder. Will you be joining us?"

"I'm afraid not. These men owe me drinks," said John, "and they seem eager to settle up." Paul took a seat. John turned and stepped into the fray of inebriated golfers, who had formed a backslapping gauntlet for him.

He took his time going through the line, as he enjoyed these men. And they appreciated him. They all knew about his past, and no one ever mentioned it. That's why he was so comfortable among them. The realization gave John an extra dose of affection as he worked the crowd. Between greetings, he canvassed the room, waving to members seated around the tables.

The bartender handed him an Aperol Spritz, made from prosecco and Aperol, its rich orange hue shining like a lantern in his hand. He took a sip, whispered the obligatory "ahhhhh," then headed toward the locker room.

It was time to show Paul what he could do.

Lepic leaned around the corner, then peeked through the glass-panel door separating the bar from the rest of the club. Robie was on the move.

He pulled back. Robie was headed toward the business office and locker room. That made sense. The office likely contained a substantial sum of money, and the locker room held the wallets and valuables of the members present.

He nodded to himself. That's why Robie was in the bar: to see who was there. The man was a noted lockpick, according to police files. A locker room would be easy for him.

Lepic moved behind a column, getting a better view of Robie, and it became clear to him; all the intrigue and notoriety surrounding Robie was misplaced. *He's just a common thief.*

John walked toward the end of the hallway, near the manager's office and the locker room. He planted himself in a quiet corner and waited. He was confident his plan would work. The bar was bursting with opportunities, more than he'd imagined. It would come down to selecting well.

After a moment, a young man stepped out from a supply closet, carrying an armful of towels.

"Javier," said John with a cordial wave.

Javier lit up. "Señor Robie. What a nice surprise."

John shook his hand, then pulled him close. "I was hoping you could help me out," he whispered. "Just a small favor..."

Lepic had his back to the column, hidden from Robie's view. But a window provided a good reflection of Robie's activities.

This was the moment. Robie had been waiting for someone, and here he was, a locker room attendant. They'd chatted closely, as if conspiring. The attendant then went into a room. He'd emerged with a small brown bag a minute later, which he passed to Robie. They chatted a little more, then Robie reached into his pocket and handed the attendant money.

Lepic thought about what he'd just seen: clearly an illicit exchange. The encounter happened in a hallway, out of sight. The young man had handed something of value to Robie, who had hidden it in his pocket. Was it possible this young man was Robie's accomplice? As an employee, he would know the cadence of revenues, how much was received, and when it was taken to a bank. He would also know where each member's locker was located. Perhaps he'd passed Robie a master key?

His heart beat faster. He reached into his suit jacket and touched his holstered pistol, a semiautomatic MAC 50, the official pistol of the French Army. If it was good enough for them, it was good enough for law enforcement. The magazine was in; it was ready.

He hoped like hell Robie gave him cause to use it.

John headed back into the bar. He handed a tip to the bartender, a thank-you for the cocktail, and they talked for a minute. He then caught Paul's attention and motioned he'd be in the shaded alfresco area.

There was no one outside; all the tables were available. He picked one right next to the manager's office, the window to which was slightly open.

He reached into his pocket and pulled out the brown paper bag. He set it on the table next to his drink, then sat down. He crossed his legs, took a long sip, then admired the fairway view. It was magnificent.

After a moment, he picked up the brown bag and emptied it onto the table. Two Montecristo cigars fell out, his favorites ever since Javier had told him about their origin. Javier's father had worked in a cigar factory in Havana as a *torcedor*, a cigar roller. That factory had employed *lectores*, readers who kept the workers entertained. And the story the workers loved the most was *The Count of Monte Cristo* by Alexandre Dumas. The factory owner enjoyed the story, too, and he would sit in while the book was read. In honor of the tale, the owner created the Montecristo brand. The workers insisted that it be the best, and it was. Javier still had family in Cuba who sent him cigars, and he was more than happy to share his good fortune with John.

John reached into the ashtray and removed a clipper and a box of matches. He clipped, then lit his cigar and relaxed into his chair.

Paul emerged, and John waved him over.

"We don't have time for this," said Paul. "I've got a lot to do."

He offered Paul a seat. "Just ten minutes. There's something I need to share. Trust me, it will be worth your time."

Paul hesitated, then took a seat. The bartender magically appeared with two Aperol Spritzes and set them on their table. John pushed a cigar toward Paul.

"Planets are aligning to make me relax. Why not?" He lit his cigar and sipped his cocktail, then turned to John. "What's on your mind?"

"You first. How did it go with Hugo?"

"Very well. He appreciated the warning, and he will take extra precautions this week." Paul took a long draw, then said, "He's aware of this type of threat; he knows it has happened before and tells me that he no longer finds himself in compromising positions."

John raised his glass in a toast. "Here's to Hugo and to phrases with double meanings."

"Double entendres," said Paul as they clinked glasses. "Your turn."

John sat up and straightened his collar. He was apprehensive, even though he had the information and was ready to deliver. But it had to be perfect. "There were nineteen men in the bar. Of the nineteen, four were from Belgium, specifically Brussels, and they're here for a long weekend of golf and gambling. One man joked about giving the bartender a five-thousand-franc chip from the Casino de Monte-Carlo, where they gambled last night. He still has it, the red placard sticking out of his pocket."

"I didn't notice. I was talking with Hugo, then I came to you."

"No matter." John rested his cigar on the ashtray lip, then took a sip of his drink. "Remember that restaurateur from Saint-Tropez? We played with him last week. Just now, he entered the bar, spotted the banker from Sainte-Maxime, and left. No words were spoken, but there was a definite tension between the two men. The restaurant isn't doing well, and I believe he owes the banker some money."

Paul was intrigued. "Okay," he said, then looked more closely at John, predicting where the conversation was headed.

John continued, "Oh, and that middle-aged man who owns the factory not far from here; he's got a date tonight. He was at the bar, freshly showered, shaved, and with an extra splash of cologne, all on a Friday afternoon. Big smile, too. In great spirits. We've seen him out with his wife, and he never cleans up like this. They're not the happiest of couples, either. The only one more miserable than him is his wife. So, a date."

"I'm following, but I'm not."

"Bear with me," said John. "Our good friend Randall, the golf pro, is also sitting at the bar. If you play him for money, I suggest you do so in the afternoon. He's three cocktails in, and it shows."

"I'll note that."

"Final point. Hugo shot a ninety-eight today; he struggled on the last four holes. And he's probably having just one drink. He's got a meeting with his accountant today at four o'clock. Right about now, you'll find him sitting in front of locker number twenty-two as he gets ready to leave."

"He did shoot a ninety-eight," said Paul. "But you weren't there when we discussed that. I don't understand. John, how do you know all this?"

He got serious. "Hugo had his scorecard, a pocket pad with an appointment, a key for locker twenty-two, and a key to his hotel room, all sitting in front of him at his table. That's how I know. And it's the same for everything else. One pass through that bar was all it took. Details reveal a lot if you don't miss them. And I don't miss a thing. Ask the bartender. He'll confirm it all." He leaned closer to Paul. "Tomorrow night, the cocktail party. You said yourself, that man we chased, the one who died. He was going to the party."

"I believe he was."

"Something important might happen there. And it'll be busy, a lot of people, a lot of press and celebrities, a lot of distractions. There's no way you can cover it all."

John kept his eyes on Paul and saw it begin to register.

"You're going to need some help," said John. "Someone with an eye for detail, someone who can see what's really happening."

"Ahhh, now I understand."

"I'm glad you do. Your odds of finding something, of getting a lead, they're much better with me on board."

Paul was silent. John watched him stare straight ahead as he processed everything. "You're right. That's exactly what we need."

They locked eyes, and John tilted his head. "What do you say?"

After a moment, Paul nodded in firm agreement.

John leaned back in his chair. It had worked! He would be going to the cocktail party as Paul's guest. No one would dare question him, and no one would turn him away. He would talk with Francie and straighten things out. He pulled a slow draw from his cigar, then exhaled. John felt tension release from his shoulders. He'd really wanted this.

They gathered their things, finished their drinks, and headed toward the parking lot. He was relieved. He would see Francie, and all because he'd read Paul's situation well. He had known what to share and more importantly, what to hold back—like the backward *N* imprinted on the invitation, and the fact that Lepic had followed them to, and through, the club. He had seen Lepic the moment he'd left his villa and tracked his every move since.

They approached Paul's car. Out of the corner of his eye, John saw Lepic at the far end of the parking lot. He was behind the wheel of his car, beating his dashboard with both fists.

He had to be very careful. Knowing Lepic, he would double his efforts. The man's ego would demand it. And that made him even more dangerous.

CHAPTER 11

John checked his tuxedo, then entered the ballroom with Paul. Immediately, he felt transported to another world. A calypso band was playing, and the soft, catchy melodies infected the crowd. He looked around. Hips swayed, smiles stayed, and laughter punctuated every conversation. Great swatches of geometric fabric climbed the walls, brightly colored and with playful prints. Impossibly handsome waiters sporting *marinière*, the iconic blue-and-white-striped sailor shirts, passed by with trays of champagne, and photographers' flashbulbs were popping like random claps. Oversized postcards on driftwood easels with beach and boating scenes were scattered around the room. He couldn't help but smile.

John looked over at Paul. "Okay, which side?"

Paul scanned the room. "I'll take the left side. Hugo is there, and some other politicians. You take the right and stay focused. We're here for one reason."

He patted Paul on the back. "Understood." He then turned to survey his side. There was a cluster of international celebrities just a few feet away—the sultry German actress, the scandalous Australian actor, an American crooner wearing a straw boater's hat, and Josephine Baker, whom John knew from their days together in the Resistance. A Black entertainer, Josephine had fled America to escape the shame of segregation and the all-too-real danger of bigotry. A Resistance mission brought them together, and she and John took to one another instantly. They'd done great work, which they never discussed. Josephine nodded to him with a sly smile. John did the same. Some secrets created deep friendships.

In the back of the room, he spotted an industrialist in a raucous conversation with the fun-loving cousin of the recently crowned Queen of England. The royal rogue had commandeered a tray of champagne glasses and offered a drink and a pickup line to every woman who passed.

To his side, John saw a man walking toward him, hand extended while holding a single champagne flute. "Monsieur, you ordered prosecco," he said. "One trip to Italy, you're like a tourist. Italian this, Italian that..."

John looked over to find a grinning waiter with shoulder-length hair, whisker stubble you could strike a match on, and arms like braided granite extending from his French sailor shirt. The man handed the glass to John, then gave him a sincere, firm handshake.

John stepped back to look at him. "Luca, I didn't know..."

"Ahhh, they needed bartenders," said Luca. "So why not?" He raised his eyebrows. "One for you, one for me, it's a good night."

They had met in prison then fought together in the Resistance. They were a formidable team. Luca Spada was the best fighter John knew, a skill he'd picked up as an *expatrié* living in South America after a run-in with French authorities. Unlike his other friends from that time, he harbored no jealousy or resentment toward John.

Luca tapped John's champagne glass with a fingernail. "I have a bottle for you. I'm at the side bar when you're ready." He turned and walked away, then looked back. "And I'll have your car fixed next week. Waiting on some parts; you know how it is."

As if a conductor had silenced them, the crowd hushed.

John looked over to see Francie Stevens.

Francie looked into the ballroom. The man at the door had told her to wait. She saw the man walk up to and speak with Marcel Julien, who looked at Francie, clasped his palms together in a champion's cheer, and smiled. He then corralled several photographers and lined them up.

Francie leaned toward her mother, then said quietly, "Fingers crossed."

"You're ready, dear. You've been ready for years."

"Sweet of you, Mother."

"And I'm sure you're ready for him, if he's even here."

"If he is, I'll approach him first. John Robie won't catch me off guard. Not tonight."

Francie felt Alex's touch on her shoulder. "It's time. Marcel just waved you in. We'll follow in a bit."

She looked down at her bright navy-blue dress, cinched and belted at the waist, the light fabric folded and breaking just below the knee. The dress slipped off her shoulders, making the neckline plunge even more. She touched her pearl necklace, loving its contrast with her tan. It was time.

The calypso band stopped what they were playing and launched into a fanciful Caribbean version of Nat King Cole's "Unforgettable." Francie entered the ballroom, passing a firing squad of photographers as the crowd focused on her. She strode right up to Marcel, who had found a microphone with a steel-grilled head that looked as big as a birdcage.

"Ladies and gentlemen," said Marcel, "Fashion Week celebrates the best of the French Riviera, with its beauty and glamour. With the sun, the sea, the beaches, and most of all, the people, the Riviera is admired worldwide. Truly an international playground, a place of great excitement and even greater possibilities." He motioned toward Francie. "And if there's one woman who captures the spirit of the Riviera, it's Francie Stevens, who needs no introduction. And who, I'm delighted to say, has agreed to represent our newest line."

A crescendo of applause rushed from the crowd like a stampede. Reporters and photographers formed a half circle around Marcel and Francie. He put his arm around her and aimed them both at the press. All smiles. She held an envelope and handed it to Marcel as the press fired off questions like a string of fireworks.

"The measurements for my mannequin," she said under her breath as she held her smile. "From Karl, the tailor."

A member of the press shouted, "What is it?"

Marcel pocketed the envelope quickly, then said, "A love note from a pretty girl." He glanced around, wide-eyed and playful. "Where's my wife?" The crowd roared as Odette Julien stepped forward and playfully punched her husband on his arm. Then, like a dancer taking the lead, Marcel posed himself and Francie for the cameras. They shook hands, stood arm in arm, toasted each other with champagne, then held hands at arm's length and bowed like a pair of figure skaters.

After the initial excitement wound down, Odette approached Francie, then held her hand. "That was your first walk as a model," Odette said, "and you were fabulous. So tomorrow won't be your first time. No need to be nervous. You've already done it."

"Thank you so much, Mrs...."

"Odette, please. And he's Marcel. No more 'Mr. Julien.' Before he parades you about, can I get you a drink?"

"There's one quick thing I have to do. I'll just be a minute."

John couldn't take his eyes off her. He hadn't seen Francie in a year, and the difference was remarkable. Last summer, she'd been a stunningly beautiful girl just becoming aware of her charm. And here was a woman, glowing with confidence, a natural in front of a very demanding crowd. He took a step in her direction, then heard a familiar voice.

"Lucky, is that you?"

John turned to find Maude Stevens, who, after a good stretch at a casino last summer, had nicknamed him Lucky. She rushed up to him with a smile, a hug, and a kiss.

"How are you?" he said. "It's been a while."

"It has," said Maude. "And you're no worse for the wear. You look great. How've you been getting on?"

"Very well. Cooled my heels abroad for a bit, but that's behind me now. How was your winter? Skiing in Quebec, right?"

"It was chilly," said Maude, rubbing her upper arms. John saw her look over his shoulder. "And it's about to get colder."

He glanced back to find Francie Stevens, marching toward him with a determined gaze.

Francie watched John turn, a puzzled look on his face.

"John."

His confusion melted away, and charm surged from him like a floodlight. "Francie, you were breathtaking," he said. "I'm at a loss."

"A loss," said Francie, "is a temporary state for a thief like you."

"Bundle up; it's a cold front," said Maude, who backed away and headed for the bar.

He looked confused again. "Those...those days are behind me," he said. "You know that."

"Do I?" asked Francie. "Last I heard, you were 'retired, not reformed.' Those were your words. That's changed?"

He seemed off-balance. "Yes, yes, I'm reformed, sure." He collected himself, then said, "I was hoping we could talk."

"About what?"

"About us. I haven't heard from you in months."

"You didn't get my message?" asked Francie.

"No. You stopped writing. You wouldn't take my calls."

She stepped closer. "That was the message."

John paused. She could see him thinking through his comments. Her confidence surged. It was working. She was in control.

"Francie, what's happening?" he asked. "Why did you stop writing?"

"Why do you think?"

He stepped back. *He's buying time and steadying himself,* Francie thought.

"Why?" he asked. "Well, except for Paul, you didn't like my friends. I remember that. And you weren't very fond of my past."

She shook her head. "You still don't get it. Those criminals you call friends, your burglar days—you blame everything around you, John. Then again, looking around is easier than looking within."

"What's that supposed to mean?"

"It means you look everywhere but here," she said as she poked his chest. "You know what your mind wants. But you have no idea what your heart needs."

"Where is this coming from?"

"It's coming from experience. You value things, not principles. You don't know what matters. I'm not sure you have any principles." Francie stopped herself. "Well, that's not true. Last summer, you showed loyalty, remember? To that girl, Danielle, but only because she was also a thief. You were never loyal to me. Only to another woman."

"Francie..."

"You treated me like another heist," she said. "Like something to acquire, to possess. If you knew me this much"—she pinched her fingers—"you'd know that doesn't sit well with me."

"It's not like that at all."

She paused for a beat, forming a thought. "It became obvious over time. You and I, we're as different as night and day." She snatched a drink off a passing tray. "But I'm glad we ran into one another. Tonight confirmed everything, and now I'm certain. I want nothing to do with you, John Robie."

A hand rested on Francie's shoulder. Alex Dandridge stepped up. "Is everything all right?"

She smiled up at him. "Yes, dear. Wonderful." He wrapped

an arm around her shoulders. Francie felt a strength she hadn't noticed before. Alex was more powerful than she'd realized, and it bolstered her own conviction.

Alex stared at John and said, "We're done here. You're done here. Am I clear?"

Francie put her arm around Alex's waist, and they walked off. She felt confident and comfortable for the first time that evening. It had gone better than expected, and taking charge had been the right approach. Yet she felt unsettled for some reason. Perhaps she had overplayed her hand, been too direct, maybe too cruel? She pushed that thought from her mind.

One thing was sure. John Robie got that message. She had no doubt.

The room swirled around John. His mouth was dry, and his heart was beating fast. He tried to swallow, and it took effort. What had happened? How could he have misread Francie to that degree?

A boisterous conga line snaked through the party, pulling people into its wake. "She doesn't understand," he muttered. John had thought about her obsessively for months, he'd imagined this conversation, but he never envisioned this. All that planning, all that anticipation, for what?

He rubbed his forehead as he tried to slow his thinking. Francie had completely misjudged him; he was sure of that. If she knew his real intentions, she'd see it differently. Another conversation would do it, and he'd be better prepared. He would set the record straight.

But what about that man? A new boyfriend, maybe even a lover. He was sure of himself, too. John had a sour feeling in his stomach, thinking about how that man had stared him down, then told John he was "done." He was lucky he'd caught John off guard. A threat demanded a strong response, and John never backed down.

No, he was far from done. He'd invested too much time into Francie Stevens, and he wasn't about to lose out on her, especially not to that boyfriend.

John swayed as if different forces were pushing and pulling him off his feet. He looked around and saw Luca behind a bar and headed in that direction.

Odette Julien was sure of what she'd heard. Francie had called the man "John Robie," then walked away when her boyfriend showed up.

And here was John Robie walking toward her, looking like he'd gone ten rounds in a prize fight.

Odette was leaning her back against the bar. She turned and said to the bartender, "I think this man needs a drink."

The bartender, a handsome brute of a man with long hair and thick forearms, glanced up. "Yeah, he doesn't look so good."

"Might want to make it a double," she said. The bartender gave her a half smile, filled a champagne glass, poured a double shot of dark rum, and put it to the side.

John stepped into the space at the bar next to her. The bartender placed the two drinks in front of him. She watched him down the shot, then motion for another.

"I don't believe we've met," she said. "I'm Odette Julien, Marcel's wife, and you look like you're having a rough night."

"I am," said John before downing his second shot. "I just need to clear my head." He put the shot glass on the bar, then ran his fingers through his hair before grabbing the champagne. He took a healthy sip, then turned to her.

"Did I hear correctly? Did someone call you John Robie?"

"Yes, and I apologize for my bad manners." They shook hands. "Nice to meet you, Odette."

She dropped her voice to barely a whisper. "John Robie, the cat burglar?"

He paused. "That was a long time ago," he said. "I paid my debt to society, and then some. That's not who I am anymore." He took another sip. "Not that it matters, but I only stole from those who could afford it. And they were insured, so there were no real victims."

She moved in a bit closer. "That's not quite true, is it?"

"Why would you say that?"

"Well, we're meeting for the first time tonight, but our paths crossed once before."

"How so?"

"Years ago, Marcel and I stayed in this hotel for one night. That was all we could afford back then."

"Go on."

"That night, someone broke into our room and stole an alexandrite ring from my vanity. It was beautiful, dark navy in color, like a sapphire."

John was listening intently. "Maybe it wasn't me. I'm sorry, I have no recollection."

"I didn't think you would. It was the smallest item you stole that night. And it was you, by the way. That came out at your trial."

"Then my apologies, by all means. I'm happy to replace it."

"You couldn't possibly replace it," she said. "It was in my mother's family, and it was the only thing she took with her when she fled her homeland." Odette looked down as the memory came back. "She said that stone brought good luck, and it certainly did for her. She was the only one in her family to survive the escape." She looked up into John's eyes. "And it was the only thing she left me."

"I'm so sorry."

"Marcel was more upset than I was. He was furious. Alexandrite brings great fortune to those in business, and he believed we needed it." She waved her hand about the room. "As you can see, he's done well without it. So a myth, perhaps."

John was quiet. He looked at her with tired eyes. "I don't know what to say."

She put her hand on his forearm. "You're upset, and I'm not sharing this to upset you—quite the opposite. You see, we all tell ourselves things to justify our actions. We do that enough, and we believe it. Then we can't see the truth, just the story we've created."

He leaned back to gain perspective.

"That's a dangerous way to go through life," she said. "Not being able to see the truth. I wouldn't want that for you."

Odette studied him for a moment, feeling more compassion with every passing second. She took hold of his hand and squeezed. "Thanks to you, I learned a great lesson back then. Never put too much stock in any one thing. Not in jewelry, a man, or anything you think you believe. Only in yourself. That was more valuable to me than any ring."

John nodded but still didn't speak.

She patted his arm. "Please don't be upset. I know you fought for us during the war, and you turned your life around. I hope our paths cross again. And that is the truth."

Odette started to walk away. She turned back and smiled. "It was nice to meet you, John Robie."

Odette was comforting him, but John was sick. A pounding muted her words in his head. First Francie, now Odette Julien. He had never considered jewels to have value beyond their sale price. He wondered how many other stolen jewels had such sentimental value. He felt queasy, feverish.

When Odette said his name, John saw a man turn around and stare at him. John glanced over, and the man's eyes searched behind him as if he were looking for someone else. That wasn't the case, and John knew it. The man slowly turned away. John looked him up and down. He'd not seen him before. He was dark and lean, and something about him made John think he was dangerous. The man walked away with the athletic grace of a boxer.

John watched him wander through the party, weaving between people until he neared Marcel Julien. The man walked up behind Marcel and whispered. He didn't appear to be speaking to Marcel, just to the space behind him. Marcel tilted his head ever so slightly to hear the man.

Marcel then scanned the room. His eyes settled on John just for a second. Then he said something over his shoulder. It was quick, only a word or two.

That's odd, he thought.

John spun around to put his glass on the bar and found Paul standing behind him.

"Had enough?" asked Paul. "Or do you want the whole bottle?"

"Paul, I..."

"I've watched you all evening, and I've discerned something. You came for Miss Stevens."

John hesitated. "I was hoping to see her, yes, but I'm here to help."

"To help yourself, not me. Just now, I was watching. How many drinks did you have?"

"Just a couple. I...we need to fit in."

He held up an index finger and pointed it at John's face. "I knew this was a mistake; I knew it. You're trying to get her back, and you used me to get in here. You had no intention of helping me."

"Not true," said John, glancing at his watch. "We've got time. Let's get back out there."

"No. You'll not disappoint me again. I'll take it from here. Just keep doing what's best for you. Like always."

He started to protest, but Paul marched off before the words came out. John walked after him, then stopped. Blocking his way was the dark, dangerous-looking man who'd been staring at him a moment ago.

"Monsieur Robie. Someone would like a word with you. Follow me, please."

CHAPTER 12

John followed the man out of the ballroom and down a long hallway.

Paul's accusation had stung. He knew Paul was right and had every reason to be disappointed. John was angry with himself. He'd planned on talking with Francie, then helping Paul. The night just got away from him.

And now this. Marcel Julien most certainly wanted a word, and he would be in a foul mood. That ring had meant a lot to both Odette and Marcel. John rounded his lips and blew hard. He had to focus; there were too many thoughts running through his mind. *One thing at a time*, he told himself.

"Where are we going?" he asked.

"Almost there."

He spotted split kitchen doors, a porthole on each side. The man strode right into the kitchen, and John followed. It was surprisingly quiet, a few white-aproned cooks off to his right. The man kept the same pace, not a step slower or faster, as he headed to the back door. He opened it, then waved John through.

"Where it is private," said the man.

John stepped through the door and found himself in an alley behind the hotel. It was dark and rank, the odor coming from a cluster of garbage cans fifty feet away. Two gaslights illuminated the area, but barely. A couple of cats turned to look at him. He looked around for Marcel but didn't see him.

Behind him, the door slammed shut, the noise reverberating through the alley. John turned and found the man he'd followed standing there, hands crossed at the waist.

"You took something from this very hotel," said the man in a deep, deliberate voice. "Something that didn't belong to you."

John held up an open palm. "If I did, I'm sorry. I'll make it right." He looked around. "Where's Marcel? We can work something out."

From behind John came the slightest noise. He would have ignored it, but both cats turned to look simultaneously. He glanced back to find a massive man with a barrel of a body, his shoulders as wide as a cathedral door. He hadn't been there a moment ago— probably hiding behind the garbage cans. *Not good.*

John knew what was happening. He stepped away from the hotel to see the entire layout of the alley. Both men began closing in.

"I'm happy to replace the ring," he said, his head swiveling from one man to the other.

"This isn't about a ring," said the first man.

John looked at him, confused. Then it came to him. When that other man had fallen from the rooftop two nights ago, John had climbed up the pipe and gone into the man's room. He'd found the man's duffel bag, with the Mauser pistol and stacks of cash, which he'd thrown over to the first balcony before making his way to the rooftop. Later that same evening, he'd gone back to retrieve it. He didn't know why. He just took the cash, then hid it under some loose stones on the floor of his wine cellar. It made sense now. Someone figured out John had taken it, and these men were here to get it back.

The massive man stayed silent. The other one said, "Give it back. I won't ask again. You understand?"

John evaluated his position. Directly in front of him was the hotel wall, sturdy brick and stone, with an old fire escape ending at the second floor. The huge man was to his right, the other man to his left. John needed to back one off and surprise the other. In full stride, he leaped onto the wall. His body collapsed into a squat, then he exploded off, aiming himself at the massive man. John slammed an elbow into the big guy's head; it cracked against his skull like a cattle whip. The big guy's eyes rolled back, then he keeled over, hitting the cobblestones hard.

One down.

He spun to take on the other man but was late; the man tackled John. The two of them sprawled across the cobblestones, causing the cats to flee in opposite directions. He broke free of the man's grasp, then got to his feet. So did the other man.

In John's experience fighting in the Resistance, it never paid to circle an opponent, figuring out the best attack. He always went at them fast and hard, and he did so now. John bull-rushed him against the wall, then threw a flurry of punches. One of his shots hit hard, and the man went slack. He was unconscious. Not dead, but out cold.

Two down.

John rose to his feet, then looked down at his tux. He was a mess, his clothes disheveled and stained.

He ran back into the kitchen, tucking in his shirt as he went. There was someone who knew what had just happened.

And that someone was back at the party.

CHAPTER 13

John exited the kitchen into a long hallway and immediately spotted Luca and two other waiters carrying cases of wine back into the party.

"Luca," he yelled, "I need a favor."

Luca set his case of wine down on the floor and rushed toward John. "What happened?"

"A little problem out back. I need to speak with Marcel Julien. He's inside, and..."

"Not anymore. I just saw him in the lobby, on his way out."

John thought for a minute. He'd just fought with two tough men over the money he'd taken from the man on the rooftop. One of the men from the fight had a secretive exchange with Marcel just before the confrontation. That wasn't a coincidence.

Things were falling into place, but John wasn't completely sure. Not yet; he needed more information.

"Do you know where he lives?"

"I don't, but the valet might. Let me see."

John leaned back against the wall. He suspected Marcel was the intended recipient of the cash, but he had to confirm; that meant doing things he hadn't done in a long, long time. But if he was right, it would be justifiable.

"Marcel has a villa," said Luca, rushing back, "but he didn't go there. He went to his yacht at a marina west of here."

"Then I'll go there."

"And I'll take you. Meet me on that side."

CHAPTER 14

SATURDAY NIGHT

Vieux-Port de Cannes, Cannes

ohn peered over Luca's shoulder as they sped down the Boulevard du Midi Louise Moreau, the sea on their left glistening like gold under the full moon. He had no idea how fast they were going, but the breezy night felt like a windstorm, causing his eyes to water. Back at the hotel, Luca had pulled up on a motorcycle and told him to get on. He should have added "hold on," but John figured that out soon enough.

"One more gear, and we'd be flying," said John.

Luca took his left hand off the handlebar, then pointed toward the sea. John saw Marcel's yacht moored just off the marina, sitting by itself in the calm water, parallel to the shoreline.

He tapped Luca's side, then said, "Pull up by that beach. I have an idea."

Luca did, and John dismounted. "Remember that German freighter in Marseille?" John said as he took off his jacket. "The one we sabotaged."

Luca nodded. "Same approach?"

"Same approach."

He stripped down to his military-green boxers, handing Luca each article of clothing as it came off.

"I'll watch from here," said Luca, hanging each item over his forearm. He patted John's clothes, then searched for something. He came out with a cigar.

"You mind?"

"Not at all."

"I see something, I'll rev the engine, okay?"

"Okay. I don't know when I'll be back."

"Not a problem," said Luca. "Beautiful night, nice cigar. I'll be here."

With that, John walked down the beach and entered the water.

John swam straight out, then stopped and looked around. Marcel's yacht was not too far down the beach. It was a bright, cloudless night, and the water was as still as glass, conditions he despised. Moonlight made it hard to hide your movements, and still water meant no ripples or peaks to camouflage his approach. John would have to make adjustments.

He swam toward the ship's bow, using slow, measured breast-strokes, being careful to keep his head from rising too far out of the water. He knew it would take him longer, but it generated less splash and allowed him to observe as he approached. He paused halfway to the ship and saw Marcel with drink in hand, talking with some crewmen on the aft deck. He was directing them to take a dinghy back to shore, then he entered the salon, the main cabin, and sat at a table.

John swam up to the anchor line, which reached from the front point of the bow down into the sea. He shook water from his hands, then got a firm grip on the thick chain. He pulled himself halfway out of the water, careful to move slowly, allowing the water to drip off his body. Using only his hands, he continued up the chain a link at a time. At the top, he pulled himself up enough to see Marcel in the salon, still sitting at the table. He lowered himself so he was hanging from the side, then pressed an ear against the hull and listened. No sounds from down below. As far as he could tell, no one else was on board.

He began moving down the ship's length. He was on the side facing the sea, shielded from folks on shore, and he needed to be near the stern. Nice and slow, a foot at a time.

He felt something stir in his chest. What was it? He thought for a moment, then realized: all those years of training as an acrobat had paid off in a way he never imagined back then.

After he approached the back of the ship, John froze.

In the distance, he heard Luca revving the engine of his motorcycle.

John pulled himself up enough to peer over the side of the yacht toward the shoreline. He saw the dinghy leaving the dock and heading in his direction. He spotted a ladder running from the deck to the waterline. That meant they'd board on his side, and they would see him in a few seconds.

He didn't have enough time to get back to the bow. John glanced at the salon to check on Marcel. The man had left his table and was heading toward the stern, the back of the yacht. John had to move. He swung one leg up and onto the deck, then flipped himself up. He army-crawled toward the bow, away from Marcel and the advancing dinghy. John spotted another ladder, took it up a level, then moved into place directly over where Marcel had been sitting. He could lean forward and see both Marcel on the yacht and the dinghy cutting through the water with the crewman seated in the back.

And seated in front was Hugo Rousseau.

John lay on his stomach as Hugo climbed the ladder and joined Marcel on the yacht. Marcel and Hugo then moved inside and sat at the table. From his position, John could hear every word, and if he leaned over, he could see the two men. The crewman in the dinghy had circled the yacht, then headed back to the dock.

Hugo spoke first. "Heading to sea, are we?"

"No such fun," said Marcel, who handed a drink to Hugo. "I just enjoy being away from land. It's very private; we can talk."

"I won't be long, but first, here's to a very successful start. You must be thrilled." Hugo raised his glass in a toast.

"I am. We'll show very well this week. I see success on several fronts."

John watched the two men. Both were relaxed as they sipped their drinks. Then Hugo said, "On the other matter, I believe you owe me quite a bit of money."

"Yes, you are right. You'll have it soon, the next day or two."

"I thought tonight."

"So did I, but we had a minor setback."

John was watching intently, and something about Marcel struck him as odd. He wasn't acting like a man who owed a lot of money to Hugo. He seemed too comfortable.

"What kind of setback?" asked Hugo.

"Our man with the money ran into a problem. We believe someone threw him from the roof of the Hotel Carlton."

A jolt ran through John. He'd been right; Marcel was involved. He shifted closer to the edge.

"And I presume the money went missing."

"It did," said Marcel. "Our man got sloppy. Why else would he be up on a roof? He knew better. His family will pay for his mistakes, but those are the rules."

"And what are you doing about this?"

"We know who took it, and my men are getting it back right now. So, a day or so."

"And if there's another problem?"

"There won't be. But if we encounter a delay, they'll send the money again. Only a more experienced courier will make the delivery. It happened once before, and trust me, there won't be any problems with that man. He's...what's the word?"

"Efficient?"

"Ruthless," said Marcel. "That man gave me nightmares." He rose from the table. "Would you like another drink?"

Hugo rose, too. "I must be going. Thank you."

Marcel nodded, took one step onto the aft deck, then waved toward shore. John could see the crewman start up the dinghy. Marcel and Hugo stood side by side, looking back toward the shoreline.

"I'll see you Monday at the first fashion show," said Marcel. "We'll know more then."

"A word of advice," said Hugo. "Keep a good watch for the next few days. French Intelligence visited me, and they suspect something is in the air."

"What do they know?"

"That's the thing," said Hugo. "They have no idea what we're doing. Tell Moscow the French haven't a clue."

CHAPTER 15

SATURDAY NIGHT

John's Villa, Saint-Jeannet

John tousled his hair, then draped the towel over his shoulders. The night was catching up to him, and as tired as he was, he wouldn't sleep. Not yet. He finished getting dressed and walked into his den.

He poured himself a stout glass of cognac and sat on the hearth in front of the limestone fireplace. He took a sip, then combed his hair back over his head with his free hand.

So much had happened, and so quickly, he hadn't had a chance to think about it all.

The first setback he'd had was with Francie. She'd accused him of being selfish. Easy for her to say. She'd never had a real worry— not with parents, accountants, and lawyers guiding her. John, on the other hand, only had himself. There was no one he could reach out to, no safety net for him. Living like that caused John to focus on himself. How could it not? He began to nod, finding conviction in his thoughts. What Francie saw as selfishness was nothing more than self-reliance. Easy mistake to make. He'd speak to her again on Monday, assuming he could get into that fashion show. He'd find a way.

Then his mind shifted to Paul, his best friend. John took a big swallow, feeling the liquor scorch his throat. Paul had also called him selfish, and that gave John pause. First Coco, then Francie, and Paul had all accused him of being self-centered.

John thought about that. Coco was desperate, so what he said could be dismissed. But Paul's comments held up. He replayed the scene in his mind and understood Paul was similar to Francie. Born into money, he never had to worry about his survival. Yes, that made sense. It was becoming clear to John. With wealth, one can afford to be selfless. When all your needs are met, you focus on others. But if you're living day-to-day, as John had since a young age, you'd absolutely think about yourself.

That's what Paul and Francie had both missed. It's what they mistook for selfishness, and that context made all the difference. John was relieved. At the right time, he would explain to Paul, but not now. Paul was too angry, and to make that right, John would share what he'd learned. He'd gotten significant intelligence on the man who'd fallen from the roof. John knew the man was delivering money to Marcel, who was to pass it along to Hugo. Why, he didn't know—not yet. But he did know Moscow was involved. And Marcel was willing to kill for that money. More importantly, that man on the roof had been ready to die because of it.

Something big was in play, and the pieces were falling into place. He would stop by Paul's first thing in the morning.

He downed the remainder of his drink, then refilled his glass. He wandered over to the front door and stepped outside, feeling the cool night breeze wash over him, neutralizing the warmth of the cognac. The gentle wind held hints of lavender and rosemary, a sweet scent that always seemed to hang in the night air. And it always calmed him.

John took a deep breath, drank more, and leaned back against the stone wall of his home. He'd avoided thinking about it all night, but what Odette said shook him. He'd prided himself on his core beliefs, specifically that his thefts were "victimless crimes." He'd assumed insurance companies covered the financial loss of stolen jewelry. He'd never considered the emotional loss. But it was real. It stayed with Odette for all those years. To her credit, she was compassionate. She'd even found a lesson in it for him—if you justify your actions with false rationale, you'll miss the truth.

John took another big swig and massaged his forehead, staring at the gravel between his feet.

What were his other flawed principles?

What else was he not seeing?

CHAPTER 16

epic swatted at a gnat hovering just under his nose, then shook his head. The dark of night was for insects and crooks, not civilized people.

The criminal John Robie was a great example. Did all his thieving at night, the cover of darkness being his unseen conspirator. *And now he leads a life of luxury.* Lepic bit his lower lip as he shook his head. There was no fairness in the system. But justice, that was another story. Justice would find John Robie soon enough, and he would never see it coming.

A noise. Lepic held his breath, then pushed aside the bushes in front of his face. Hard to see anything at this hour, so he listened closely. The front door opened, and out stepped a man.

The man leaned against the wall next to the door, took a big swig of a drink, then hung his head. He'd had a rough night. Lepic shifted a bit to get a better look.

It was him.

Lepic stepped forward from the bushes. The man was startled but didn't move. Defiant, this one. He walked straight at him.

"They call you Coco, do they not?"

Lepic saw recognition on the man's face as he turned away from the inspector. "Stop!" he shouted. "Don't ever turn your back to me."

Coco stopped, spit liquor to the ground, then faced Lepic.

"You know who I am?" Lepic asked.

Coco nodded.

"Then you know I can ruin your life on a whim, right?"

Coco nodded again. Lepic stepped right up to the man.

"I can also change your life for the better. I'll bet you didn't know that."

That got Coco's attention. His grizzled sneer softened, and he gave the slightest nod. "Go ahead. I'm listening."

"I saw you the other night at the hotel. You had words with John Robie."

Coco shook his head, denying any conflict, and started to say something.

Lepic cut him off. "Don't lie to me; I saw you. You were at odds." He loosened up, taking a few relaxed steps to the side as he emphasized his words with hand gestures. "I, too, have a problem with him."

He moved in a half circle around Coco. "My friend, you have a big problem." He wagged a finger in Coco's face. "Yes, I know about it. You are in serious trouble with a gangster. Gambling debt, I believe."

He paused in front of Coco, offering his best benevolent smile. "All of this got me thinking. I will make your trouble disappear if you help me with my John Robie problem."

Coco was listening. He hadn't dismissed Lepic, so he continued. "As an inspector, I have many cards to play. Everyone owes me, even your gangster friend. You understand?"

Coco nodded.

Lepic reached into his pocket and pulled out a small brown bag. He handed it to Coco. "Okay," said Lepic. "Here's where we begin..."

CHAPTER 17

SATURDAY NIGHT

Hôtel Belle Rives, Antibes

Francie sat on the beach blanket, her back to the hotel. She warmed her hands by the campfire, its flames lapping the cool night air like a thirsty dog.

She looked out over the sea as a private smile graced her face. She had done it. Her introduction to the fashion industry, press included, was fabulous. Francie closed her eyes and replayed the highlights of the evening. She'd been calm and confident, even with John Robie there. Another reason to be proud. She'd dealt with him head-on.

But something was bothering her. She couldn't put her finger on it, but something was off.

Francie heard something behind her. She turned to see Alex walking toward her, carrying an open bottle of champagne and two elegant glasses. He sat next to her.

She gave him a playful backhand to the shoulder. "I thought you went back for a sweater."

"Celebrating you is more important." He poured her a glass, then one for himself.

"Congratulations, Francie. You were superb. All eyes were on you, and you were magnificent. All those designers, models, and you stood out, so poised and full of fun. Even with your ex there."

"He did add to my nerves." She waved away the thought, then kissed Alex on the cheek. "This is so thoughtful of you. I must say, they raise boys right in...where were you born?"

"A small town in the Carolinas," he said. "The Deep South. Born and raised."

"Southern manners and Southern charm."

"The manners, for sure. Don't know about the charm, but I was raised to be respectful."

"And thoughtful," said Francie. She paused, then asked, "What was it like growing up there?"

He put an arm around her, and she leaned into him. "It was wonderful in a lot of ways," he said. "The people, the country, and the values made it a great place to grow up. But I haven't been back there in years."

"Why is that?"

"My family had a big piece of land," he said. "The kind that takes generations to acquire but only one generation to lose." Alex looked down. "It left a bad taste in my mouth. I'm in no rush to return to the States."

Francie hooked her arm through his. "I'm sorry to hear that."

"It was fine for me. I'd always had ambitions beyond that town. I wanted to see the world, meet interesting people." He kissed her on the side of her head. "I couldn't be happier."

Francie was quiet, then said, "I'm in no hurry to go back, either, but for different reasons."

"What might they be?"

"I never fit in. Old wealth thinks I'm a hillbilly, and the new-wealth folks are so ostentatious, so showy, which is much worse. On top of that, everyone wants your money—the government for sure, but even old friends and new acquaintances. Hands are always out. It doesn't matter how charitable you are or whether or not you believe in their cause. They want more. It's how they see the world, and it's reflected in every discussion, every action."

Like John Robie, Francie thought. Was John's view of the world and himself simply a reflection of his circumstances? If that were the case, had she handled it the right way?

She hadn't, and that was it. That was bothering her. She'd been too confrontational with him. Yes, he needed to hear what she'd said. He'd earned that. But there was no need to embarrass him so publicly.

Francie caught herself. Why was she so concerned about John? He wouldn't return the favor. He'd think only of himself. Perhaps she should use John's standards with him. She took a sip, then a deep breath. No, she told herself. She'd be considerate to everyone, even John. If she saw him again, and that was a big *if*, she'd be less aggressive. She would hold firm, but she'd be more understanding.

Alex took the empty glass from Francie. "Big day tomorrow. You need to rest," he said. "I'll walk you to your room."

Francie kept her eyes on the sea. "Just a minute, dear. I want to remember this."

CHAPTER 18

SUNDAY MORNING

Paul's Estate, Saint-Tropez

John looked out the window and saw Paul's stables and a procession of muscled horses being led out of the barn. He sighed. The hard part was behind him. Paul had been angry, but he heard John out, which meant he was calming down. He crossed his arms, as solemn as a churchgoer. All John had to do was show a little contrition, then he could transition to what he wanted.

"You were right," said John. "I misled you, and I apologize."

Paul came around from behind his desk. "All you had to do was ask. I would have gotten you in."

"That's very noble of you," said John. "No pun intended. You're a great friend."

"I was counting on your support, but you were there for her, not me."

"I was there for her, but what I learned helps you."

Paul stopped. "What do you mean?"

John began to speak when the door to the study opened. In strode a short, well-dressed man with thick glasses and a balding head. He was carrying a stack of papers in one hand, a cup of coffee in the other.

"This is Armand, my associate. He's helping me," said Paul. "And this is John Robie."

At the mention of John's name, Armand stepped back. He looked him up and down. "Seriously, you are John Robie? The infamous cat burglar John Robie?"

"That was me. A long time ago."

Armand put down his coffee and vigorously shook his hand. "It's a great pleasure. Paul speaks of his friend 'John,' but I had no idea."

Paul motioned toward a chair. "Have a seat. John has something to tell us."

"That's what happened, and that's what I heard." John thought for a minute. He'd covered everything, except for the money he'd taken. No need to bring that up. Not now.

"You're sure it was Hugo?" asked Paul.

"Absolutely."

"And it wasn't blackmailing?" asked Armand.

"There was no threat, no intimidation. Both Marcel and Hugo acted like partners."

"This is great. Thank you," said Paul. He then turned to Armand. "What are they up to?"

"Something serious. What it is, we don't know."

"And who else is involved?" asked Paul.

Armand shrugged his shoulders.

John chimed in. "One more thing. Marcel and Hugo will both

be at the fashion show Monday night. Marcel said, 'See you at the show.' Something like that."

Paul nodded, deep in thought.

John looked back and forth between Paul and Armand. "So, Monday night is the next time they'll be together. How can I help?"

Paul waved John off. "Best if you don't come. Marcel saw you and Francie at the party Saturday night. Everyone did. He'll assume you'll approach her again, and they'll be waiting after what happened in the alley. If you show up, you'll be their focus. We want them focused on anything but you. We want them relaxed to see who they associate with."

John was surprised. He'd planned on going Monday to try to see Francie again. If that were off the table, he'd have to visit her at the hotel, and she would avoid him. *No,* John thought, *I have to go on Monday.* An idea came to him.

"You want Marcel and Hugo relaxed," said John. "If their guard is down, you'll learn a lot. But if they're concerned, you'll learn even more. And I can make them very concerned."

Paul thought about it, then said, "I don't know. The risk to you—"

Armand interrupted, holding up an index finger. "What did you have in mind?"

"I'll drop some comments based on what I heard. Remember, Marcel and Hugo thought they were alone."

"And?" asked Armand.

"And when they realize I overheard them, they'll be very concerned. That might drive them to warn an associate. And you two follow them, see who they go to." He paused; both men were listening. "But it has to come from me."

"What you overheard," said Armand, "it was vague enough to deny."

"It was," said John, "but I can throw in a threat or a demand. Something to add pressure."

Armand thought for a moment. "It might work—but it is a clear provocation."

John nodded his agreement. "There is risk, but remember, Marcel had men attack me because he thinks I threw his man off the roof." There was still no need to mention the cash; besides, a partial truth never hurt anyone. "I know men like him, and he'll come for me again, whether I'm at the show or not. This way, I'm in control." The plan, and his belief in it, made sense. "I'm going to take action, one way or another. This way helps you, too."

For a long moment, Paul said nothing. "We don't have much to go on," he said, then turned to John. "If we say no, you're still going to do something?"

"I am."

John could see Paul struggling with the dilemma. He didn't want to put John at risk, yet he also needed more information.

Armand spoke up. "He's right. Scatter the rats. They run to their nest."

"Okay," said Paul. "But if anything goes wrong, we step in right away. That's not negotiable. And, John, you need to think this through. If you provoke them, this is only the beginning."

"I know," said John. "But I have to end this, and my best chance is for you to arrest them. Maybe this leads you to something."

"Let's hope so," said Paul. "We'll meet before the show and go over everything."

John shook hands, then headed out. It was a good plan. But

Armand had been right. What John knew would startle the men, but it was vague enough to be explained away. Both Marcel and Hugo were too seasoned, too intelligent. He needed more.

John smiled. With what he'd seen at the golf club, he knew where to start.

CHAPTER 19

John knelt on the floor of his wine cellar, grabbed a bottle rack, and slid it away from the wall. He then grabbed a flat-head screwdriver.

The stones lining the walls of his cellar were large, easily two feet across and two feet high, and also deep. John wedged the screwdriver into a space between two stones, then began working the tool. Gradually, one stone began to separate from the wall; it was only a half-inch deep, unlike the others. John removed the stone and placed it face down on a blanket near his feet. Scuff marks on the front would be an easy clue for someone, and there was no need to make it easy.

He needed more information on Hugo and possibly Marcel, and he wasn't going to be careless about getting it. He reached into the wall and pulled out a long crate. John opened it and saw the contents as he had left them.

Knives and handguns were lying on top. He moved them aside.

TO CATCH A SPY

He disliked guns of any kind, but knew they were sometimes necessary in his world. He then set aside several thick stacks of cash, a couple of passports, a small bag of loose diamonds, and his father's wedding ring, John's only keepsake. Below that were several canvas sacks.

John removed the first sack, then reached inside. He pulled out a pair of dark-gray flannel pants and a black long-sleeved shirt. At the bottom of the bag were two pairs of crepe-soled shoes, thin gloves, and leg straps with various holding compartments. These were his burglar clothes. He'd always preferred gray and black, as they blended with shadows. The shoes were silent, the gloves left no fingerprints, and the leg straps held lockpicks, a thin roll of tape, a compact glass cutter, and even a small suction cup.

He looked into the other sacks in the crate. One held different police uniforms, another contained various trade coveralls, and a third one had different hotel uniforms—valet jackets, concierge caps, and well-creased pants. John wanted that one. He took some items, repacked the crate, then put it back into the wall.

He paused. Why had he kept these clothes, these tools? He told everyone those days were behind him, so why hadn't he tossed it all? Had he known he'd use them again? He considered that, then dismissed the thought. Everything was easily replaced, so not that; it was something more profound. He thought for a moment, remembering when he'd worn the clothes and used the tools. He'd been excited and alive and very much in control of his life.

And that was it. To him, these items were a symbol of a significant accomplishment. He'd had a sense of pride for what he'd done, but he kept that to himself. Was it wrong to think of thefts as accomplishments? John suspected it was, but he couldn't deny his feelings.

He looked at his watch. He was running late. John put the stone back in place and then moved the wine rack against the wall.

Time to get to work.

CHAPTER 20

John casually strolled down the street and looked out over the sea, two blocks away. The sun had an hour or more until it set, and it was in no hurry. There were a few stragglers on the beach, the breeze was warm, and traffic was moving slowly. There was a touch of laziness in the air, and it felt suitable for this time of day.

The hotel was up ahead. Just in front, John saw a man in a twill jumpsuit and matching cap painting the post of a streetlight. John kept a leisurely pace, periodically switching the bag he held from hand to hand.

As he approached the painter, the man turned, looked around, then faced John's direction.

"He left his room," said Luca, pulling down the brim of his cap. "312, just like you said. His assistant is right next door, so be careful."

"Where did he go?"

Luca continued with his painting, seemingly paying John no attention. "Out to dinner, I think. He was wearing casual clothes. A man picked him up. Then they drove away."

"Thanks, Luca. You're a good friend."

"And a good painter. Look at this pole. Hey, you still need me?"

"Fifteen more minutes, in case he comes back," said John. "If he does, hold him off if you can."

John headed into the hotel lobby. He strode over to the elevator, then took it up to the fourth floor. He walked down the hallway, found a storage closet, and stepped inside. He opened his bag and took out a concierge jacket and hat, the same color worn by the hotel staff.

He donned the outfit and removed a set of lockpick tools from his bag. John selected a tool for each hand, then grabbed a big armful of towels and swung them up onto his shoulder, positioning the towels to hide his face, just in case he passed anyone. He went to the stairs and headed down. He exited the stairwell on the third floor and made his way to room 312—Hugo's room.

He noticed the trim on the doorframes, the slight scent of disinfectant, and the patterns in the carpet. All his senses were magnified. When that happened, John felt nothing could go wrong.

He placed the towels on the ground, then moved fast. He inserted the two lockpick tools—a tension wrench and a rake pick—into the door, and in less than ten seconds, he had it open.

He slipped inside, ensured the room was empty, and immediately scouted out an emergency exit—the balcony—and a hiding place—under the bed. He opened the door to the balcony and looked outside. Nothing in his way if he had to escape.

John reentered the room but kept the balcony door ajar. Across the room was a small desk with stacks of files on the left and right. He scanned through the documents, finding economic reports labeled *"Classé Secrete,"* one on shipping, and one newspaper article on French airports. Other than the airport article, every document had a cover page denoting the issuing committee in the French Parliament. He stood over the reports, thinking. There were no common themes here and nothing on Russia. Then he checked the desk drawer. Nothing there.

John froze. He heard people talking in the hallway, and they were getting closer. He moved next to the bed, just in case. Their voices carried right up to, then past, his door. A few seconds later, he heard someone fumbling with a key down the hall. A door opened and closed, then the voices stopped.

Back to work.

Next to the desk was a briefcase. John placed it on top of the desk and looked inside. Just newspapers and periodicals, some domestic train tickets, and a well-worn novel by Camara Laye. But nothing concerning Russia or French Intelligence.

Just then, he heard something at the door. A key chain jangling. He moved fast. He closed the briefcase, took one quick step away from the desk, dropped to the floor, and hid under the bed.

The door opened, and in walked a hotel maid. In her arms were the towels John had left by the door. The maid glanced around, straightened the bedsheets, then headed into the bathroom. He turned his head to follow her feet, and next to him, under the bed, was another briefcase.

This one had a lock.

The maid left the bathroom, looked around, and then left the room, gently closing the door behind her. John waited a beat, then got to his feet, briefcase in hand. He laid it on the bed. It had a Yale lock. He was relieved; his lockpick tools would work.

John unlocked the briefcase. Inside were two reports, one an overview of the political situations in the French territories and the other an in-depth analysis of the Suez Canal. Both looked very different from the reports on Hugo's desk. No government committee cover pages, no attributions at the beginning or the end, and a much lower paper grade. He flipped through the reports, both densely written. Neither contained bookmarks, dog-eared pages, or handwritten notes.

John put them back into the briefcase, locked it, and replaced it under the bed.

Hugo was hiding these reports, so they were critical to him. Exactly how, John didn't know. But between what he'd overheard on the boat and what he'd just seen, he certainly had enough to get Hugo's attention.

CHAPTER 21

John peered through the window of a tiny café, which looked smaller than some closets. Paul and Armand were sitting at a round table the size of a dinner plate. They saw John and waved him in.

John hurried through the door. He was excited; today he would help Paul and then speak with Francie, reversing the order from the other night. That way, Paul couldn't criticize him, and he'd explain himself to Francie, which was the key first step to getting her back on board.

He grabbed a cup of coffee, American-style, and joined them. An assortment of *cannelés*—turret-shaped pastries the size of shot glasses and flavored with vanilla or rum—covered the small table. An army of crumbs surrounded Armand. They were every-where—on the table, on Armand's pants, on his fingers, even on his coffee cup.

"Move fast if you want one," said Paul. "They won't last long."

John helped himself, then huddled in close. "As I said on the phone, I have news."

Paul gestured, giving him the floor.

"To provoke them into action, I needed more information about Hugo and Marcel. More than what I heard on the boat."

Armand, his mouth full, mumbled something along the lines of "I told you that."

John handed Armand a napkin, then continued. "So I got more information."

Paul started to speak. John held up a finger, asking him to wait. "Hugo keeps a secret briefcase in his hotel room. Hidden and locked. Different reports are inside that briefcase."

"What type of reports?" asked Armand.

"One had to do with the French territories."

"Makes sense," said Armand. "Hugo's committee oversees them."

John nodded. "That's true. But on his desk, just lying there, he had other reports, some about the territories. All those reports were labeled 'classified,' and all were official documents of the French government. But this report, the one hidden away, wasn't. It was anonymous. Impossible to know who issued it. And it had to do with the politics of each country. Which parties were in power and which were in opposition. It listed indigenous groups for and against France and had lists of local professors, journalists, and radio personalities."

"Interesting," said Armand.

"Yes," said John. "Very interesting."

"And what about the other report?"

"That report focused on the Suez Canal as a trade route for France."

TO CATCH A SPY

Armand pulled back. "Everything runs through the canal."

John nodded. "That was the gist of the report."

His hands folded on the table, Paul asked, "How did you come upon this information?"

He gave Paul a firm stare. "How do you think?"

"So we're back to thieving, are we?" Paul shook his head, disappointed. "I knew this was a bad idea."

"Listen to me. These men threatened my life. And I have a chance to help you stop them and do it the right way—by bringing you the intelligence you can't otherwise get." John was simmering, but he kept going. "Tell me, how do you think your spies get information? Do you think they look it up in a library? Not a chance. They do what I did. And just so you know, I took nothing. So no, I'm not back to thieving."

Paul's face turned red. He lowered his eyes, then said, "I hear you, and I apologize."

After an awkward moment, John said, "Accepted. And one more thing. This will never roll back on you. I'm very good at what I do."

Armand rocked in his seat with a broad smile. "This, I never imagined. Working with John Robie," he gushed. "We are like partners."

John clasped Armand's forearm, grateful for the support. "We are partners, and we'll stick to the plan. It's going to work. You'll see."

Paul and Armand got up. "We'll head over first," said Paul. "No offense, but people can't see us with you."

John watched the two men leave the café. He waited a while, drinking his coffee and eating the last *cannelé*. After several minutes, he checked the clock on the wall.

It was time.

CHAPTER 22

To Francie, the layout for the show was very clever. The audience and the runway were on the boardwalk, and the models' staging area was on the beach. Each designer had a large tent to house the models, stylists, and designers. Francie grinned. The tents, and the walkways between them, were buzzing with excitement.

She looked up at the boardwalk. A steel drum band was playing, their soft, catchy melodies adding a rhythmic bounce to the ambience, and a land breeze carried the familiar scent of sun-seared boardwalk planks. The VIP chairs on each side of the boardwalk were filling up, and the press was everywhere.

Francie bit her lip. There had been press at the cocktail party, but not like this. If she was going to distinguish herself, she had to be careful. Whatever she did, good or bad, would end up in every newspaper in Europe.

Marcel walked up behind her and placed his hand on the small of her back. He said, "Francie, I must show you something."

"Before I forget, more measurements from Karl." Francie handed him the envelope.

"Thank you. This way, please. You must see." He led her over to the tent opening, then pointed outside. "You start here on the beach. Then you walk up these steps to the boardwalk. You must walk twenty-five meters down the boardwalk before the runway starts."

"Okay..."

"I tell you this because of the stairs. Models rarely use stairs. Too risky. You slip, you trip, and everyone sees. The press remembers the stumble, not the fashion. Or worse, they blame the clothes. So stay close to the handrail, and grab if you must."

"Good to know," said Francie.

"And when you reach the boardwalk, be careful of your heels. They get stuck in the cracks between boards. When you walk, always step in the center of each board. Stay away from the cracks. Once you reach the runway, no more problems."

"Got it."

"Keep it simple," said Marcel. "No deviations today."

Just then, Francie's mother appeared, with Alex and Odette Julien in tow. "Francie, darling. Would you care for one of these champagne cocktails?" She turned to Alex. "What's it called again?"

"Mimosa."

"That's it. Mimosa. Invented by that British director, the one with all those thrillers. They say he made the first one right here at the Riviera."

"Cheers to that," said Alex as he clinked Maude's glass.

"Aren't those brunch drinks?" asked Odette.

Maude laughed. "We got a late start."

"They look delightful," said Francie. "I would love one. After the show, though."

"Always sensible," said her mother. "Better you than me." She downed the last of her drink, then stared at her glass. "I must have spilled some on the way over."

"Would you like another?" asked Alex.

Maude beamed. "I would."

He glanced around, then spotted a beach bar near the tents. "Be right back."

"Make that two," called Maude.

Up on the boardwalk, Francie spotted a commotion. In unison, the crowd went silent, and the steel drum band began playing a familiar song. Francie listened for a moment. It was "Hymne Monégasque," the national anthem of Monaco, played island-style. She saw the Prince of Monaco enter, leading a sizable entourage.

Odette smiled. "What a surprise."

The prince took a seat at the far end of the runway. He settled in as photographers circled him, catching his every move.

Just what I need, thought Francie. *More pressure.*

Alex appeared, then handed the first mimosa to Maude. "If more spills, we have a backup." He raised his hand with the second drink.

Maude downed the first in two gulps, then took the second one from Alex. With her eyes on the prince, she said, "I think I'll take my seat."

Francie saw Christian Dior's model step out of a tent. She was first up, and her outfit looked fantastic. The model had a tiny waist, like all Dior's models. Francie was curious how he'd design

Capri pants with his signature flair from the waist down, and now she knew. The pants had wider openings like a bell at the bottom of each leg. She looked around again. The excitement was palpable. To the side, she saw another designer, Coco Chanel, peek out from a tent, gauging the start time.

"I've got to get ready," said Francie.

She kissed Alex on the cheek, then headed to her tent. On the way, she spotted John's friend, Paul Du Pre, up on the boardwalk, walking with another man. Francie squinted. She couldn't see who the other man was. Then the crowd shifted a bit, creating a small opening.

It wasn't John.

For the best, she thought. John would distract her, and she needed to focus on what she had planned.

CHAPTER 23

The woman found John's name on the registered guest list, handed him a program, then signaled the security guard. The guard opened the rope line and let him in.

He moved through the crowd, taking his time. Across the way were Paul and Armand, deep into what appeared to be a casual conversation. John knew better. He saw celebrities, art patrons, and politicians brimming with anticipation.

Off to the side, he saw Hugo standing with a few men, all of them looking monied and polished. John grabbed a drink off a passing tray, then headed over.

He came up behind Hugo. "We meet again."

Hugo turned, a look of surprise on his face. "I didn't expect to see you here."

"See me here, or see me at all?"

John watched Hugo's eyes slowly sweep around, then settle on John. Hugo took two steps back and away from the other men. "That's an odd thing to say."

"Not after the weekend I've had," said John. "Your friend down there doesn't like me. I thought he might have said something."

"You mean Marcel? He's a friend. We talk. Never about you, though."

"My mistake." He waited a moment, then asked, "What do you talk about?"

Hugo laughed without smiling, then said, "None of your business."

"We disagree. It is my business."

"What is?"

"Your missing money."

Hugo feigned confusion. He looked down onto the beach, then said, "I'm not sure I follow."

"The Hotel Carlton," said John. "The man who fell from the roof... Marcel thinks I have that man's missing money."

"I read about it in the papers," said Hugo. "A hotel, missing money." He turned up his palms, then shrugged his shoulders. "A famous thief like you..."

John waited a moment, then said, "It was in the papers, but they never mentioned the money."

The back-and-forth stopped. He watched Hugo bow his head as he thought about what to say next.

"I'm humoring you," said Hugo. "Just playing along. And, no, Marcel never mentioned any of this." He turned away. "We're done talking."

It was John's turn to feign confusion. "Marcel never mentioned it? Not at the cocktail party, not on the dock? Not even on his yacht when the two of you were sitting in the cabin?"

Hugo's face flashed anger. He shot a look at John, then turned away. "I've had enough. I don't know what you're up to..."

"Too bad," said John, "because I know what you're up to."

Hugo shook his head. "You have no idea."

"But I do. Unlike the French, I have a clue."

Hugo stood still as he tried to recall that phrase. Then it came to him. John saw the hubris drain from Hugo's face. The man took a step back, genuinely confused.

John took a chance. He didn't know what the files in Hugo's room meant, but he didn't have to know. He leaned forward, then whispered, "Will it be the territories? Or the Suez Canal?"

Hugo stood there, his eyes shooting left and right. John could see he was shaken.

"Harder without the money," said John. "Wouldn't you agree?"

"Enough!"

He stepped back, giving Hugo space. "You look like you've seen a ghost."

Hugo glared at him. "A dead man, not a ghost."

With that, Hugo peeled away and headed for Marcel's tent. John looked across the boardwalk and saw Armand moving, getting in position to follow. After a minute, Hugo stormed out of Marcel's tent. Armand trailed him from a safe distance.

One down.

One to go.

CHAPTER 24

rancie's heartbeat jumped. She was up next, the last model in the show.

She took a final look in the mirror. Her Capri pants were higher-waisted than those of the other designers, accentuating her shape. Francie pinched the pants all around her waist and upper thighs, and there was no gap. She smiled. Karl's measurements had been perfect.

She put her hands on her hips, then turned to see her side view. Her bright-white pants had pink piping down each side, and her tanned arms complemented her pink cap-sleeved blouse. The silver and diamond jewelry added elegance to the otherwise casual outfit. And her white, silver-trimmed sandals, with more heel than she liked, tied it all together.

Outside the tent, Francie saw Marcel on the boardwalk, addressing the crowd and sharing his vision of Riviera Casual, clothing fit for "sea, sand, and land."

Now was the time. Francie took off her shoes, and with a wet towel, she patted her exposed lower legs. She stepped outside the tent, grabbed some sand, and pressed it onto the wet spots on her legs.

Marcel called her name, and Francie sauntered up the stairs, her sandals dangling from her hand. As she reached the boardwalk, there was a quiet hum of curiosity from the crowd. Francie paused, then looked down at her legs. She started to brush off the sand, then, with a playful smile, she waved the task aside. Francie didn't care, and neither should the audience.

She made her way down the boardwalk with an energetic and effervescent pace, stopping and spinning every few steps. She followed the technical instruction provided—elbows out, hands on waist, hip cocked, knee bent—to focus attention on the fashion. From the eyes of the crowd, she knew it was working.

At the far end of the runway sat the Prince of Monaco. As she got closer to him, Francie, eyebrows raised, gave him a sultry smile. The crowd oohed, an odd sound pairing an appreciation of her playfulness with an unspoken warning: Do not proceed.

Francie pranced toward the seated prince, barely able to contain her smile. She stopped before him, twirled around, pretended to lose her balance, then dropped onto his lap. She threw an arm around his shoulders, then kicked up her feet. There was a pause as the audience held their breath, then the prince roared with laughter. He played right along, brushing sand off Francie's leg, then whispered in her ear. Francie sat up straight, turned to the crowd, and then put a hand over her mouth. The audience erupted.

Photographers circled Francie and the prince, and the two continued their charade long enough for pictures. Francie whispered, "I hope you didn't mind."

The prince beamed. "The most fun all summer," he said as they both got up and stood side by side. The prince motioned for Francie to take a bow.

Reporters rushed toward them. Members of the prince's entourage stepped in, holding the press at bay and directing the prince off the boardwalk. Before he left, he looked back at Francie, smiled, then gave her a slow, suggestive wink. The photographers caught the moment as the crowd cheered.

Francie nodded her gratitude to the prince and mouthed "thank you." Reporters moved in and began firing questions. Behind the press, Francie saw Odette Julien, shaking her head in joyful amazement. She blew Francie a kiss.

And toward the back, moving through the crowd, was John Robie.

CHAPTER 25

John saw an opening in the flow of people. He slid in, moved with the crowd, and stepped out next to Marcel Julien.

Marcel was startled but didn't look over. "Well, well," he said in his deep, timbered voice. "Look who it is. John Robie, legendary cat burglar and now eavesdropper."

"You spoke with Hugo."

"I did," said Marcel, keeping his eyes forward. "How did you hear us, by the way?"

John dismissed his question. "Another time, perhaps. How are your men, the ones from the other night?"

"Coming around. Had you given them what they wanted—"

"What they wanted was some missing money. And me dead."

Marcel glanced at John, then went back to looking forward. "No theatrics. Not here."

"We're just having a conversation," said John. "About you trying to have me killed."

"Keep your voice down." Marcel looked around, calmed himself, then said, "You could end this now. Just give it back."

"It's not that easy."

"Why is that?"

John turned up his hands. "You're not one to forgive and forget. That's not your style. People need to pay. Like me, for instance, and that man on the hotel's roof. He knew what was coming."

Marcel folded his hands together. "You do have it."

"The money? I never said that."

"You didn't have to." Marcel glanced at his watch. "Before you become tiresome, tell me what you want."

"Who says I want anything?"

Marcel turned to face him. "This is interesting. You spoke with Hugo, and you didn't ask for a thing. Not the money, not a finder's fee, not even a favor. Nothing. And here you are, doing it again."

"So what."

Marcel smirked. "So there's another reason for your visit. There must be." He looked, rubbing his chin. "You're not here to negotiate. So why are you here?"

"To discuss the other night. Accusations, assaults, fighting in alleys—we can't have that."

"No, that's not it. You come, you want nothing, yet you play these insinuation games with Hugo, then me." Marcel closed his eyes for a moment, then shook his head. "Ahh, yes. I know why you're here."

"Do tell."

"You are here to incite panic. You hope to enrage us, to send us scurrying. You want to see where we go, to whom we turn. And that is very informative."

"That's not it, but tell me, how is it informative?"

Marcel smoothed the front of his tuxedo, then straightened his lapels. "It tells me you don't know anything, despite your little performance with Hugo. But, if you can identify others—our co-conspirators, if you will—they might lead you to something."

"Not true," said John. He caught his breath, then tried to calm himself. Marcel was taking control, and John hadn't anticipated this.

"Wait," said Marcel. "There's more to your plan." He wagged a finger in John's face. "You frighten Hugo, and he runs off. Why? To follow him, see where he goes. Then you approach me, hoping to do the same. That begs the question—who is following Hugo? Not you. You're right here. We both know what that means. You are working with someone else. At least two others, I think. One to follow Hugo, one to follow me."

John shook his head. "I work alone. Always have. You're speculating."

"I'm not, and I'm not panicking, either. I'm curious, though. Who followed Hugo? One of your criminal friends? No, they wouldn't fit in here. Who, then?" Marcel looked over the crowd. "Whoever it was, he's gone. Following Hugo, of course."

"About the other night," said John. "Surely—"

Marcel cut him off. "And who was to follow me? I haven't run off, so that person is still here."

Over Marcel's shoulder, John saw the figure of a woman approaching. She walked around Marcel, then stopped abruptly. It was Francie, with a look of surprise and concern. He started to speak to her, then stopped. Francie backed off, still very confused, then walked away.

Marcel turned just in time to see Francie disappear into the

TO CATCH A SPY

crowd. "Ahhh, Miss Stevens. I'd almost forgotten about the two of you." He was quiet for a moment, thinking. Then he said, "You've taken a lot from us. It's time we took from you."

John stood there, silent. What was Marcel saying? What did he mean?

As calm as the evening weather, Marcel said, "Thank you. I've learned quite a bit." He excused himself and walked toward his chauffeur, the dark, brooding man from the other night. Marcel whispered in the chauffeur's ear, then led the man away.

John made eye contact with Paul, who was ready to follow Marcel. John shook his head, warning Paul off. *Don't bother.*

John was sweating. He patted his forehead, unsure of what had happened.

Unsure of what he'd just done.

He stepped away from the crowd, then tugged on his collar. His mind was darting; he had to settle down.

He went to the rail, then looked out over the beach. John shook his head. That hadn't gone according to plan. He knew his approach was risky and that Marcel would eventually counter—he would send men after John, maybe try to ambush him. Some sort of low-level reprisal. Not now. After tonight, Marcel would come at him hard. The man hadn't been worried. He walked away confident, not defensive at all. He even taunted John, saying he'd learned quite a bit.

But what had John learned? For one, Marcel didn't deny anything. Quite the opposite. He treated it like a business conversation. That meant he didn't fear the law. Why should he? Marcel had protection—connections, resources, even dangerous men at his disposal.

He also learned Marcel was sharp, a quick thinker. He'd pieced John's plan together fast, even knowing an associate of John's was supposed to follow him. And worst of all, just as that realization crossed Marcel's mind, Francie appeared. He made a connection, then threatened to "take something" from John. Was he threatening Francie? Hard to say, but it didn't seem like a coincidence.

Assuming it was a threat against her, what would Marcel do? John considered a few possibilities. The easiest was for Marcel to turn Francie against John. A few comments and lies would be enough to eliminate his chance at reconciliation. And easy enough to do. Marcel would be around her all week.

But it was more than that. His tone implied something serious. What could that be? Would he physically hurt Francie? That was unlikely to happen—the newspapers were praising her; Marcel wouldn't hurt her. He was a businessman, and she was good for business.

John was stuck. If not a physical threat against Francie, or slanderous comments about John, then what? He had no idea, which meant he needed more information. And information, like jewels, was something he could get. He knew that Marcel, like Hugo, was sheltering secrets. That much was clear. But where? Lots of options with a man like Marcel Julien. It had to be private, where he believed secrets would be safe. The yacht was compromised, so not there. As far as John knew, Marcel didn't have a local office. That left Marcel's villa, which was probably very well protected.

To his surprise, Armand stepped out from the crowd.

John looked puzzled. "Aren't you..."

"...following him?" said Armand. "Yes, I did. After he left, Hugo went to his car, not his hotel room; I didn't expect that. He got in the back seat, and the driver took off. It happened fast; I couldn't follow him."

"Did he speak to anyone on the way out?"

"You saw him with Marcel. After that, a few words with Marcel's man, his chauffeur, I believe."

"He's more than a chauffeur," said John. "He's a thug, a killer. Marcel spoke to him, too, and I would expect that. But why would Hugo speak to him?" He turned to face Armand. "Looks like we have a connection. Not strong, but one to consider."

Armand agreed. He was pleased with himself.

John clapped him on the shoulder. "We did well; we're a good team. Listen, I have to speak with someone, but I wanted to ask a favor before I go. I'll be paying a visit tonight, and there's something I need."

CHAPTER 26

rancie couldn't wait to see Alex. She'd done well; it was clear from Odette's reaction. But Alex being in the audience had an added perspective, and she wanted his take.

She handed her Capri pants, blouse, jewelry, and shoes to one of Marcel's fashion designers. Then she inspected her outfit, tucking her blouse and checking her pants for glaring lines. Francie stepped outside the tent. She looked for Alex on the beach but didn't see him. She went to the boardwalk and ran into a squad of reporters at the bottom of the stairs. They rushed to her, lobbing questions from every direction. They cared about the prince, no one else. Was it planned? Did she know him? Will she see him again? What had he whispered? The press was relentless. They couldn't get enough.

Behind the mass of reporters, Francie saw John step out from behind a tent. She could tell with a glance that his demeanor was serious, even contrite. John stood to the side, waiting for her, and she acknowledged it with a half-raised finger. Just a minute.

Then she heard a deep voice call her name.

CHAPTER 27

John was eager to explain himself, and he'd rehearsed it several times. But he had another reason to talk with Francie. He needed to warn her about Marcel. Not too strongly; that might work against John's interests. Just a hint for Francie to keep her distance. Enough to show he wasn't self-centered.

He walked between the tents, moving at a cautious pace. To his side, John heard a commotion. He looked around a corner, and there was Francie, encircled by reporters.

Francie looked over and held John's glance for a second. He thought he saw her hold up a finger as if asking him to wait.

Then a low, timbered voice called her name. John knew that voice. He'd heard it just a few minutes ago.

Marcel Julien.

John slipped back between the tents and caught a glimpse of Marcel approaching Francie. *Damn*. He could have talked to her and warned her about Marcel if he'd come a few minutes earlier.

But that window had closed. Approaching her now would lead to a heated exchange with Marcel. Or worse.

John was angry with himself and with the situation. He looked out again and saw Alex approach and kiss Francie. The two of them held hands as Marcel appeared to be giving them directions. As Marcel spoke, John saw Francie look over. She made eye contact with him, and the look on her face was neutral, maybe even warm. John watched Marcel wrap up, then head back to his tent. Alex put his arm around Francie and led her away.

John slumped his shoulders, looked to the ground, then shook his head. What a disappointment. He'd gotten into the show, done exactly what he'd told Paul he would do, then missed out on his chance with Francie. It wasn't a total loss, however; his brief interactions with her were curious. He half expected Francie to shout accusations again. But she hadn't. Before Marcel showed up, she asked John to wait, then gave him a warm glance before she left. All good news. He'd prepared for confrontation, but their next chat would be civil. Maybe, just maybe, she would hear him out. That was all he needed. He just had to figure out when to approach her.

With that, he turned to leave.

Standing right behind him was Inspector Lepic.

CHAPTER 28

epic spotted the back of John Robie, who was watching someone but hiding from view. He slowed his approach.

He'd envisioned this moment, and he wanted to enjoy it. He'd gotten a haircut and even bought new clothes. He straightened his double-breasted jacket, adjusted the silk cravat around his neck, navy blue with white pinstripes, then glanced down at the sharp creases in his pants, as straight and aggressive as the blade of a sword.

He moved in behind John Robie just as he turned around.

"I knew I would find you here," said Lepic. "Looking for your next victim? Or stealing a glimpse of Miss Stevens changing her clothes?"

"Neither," said John. "And I don't appreciate the insinuation."

"A pecking order emerges. A thief looks down on a voyeur." He bobbled the thought around in his head. "It makes sense."

John moved to go around Lepic. "I don't like your tone," he said. "I'm leaving."

"No, you're not! I'm not done with you." He waited a moment, then said, "You're an arrogant man. You flaunt your stolen wealth while citizens like me pay the price for your crimes."

"What price have you paid? Unless you were referring to your demotion last summer."

Lepic pointed at John. "My demotion was due to your...your... insouciance."

"Not true. Had you been respected by your colleagues, even a little, it would never have happened." John waited, then said, "It wasn't the events of last summer that set you back. Not at all. Last summer brought out your arrogance, your unbridled ambition. And that is on you, Inspector. Not me."

Lepic fumed. As his anger rose, his lower lip quivered. "I can arrest you right now."

"And with a single phone call, I'll go free. And you'll look foolish, once again."

John tried to step around Lepic, but he cut him off. Over John's shoulder, Lepic spotted Coco, the other detestable crook, watching from up on the boardwalk. Lepic nodded subtly, more with his eyes than his head. The inspector saw it register with John, who looked in that direction just as Coco turned and walked away.

John gave Lepic a curious look. "With all due respect, I've had enough. I'm not going to defend myself every time I see you. Arrest me or leave me alone."

"I may have nothing on you," said Lepic, "but we both know fortunes can change." He snapped his fingers. "As quick as that."

John pushed his way past the inspector. "I'm going home."

Lepic watched him walk a few steps, then said, "Till we meet again, John Robie." Then to himself, he whispered, "Soon, very soon."

CHAPTER 29

John sat at his kitchen table as he threaded a new shoelace into an old, weathered shoe with a paper-thin sole. The lighting inside was weak, making the task harder than it should have been. He looked up and blinked hard to refocus his sight. At that moment, Vittoria walked outside, past the open kitchen window. She doubled back, then looked in at John.

"What are you doing?" she asked.

"I'm fixing this shoe."

Vittoria poked her head through the window, then glanced around the kitchen. "That shoe belongs in the garbage, I think."

John kept his attention on his project. "It's old but good."

"I'm afraid to ask the question," said Vittoria, "but I must. To who it belongs?"

"It's mine."

"That is why I was afraid." She rolled her eyes. "I heard of some men, you know, with the lady shoes, but a little ballet-girl shoe. That I never heard."

John sighed. "It's not what you think. Is there something on your mind?"

"Yes, I must tell you," said Vittoria as she started to climb through the open window.

"We have doors," said John, pointing. "They're not far."

Vittoria dismissed John's remark, then popped herself through the window, landing gracefully. "Just before you come home, this smelly man sneaks up to the house." She pulled up a chair across from John, then leaned toward him and said, "An ugly man, dirty, his breath like *culo di maiale*. You know this, a pig's ass?"

That got John's attention. He put the shoe aside. "That's Coco; what did he want?"

"He didn't come inside, he..."

At that moment, there was a loud knock on the door.

John stood to the side of the door, his back to the wall, and asked, "Who's there?"

"Take a guess."

He opened the door to find Lepic standing with two detectives. The inspector took a deep breath, seemingly savoring the moment. "May we come in?"

"You may not," said John.

Lepic pulled a folded paper from his jacket pocket. "I was being polite," he said as he waved the form in John's face. "I didn't have to ask." He pushed past him, then noticed Vittoria, half-hidden behind a column.

"Who is this?" asked Lepic.

"None of your business," said John.

Lepic looked her up and down, then said to the two detectives, "A maid or a cook, she is of no consequence to us."

John watched Vittoria. She angled her head as she stared at Lepic, then raised her eyebrows in amazement. She moved toward Lepic, a tight bundle of determined harm.

John stepped in front of her. "Not now," he whispered. "Police."

Vittoria understood. She stopped. "Okay, I'll be scared," she whispered.

"I have it on good authority," announced Lepic with all the flourish he could muster, "you recently stole some jewels, and you have them hidden on your property."

"I've done no such thing."

Lepic shot a hand toward John, palm out. "Stay where you are," he demanded.

"I wasn't moving."

Lepic wasn't even listening. "This won't take long." He nodded and the detectives moved in opposite directions, one going outside and one inside.

John looked at Vittoria. Her fists were bunched in front of her mouth, concern on her face. She glanced at him, and ever so subtly, she winked.

What was that about? He kept his eyes on Vittoria, and once Lepic turned his back, she patted the air, motioning him to stay calm.

John watched one detective enter the kitchen. The man went to the counter, near the open window, then hovered over some containers. The officer opened the lids, inspecting the sugar, the flour, and the salt. He reached into the salt and came out with a small paper bag.

Lepic stood back, a smile creasing his face. He pivoted on his heels and headed outside. John followed. The other officer was moving a wide planter spilling herbs over its rim. Once the planter was aside, the officer dug with his hands. He, too, came out with a small paper bag.

Lepic raised his arm and beckoned with his hand without looking at the detectives, summoning them both. He took the first paper bag and emptied it into his palm. Out rolled a single coin. He stared at it, then held it up. "Lira?" he said. "An Italian coin?"

John could tell it was not what he expected.

"Not a jewel," said John. "But valuable. Worth about..." His eyes tilted up. "About one lira, I'd say."

Lepic grabbed the other bag and emptied it into his hand. Out tumbled a small bracelet with no jewels, just a tiny red horn and a tiny black hand, with only the index and pinkie fingers extended.

"*Mio cornicello*," said Vittoria. "*E mio mano cornuto*." Her good luck amulet and her good luck hand. "Is mine." Vittoria snatched it out of Lepic's palm, then gave John a mischievous smile as she dangled both charms. "*Due è meglio di uno*." Two are better than one.

John watched Lepic. With each breath, his fury rose. The inspector looked around the grounds, then swiped at a pair of garden hoes leaning against the house, knocking them into a flower bed. He kicked over some planters, then rushed inside. Everyone followed him into the house. Lepic pulled drawers from a credenza, spilling the contents onto the floor. Then he entered the kitchen and plunged his hand into the flour container.

"You have pulled a trick," he shouted. "I know they are here, the stolen jewels."

John said, "I'm no longer a jewel thief, Inspector. You won't find any stolen jewels on my property."

Lepic stopped digging in the flour and rushed at John, pointing a powdered hand. "Once a thief, always a thief. You...you...!"

Lepic pulled back his flour-covered hand to slap John. Instantly, John held up a finger. "Don't," he said. "I put up with a lot. But not that."

Lepic lowered his hand; then, with his jacket sleeve, he wiped some drool from his lower lip. "Know this, Monsieur Cat Burglar. Your nine lives—poof!" He blew into his open palm, creating a small cloud of flour. "They are gone. Used up, all of them." With that, he stormed off. The two detectives looked to each other, then to John and Vittoria. One shrugged. The other shook his head. Then they followed after Lepic.

John turned to Vittoria. She let loose a giggle. "Now I tell about that smelly man."

"This Coco, he hides the jewels because he knows this"—she motioned toward the door, where Lepic had been—"this *buffone* will come to find them," said Vittoria.

"You saw this?"

"Yes, I saw, but Coco didn't see me." She shook her head. "Idiot, that guy."

"And?"

"And he finished, then I removed the jewels."

John reached out and squeezed her hand. "You saved me from jail."

She brushed off the comment. "Is nothing," she said. "And I take care of the jewels, don't you worry."

"Listen, it's going to get dangerous here. Remember that man I told you about, Marcel Julien? He'll come for me here."

Vittoria didn't flinch. "That would be his big mistake."

"I'm sorry, but you must leave," said John. "You can stay with a friend of mine for a while."

Vittoria laughed. "What, you telling jokes? You do comedy for me?" She shook her head, amazed at his naivety. "No one will bother us here, trust me. I already take care of that."

"What do you mean?"

"What I mean," she said, "is you take your little-girl dancing shoes and go do your business. When done, come home and sleep like a *bambino*. You no worry." She pushed him toward the front door. "You'll see."

John smiled. He grabbed his things and rushed out the door. He straddled the motorcycle Luca had lent him, started the engine, then sped off.

CHAPTER 30

John was motionless as he peered through the bushes at Marcel Julien's villa. The home was like a movie set, with beautiful stone walls, thick columns, and wide, rough-hewn arches. It was two stories tall, with a second-story wraparound balcony on the sides and back.

Most importantly, it was a cloudy night with a steady breeze. The clouds were important—it was easier to avoid detection with less light—but the wind was critical. It caused the shadows of shade trees to sway against the villa's walls. The shifting shadows would help him blend in with his gray and black clothing. And the rustling leaves would mask any sounds.

All in all, a perfect night for what he'd planned.

He kept his eyes on the second story. He'd been watching for an hour, and so far, nothing. He needed information to implicate Marcel further, and anything secretive would be kept on the second floor, away from visitors. But where? A bedroom or an office were the most likely places. If John could spot one of those rooms, he would give it a thorough—and silent—inspection. Whatever he found, he'd give to Paul. And that would serve two purposes—remove Marcel as a threat to John and a potential threat to Francie.

The Juliens were hosting a small party on the first floor—over the past hour, several guests had trickled in, but arrivals had slowed.

Just then, on the second floor, a light went on. John saw Marcel enter a large room. He walked around, then stopped behind what appeared to be a desk. He took a seat, then started reading something.

John sprinted across the lawn to a tree next to the house, then leaped up and wrapped his arms around a thick branch. Quickly, he swung his legs up, then flipped himself over to lie on top of the limb. Once sure he was safe, he started up the tree, one branch at a time, hugging the trunk as much as possible. He carefully moved his body in cadence with the breeze and shadows; no sharp, quick movements that might draw attention. When he was level with the second story, John slowed even more. He moved an inch at a time and kept his eye on Marcel. A few minutes passed, then he saw Marcel exit the office and close the door behind him.

John slid off a branch and onto the second-floor balcony. A soft, silent landing. He bent forward so his back was even with the railing, then headed toward the office, again moving in time with the shadows.

The room had French doors opening out to the balcony. John turned the knob: locked. He pulled some lockpick tools from a leg strap and opened the door after a few seconds. Standing against the wall, he scanned the room. As always, he looked for places to hide, just in case. To his left were drapes, running floor to ceiling, off the wall enough to hide him and his feet. There was also a reading chair in one corner and a love seat large enough to conceal him across the room.

John pulled a wide piece of tape off his pants, then used it to hold back the bolt on the door. He pushed the door closed, and it stayed in place. Perfect. If he had to get to the balcony, he could do so quickly, with no turning of knobs, no clicking of bolts.

Finished with the door, he looked for places that might harbor confidential materials. He saw a desk, a credenza, and a bookcase.

To the desk first. John tested the drawers, and none were locked. He searched the contents of each. Nothing but invoices, sales reports, and a few business contracts. He felt underneath the open drawers for packages taped to the bottom. Nothing.

Down below, he could hear partygoers. Soft music, the dull rumble of dozens of voices, and a periodic laugh. Now and then, he heard a distinctive voice, which rose above the din, then slipped back into the cacophony.

He moved to the credenza next. Its drawer held several odds and ends—eyeglasses, a thin tape measure, some empty candy tins now containing buttons, and a pin cushion. He felt behind the credenza for folders or packets but found nothing.

Then, from down below, a vibrant, laughing voice. John stopped. He knew that voice. He opened the door a crack and looked downstairs.

Francie Stevens had joined the party.

CHAPTER 31

Francie, her mother, and Alex entered the Juliens' villa, bickering over an earlier disagreement. Across the foyer, Francie saw Odette separate from a group of guests and head toward her, her smile growing with every step. Odette reached out and held both of Francie's gloved hands.

"Thank you for coming," said Odette, "and thank you for a wonderful show. You were terrific."

"I'm so sorry we're late," said Francie. "I don't know where the time went."

Maude huffed. "I know," she said. "How many outfits did you try on, princess?"

"Not again," said Francie.

Odette interrupted. "Well, you're all here now, and I'm delighted. Can I get you something to drink?"

Maude's eyes widened. "Something strong would be good. Something fast would be better."

Alex signaled a passing waiter, who approached with a tray of champagne cocktails. "Allow me," he said, handing one to Francie, one to her mother, and taking one for himself. "That's better." Then he led them in a toast. "To you, Francie. May the rest of the week go as well as today."

There was a loud exchange of voices in a room off the foyer. Francie turned to listen, then asked, "Is that Marcel?"

"I'm afraid it is," said Odette. "Weeks like this, so much tension."

Francie reached into her purse and pulled out an envelope. She was about to hand it to Odette when Karl the tailor burst out of the room, followed by Marcel.

Karl was red with frustration. He spotted Francie, then waddled toward her. He pointed at Marcel with his thumb and said, "This man, he doesn't listen. I recommend, he ignores."

"Now, now," said Marcel. "Let's not upset the guests."

Francie watched Karl look around the foyer, then settle on Maude. "Ahhh, you are the mother, yes?"

"Yes. Lucky me."

"Your daughter is a delight," said Karl. "This man, not so much. At the last minute, he changes everything."

She smiled. "I know the feeling."

"Then you'll excuse my bad manners," said Karl, who lifted the glass out of her hand and downed it in one gulp. "Men like him, they drive you to drink!"

Maude giggled. "Perhaps I should meet one."

Karl wiped his mouth with his palm, then turned to Alex. Under his breath, Karl said, "This imbecile once designed a dress for standing. Not walking, not sitting, just standing. Why?"

Francie saw Marcel approaching, barely containing his amusement. Karl moved behind Francie, using her as a shield.

"That's enough," said Marcel. "You've had too much to drink."

"Or not enough," said Karl, looking left and right. "Where do you keep the bottles?" Maude laughed out loud. Karl noticed the envelope in Francie's hand. "Ah, you have the measures. Good. Be sure he gets them." Then, with a raised voice, "What he does with them, no one knows."

"Okay," said Marcel, "Time to leave."

"Good idea," said Karl. "Front door is over there. I go, you stay."

Francie watched Karl head out, grabbing and downing another drink on his way.

"If he wasn't such a great tailor," Marcel said, "I'd throw him down a sewer. He's impossible."

Francie handed her envelope to Marcel, then said, "He's a nice man, always looking out for me."

"That's very true. And despite what he says, I do listen. With a personality like his, you have no choice. By the way, you were outstanding today, and do you know why?"

Francie grabbed Alex's hand. "I don't."

"You brought our couture to life. You showed the audience what's possible. Not through actions; any model can do that. You revealed an attitude, one that balanced fun with sophistication. One that every woman wants," said Marcel. "Orders are pouring in."

"Speaking of pouring..." said Maude, extending her glass toward a waiter with a champagne bottle. She took a big sip, then spotted someone across the room. "That's Freddie. He's friends with that Australian star, the handsome one. Oh, what a scoundrel, what a charming scoundrel. If you'll excuse me." With that, she slipped away.

Marcel turned to Alex, who had his arm around Francie. "I can't thank you enough for bringing Francie to my attention. You have excellent instincts."

Alex blushed. "I simply made the connection. I had no idea it would go so well." He pulled Francie in close. "But I'm not surprised."

"Neither am I," said Marcel. He tapped the envelope in his hand. "Let me put this away so I don't lose it. I'll be back. Enjoy the party."

Marcel kissed Francie's hand, then excused himself.

CHAPTER 32

ohn could see Marcel at the bottom of the staircase. The man worked the party like a professional as he moved across the room. Then he started up the stairs.

That wasn't good. John eased the door closed, then moved quickly across the room. He'd been in situations like this before, and the key was to be decisive and calm. And absolutely silent. Motion meant noise, so stillness above all else. John got behind the love seat, then dropped into a crouch. He moved to one side. From where he was, John had a good view of the glass balcony doors, which meant he had a good view of the reflection on those doors. And that was the area around the desk. Reflections worked both ways. If John could see someone, they could see him. So he backed himself up, then stopped when his view of the reflection was but a sliver.

There was noise at the door. John saw Marcel walk in, then shut the door behind him. Marcel went right to the desk. Behind the desk was a countertop with several decanters on display. On the wall above the decanters hung a large Impressionist painting of fashionable patrons milling about a Parisian bar.

Marcel reached under his collar with an index finger, pulled out a necklace chain, then lifted it up and over his head. It held a single key. He reached up to the painting and pulled one side off the wall, opening it like a cabinet door.

A wall safe was behind the painting. John wasn't surprised. He always checked desks and drawers first, then looked for safes. He watched as Marcel took the key and opened the safe, then did a slow, methodical inventory of the contents. Then a voice called out from the hallway. Marcel moved fast. He tossed something inside, closed the safe, then put the painting back against the wall. He started to put the necklace over his head when the door opened. Marcel stopped, then dropped the chain behind him among the decanters.

Odette peeked into the room. "Honey?"

Marcel sighed. "I thought you were a guest."

"Speaking of guests, a couple of buyers are asking for you. They're excited."

Marcel beamed as he stepped from behind the desk. "Let's write some orders," he said, rubbing his hands together. "Shall we?"

Together, they headed back to the party. Marcel locked the door from the inside on his way out, then pulled it shut.

John waited several minutes. Then he made his way over to the bar and moved the painting aside, just as Marcel had done. He found the key chain lying between decanters and memorized its position. He picked it up and opened the safe. Inside were several banded packs of currency, a stack of passports, one folder, a handful of envelopes, and a handgun with a silencer.

He reached into his pocket and pulled out a small Minox camera, a spy camera, given to him earlier in the day by Armand. As long as his palm, the camera was rectangular and one inch wide, with a single strand of chain attached to one end. Armand had set it up and shown John how to use the tiny knots on the chain for focal distances.

He started with the passports. They were all crisp and in pairs, one for Marcel and one for Odette. That's interesting, he thought. He hadn't considered Odette and wondered if she had any suspicions about Marcel. John laid the passports down two at a time and photographed them all. None were Russian, but two were Bulgarian, Russia's staunchest ally. And all had different names.

After that, he photographed the file folder's contents, moving quickly through the pages, all of which seemed to be encoded. No writing, no illustrations, just random numbers. John then took out an envelope, removed the letter inside, then snapped a photo of both items. He noticed the writing on the envelope—"FS, La Mesure." *Francie Stevens, measurements.* He smiled to himself, then put it back in the safe. No need for Paul or Armand to see that.

Finally, John removed the gun. He didn't recognize the make or model, and it had no manufacturer's name anywhere. But it had a silencer, which meant the gun wasn't for Marcel's personal defense. It was also very utilitarian, just dull black metal with no detail. That, too, was odd. A man like Marcel would want functionality and design on everything, even a gun. He laid the gun and silencer on the counter, then snapped a picture.

When finished, he put everything back exactly as it was, closed the safe, put the painting flush against the wall, and replaced the key chain. He then walked around the room, looking for other hiding places. He lifted the corners of rugs, looking for loose planks and lockboxes, felt the undersides of furniture for secret compartments, and checked the bookcases for false fronts. Nothing.

John headed toward the balcony, then stopped. He could still hear Francie's voice downstairs. He cracked the door open, hoping to steal a glimpse of her. Francie was leaning against a back wall, locked in a passionate kiss with Alex. John watched for a moment, then turned away as a penetrating doubt descended on him. He quietly closed the door.

He took a couple of steps in one direction, then the other. John felt as if he'd walked into a column. He had been so focused on his own situation that he hadn't considered others. Was her relationship with her new boyfriend serious? The way she draped her wrists over Alex's shoulders, the affection in her eyes—that was how she used to be with John. What did it mean? His mind kept freezing on that question, and he had to move. One thing John did know—time was running out, and he needed to speak with Francie soon.

CHAPTER 33

Once again, John checked his watch. Across the table, Paul was reminding the waiter they were pressed for time. The waiter and Paul were approaching a mutual understanding, their overlapping voices blending in with the familiar sounds of the seaside—merchants haggling, sea swells beating a rhythmic cadence against the boats, and gulls gawking insults at fishermen with shouldered nets.

John wanted to wrap up and head over to Francie's hotel. Seeing her with Alex the night before had left him feeling very unsettled. That morning, he'd called and left messages for her with the front desk but hadn't heard back. He had a bad feeling, and it was getting worse. He had to talk to Francie face-to-face.

But Paul wanted to discuss John's actions from the night before, and a late lunch worked for everyone. Paul suggested a favorite restaurant that served *aïoli garni*, a traditional French dish with salted codfish, boiled vegetables, and a thick garlic sauce. This restaurant included sweet peppers and *panisse*, a fried chickpea-flour patty, and Paul had convinced John and Armand to try it.

While waiting for their lunch to arrive, John finished his update and handed Armand the Minox camera. "It has photos of the passports and the encrypted file."

Armand took the camera. "I'm familiar with the Russian codes. It won't take too long."

"Was there anything else?" asked Paul.

"Yes, there was a gun in the safe."

"What kind of gun?"

"One with a silencer."

"Do you know the make of the gun?"

"No, I've never seen one like it before. It was sturdy and simple, almost boring. I took a picture."

"Good," said Paul. "If it's Russian or Eastern European, that tells us something."

"As does the silencer," said Armand.

John looked over at Armand. "A silenced gun is to attack, not defend."

"Indeed. A loud bang is the best defense. It sends burglars running." Armand realized what he'd said, then looked at John. "No offense."

"None taken. And you're right." He rechecked his watch just as their lunches arrived.

Armand dove in first. "This fish with the sauce..."

"It's delicious, isn't it?" said Paul.

John started on the vegetables, then checked his watch again. He had to leave. Next to him, a series of contented moans and mumbles came from Armand.

"Try the sauce on the panisse," Armand said. "Who knew?"

Paul turned to John. "Was there anything else you can think of?"

John shook his head. "I told you about the safe, I took pictures of what was inside, and you have the camera. That's it." He pushed back from the table.

Paul, his mouth full, held up a hand, asking him to wait. "What about his desk? Those invoices. Anything look odd to you?"

"Not really, but I didn't look too closely. Time was short, so I focused on the safe." John rose from the table. "My apologies, but I have to run."

"Of course," said Paul. "And thank you for this. Excellent work."

Armand, his eyes wide and cheeks full, pointed at John's lunch with his fork. John nodded, then Armand swooped in and removed the panisse.

With that, John excused himself. He found the manager, paid the check, then headed out into the warm sunshine.

Time to see Francie.

CHAPTER 34

As he approached the front desk, John saw the manager look up with a practiced, polite countenance.

John had looked around the pool, the beach, and the lobby for Francie, and he hadn't seen her. An unannounced visit to her room was out of the question, so he tried the next best thing—the hotel manager.

Still fifty feet from the front desk, John smiled his most charming smile. "Excuse me," he said. "I'm meeting Miss Stevens, and I can't find her. Did she go ahead without me?"

The manager pursed his lips. "I think not. After dining, she went to her room, and I've not seen her since." The manager had a thought. "Let me check something."

John waited at the desk and, once again, ran through what he'd say to Francie. He'd practiced it several times and was sure it made sense. He was less confident, however, about discussing Marcel with her. What would he say? He couldn't tell her Marcel was a traitor. The full context of his actions was still unknown, and nothing had been proven. Also, Paul's investigation was ongoing. John couldn't jeopardize it. So where did that leave him? At most, he could tell her Marcel was a dangerous man. But he had to be careful with his wording. Said the wrong way, it could come off as the jealous act of a desperate suitor.

The manager returned. "I checked with the hotel's concierge," he said, resuming his place behind the counter, "and he did not see her leave." The manager picked up the phone. "Perhaps a call to her room..."

Behind him, John heard a series of oohs and aahs from the lobby. He turned to see.

Francie Stevens was coming down the stairs, dressed like a movie star.

And she was alone.

154

CHAPTER 35

As soon as she descended the stairs, the other hotel guests voiced their approval, and Francie beamed. They loved her outfit, a white strapless chiffon dress with a crisscross pattern below her chest, tight through the body and relaxed below the high, cinched waist. She'd tortured herself selecting the perfect outfit for an evening with Alex, and the guests' reactions put her at ease.

She wanted tonight to be perfect. The more time she spent with Alex, the more she discovered how wonderful he was, devoted and giving. She had a good feeling about them and wanted their relationship to deepen. Francie looked around for Alex but didn't see him. She looked toward the front desk as she got to the bottom of the stairs. There was John Robie, walking toward her. He looked sure of himself, and her confidence began to erode immediately.

"Francie," said John. "I was hoping you had a few minutes."

She looked around the lobby for Alex again. Still no sign. "I don't, John. This isn't a good time."

"Hear me out, please. I've been thinking about what you said at the cocktail party."

Francie checked the front door. No Alex. "I may have been too harsh, but this is a bad time, and I—"

"I'm glad to hear you say that, I've given it a lot of thought, and I might come across as selfish, but I've been alone all my adult life, with no one to depend on. Except myself."

Francie held up a hand. "You're putting me in an awkward position. This isn't the time nor place for this conversation."

"The context is important, though. Considering I've had no one to rely on, it explains why you see me as—"

"Selfish?" she interrupted. "Is that what you were about to say?" Francie shot a look at the entrance. Once again, no Alex. "It's not my perception, John. It's reality." She saw him step back, confused.

Francie continued, "I've told you twice, three times—this isn't a good time for me. And here you are, forging ahead with what you want to say."

"But—"

"But that's the issue," she said. "It's who you are; it's how you think. Always about yourself, what you want, and never about me. I couldn't have been more clear to you."

"I...I...didn't realize..." he stuttered.

"You never do. How could you, when all you think about is yourself?"

"Francie, I'm sorry. I didn't think I'd get another chance."

"You mean with Alex in my life? That man is good to me, good for me, and in ways that are important to me."

John stepped closer, then placed a hand on Francie's shoulder.

Just then, another hand grabbed John's wrist.

"Don't touch her!" said Alex. "What makes you think you can lay a hand on her?"

John snapped free of Alex's grip, then glared. "Lay a hand on me again, and I'll break it."

"Francie was clear the other night. What don't you understand?"

"I understand plenty," said John. "And I want to speak with Francie. Not you."

"Then you're out of luck, because I'm not going anywhere. So leave, or be a man and say it in front of me."

John glared. "Careful now, because this man can hurt you."

"Be my guest," said Alex.

Francie stepped between them. "Please, not here," she pleaded. "Stop it, both of you!"

"This is the biggest week of your life," said Alex. "You've got a lot at stake, Francie, and I'm just trying to help. The last thing you need is a distraction."

"I know, dear," she said as she rested her palm on Alex's arm. "And I appreciate that."

John gripped his hands into solid fists. He couldn't believe it. Last night, he was embarrassed when she and Alex kissed. And now they were talking about him being an intrusion. He glared at Francie.

"I'm a distraction? Is that what you think I am?"

She hesitated, then said, "I tried to tell you this wasn't a good time. But you wouldn't listen."

"I'm listening now. Is that how you see me? As a distraction?"

Francie looked back and forth between Alex and John. "We... I...I wanted a quiet night with Alex, and I tried to avoid a confrontation for this very reason. So what do you think, John? Is this a quiet evening? Would you say you're being a distraction?"

He stood there as his face flushed red. After a moment, he said, "I apologize. I see it now."

"Then please leave," said Francie. "Or better yet, let us leave." She put her arm through Alex's. "We have plans, and I'd like to keep them."

With that, Francie steered Alex away.

CHAPTER 36

John slowed the motorcycle to take a turn, then looked straight ahead. Nothing on the road, as far as he could see. He looked backward, and it was the same. Not a car in sight.

The night air was thick as if it were pushing on his body, keeping him exactly where it wanted him. That all-too-familiar terror of being alone was kicking in the door of his heart, and he struggled to keep his eyes on the road.

John had to admit that Francie was right. Even though she'd told him several times, he hadn't been listening. But her opportunities weren't slipping away by the hour; she wasn't feeling that pressure. John was, and in his mind that justified his actions.

Not that it did any good. Francie had sided with Alex in word and action. John ran through it again, reliving every slight, including the ultimate humiliation—she'd left arm in arm with Alex, leaving John standing there like a lovestruck, oblivious schoolboy.

Damn, he was angry with himself! Why couldn't he listen?

When Francie entered the lobby in that stunning evening gown, he knew she had a date with Alex. But he ignored it. Why? Was it because, in his mind, his needs were more important? Or did he just not care?

John saw the entrance to his driveway up ahead, then took the motorcycle down a gear. Whatever chance he'd had with Francie was gone; he was sure of that. He was nothing more than a distraction to her. She'd said as much. It was over. He had lost her, and it was time he faced reality.

He turned down his driveway and glided to a stop. John put the kickstand down, then turned the motorcycle off. He looked around. What a quiet night. Not a person, a breeze, or even an insect's buzz. Nothing.

Just then, something shattered a window of his villa, spilling broken glass onto the driveway.

Someone had thrown something from inside.

CHAPTER 37

John burst through the door. Vittoria was lying on the dining table, her dress pushed up around her waist and her underwear tangled around one knee. One man was at the end of the table, near her head, pinning her arms. Another man was standing between her legs, trying to restrain her kicks. Vittoria, speaking as if she were in control, was slinging a series of Italian and French curses at the two men, one of whom had a bloody nose, and the other had three deep scratches across his face.

John rushed to the man with the scratches at the head of the table, who let go of Vittoria's arms, then pulled a knife. He turned to face John, holding the knife close to his hip, his arm cocked at ninety degrees, ready for short, powerful stabs. John grabbed a chair and hurled it at the knife-wielding man without losing a step. It arrived an instant before John, and the man raised his arms to block the chair. John grabbed the man's wrist with one hand, keeping the knife at bay. He punched the man in the stomach with his free hand, doubling him over. The man bull-rushed John back into the front door, slamming it shut. Using his fist like a hammer, John thundered blows down on the man's back. He heard ribs crack as the man sank to the floor, then he kneed him in the face. The man dropped the knife, ceased all movement, then collapsed. He was out cold. John kicked the blade aside, then turned.

Across the room, the attacker with the bloody nose was staggering about with Vittoria mounted on his back. She wrapped one of her arms around her attacker's neck, and her other hand held a candlestick. She was jabbing it into the man's face, moving it around to avoid his blocking hands. John ran to them, and the attacker saw him coming. He swung his body fast just as John got there. The spin caused Vittoria's body to hit John, knocking him into the kitchen. He lost his balance, staggered backward, then fell. His back hit the stove just as his butt hit the floor. John rolled onto his side, then looked up and saw a huge pot of boiling water wobbling on the stove's edge.

With Vittoria hanging on his back, the attacker moved near a column separating the kitchen from the dining room. He rocked himself backward, causing Vittoria's back to pound against the column, once, twice, three times. John saw her head slam into the column, and she slipped off the man's back and fell to the floor.

John got to his feet and rushed the bloody-nosed attacker, just as the man charged him. They collided like rams in the middle of the kitchen, then tumbled down, the attacker emerging on top. John looked up and saw the boiling pot, perched and rocking. The man was straddling John's chest. He cocked back a fist to hit John but hit the stove with his elbow. The pot rocked again, launching a palm-size pool of steaming water into the air. John turned away as the boiling water landed near his head, the splatter hitting him like a pack of red-hot nails. The attacker switched hands and punched down at John's face with his other fist. John twisted to avoid the blow, but it caught him and knocked his head against the floor. His vision went black for an instant, but he held on as best he could. Then the man stopped. John opened his eyes and saw the man straighten up, then groan. Vittoria was standing behind the man, digging a paring knife into his back. The man growled, flailing his arms over his shoulders, trying to stop her.

"How you like?" she hissed. "Not so good, huh? I got more for you, my friend." Vittoria grabbed a fistful of the man's hair, cranked his head back to expose his throat, then reached around with the knife.

Over Vittoria's shoulder, John saw the other attacker grab Vittoria under her armpits, yank her up, and swing her sideways into the cabinets. She landed face-first on the floor.

John was still on his back, with the bloody-nosed attacker straddling his chest. He shot an open palm straight at the man's chin; his head snapped back, and he keeled over. John shoved the man off, then got to his feet. To his side, he saw Vittoria scramble to her feet.

At that moment, someone kicked open the front door.

CHAPTER 38

John looked over and saw a half dozen men rush through the front door, dressed in dark trousers, black henley shirts, gray vests, and flat coppola caps. The men were lean and aggressive, armed with knives, clubs, and luparas, the legendary short-barrel shotguns. They moved like a coordinated military squad, swarming the two attackers and pinning them to the floor.

Vittoria threw down the knife in her hand, then pointed at one of the men. *"Dove diavolo sei stato?"* she screamed. *Where the hell have you been?*

Then it hit John. The men were Vittoria's brothers. One was wearing a wide belt with shotgun shells. He approached, his face turning from a severe stare to a gleaming smile. "Gianni," he said. "Good to see you again. It's been a year, no?" He threw his arms around John, hugging him tightly.

"Matteo," said John. "I owe you."

"You owe nothing," said Matteo, "not after what you did for us."

Vittoria marched herself over, glaring at Matteo, her anger rising. Before she could speak, Matteo said, "It was dark. We no see the roads, so we go slow. But we're not late. We got here in time." He looked around the kitchen. "You're late, I think. You said you'd have *il banchetto*, a big feast. I see nothing."

Vittoria kissed him on both cheeks. "Give me a few minutes," she said. "How many? Did everyone come?"

"All the boys," said Matteo.

Vittoria smiled, then caught John's eye. "Don't you worry," she said. "My brothers won't bother you."

"That's not it," said John. "It's not safe."

"It is now," she said. "They'll watch the house, the vineyard, all around. They are excellent. We do this many times back home. Have to."

John nodded, then looked around. "What happened?"

"I was out, taking care of business," said Vittoria. "I come home, and five minutes later, these men break in. I was telling them to leave when you showed up."

John started to say something, paused, then said, "What business?"

"Not to worry," said Vittoria, brushing aside John's question. "Listen, those bad men try for you in the alley, and tonight, they try for you here. They won't give up. I know this, so I ask my brothers to come. They stay until we fix this. They keep the three of us safe. You, me, and your long-haired friend, Lucy."

"His name is Luca, not Lucy."

Vittoria frowned. "That's what I said, no? Anyway, I asked that one to stay here. The three of us, we can fight. But if your enemy sends many men, it's no good. Now it's good."

Her brothers had the two attackers on their feet. Vittoria screamed at them, a blur of languages, words, curses, and predictions.

John leaned toward Matteo. "What's she saying?"

"Nothing to concern you," whispered Matteo. "She wants us to cut that guy's throat, the one with the bloody nose, and let him bleed out on some vines. Then she'll make wine from those grapes and drink it on holidays."

"What?" John was horrified.

"As I said, it's nothing. But she's the boss. We do what she says." Matteo took charge of his brothers, who dragged the attackers outside. Matteo began clearing the broken items. Another brother straightened out the furniture, and another cleaned the blood on the floor.

Vittoria took John by the arm. "Come with me." Together, they walked into the kitchen. Vittoria got to work, grabbing some towels, straightening the pot, and adding pasta to the boiling water. After a minute, she leaned close to John, then said very quietly, "Did you see anything? When they had me on the table?"

John was surprised. *After all that just happened, that's what she's asking about?* He thought for a moment. John didn't want to embarrass her, and he didn't want to lie. Finally, he shook his head. "Nothing. Well, maybe something, but I can't be sure. Now that I think of it—"

"I knew it," said Vittoria. "Men see this, and they get thoughts." She shuddered, then pointed at John. "Listen to me. Get those thoughts out of your head," she said. "Focus on that American girl you like so much. What's her name, Fannie?"

"Francie."

"That one." Vittoria added salt to the pot, saying, "Will be hard, but you must forget what you saw. And you say nothing."

"Vittoria," said John, "it will die with me."

She stirred the pasta. "You got that right." Then she patted John's arm. "You good man. So no worry."

Just then, there was a loud commotion at the front door.

CHAPTER 39

Odette poured herself another glass of wine as the moonlight reflected off the pool, giving the water a glazed sheen. She tilted the bottle over Marcel's empty glass across the table. Marcel held up a palm. Then he got up and started pacing across their patio.

"Our business has had problems before," said Odette. "And you've always figured it out. Remember that contract for army uniforms? That one general was holding out, but you got through to him."

"This isn't like that," said Marcel. "In the past, money cleared the way. Not this time."

"You're sure?"

He nodded. "Very sure. This could hurt us."

"Do you want to talk about it?"

"Not really," he said. "I have a plan."

Odette filled Marcel's glass anyway. She got up from the table, then stepped in front of her husband. He was startled, then he let out a deep breath and thanked Odette before taking a sip.

"Then tell me about your plan," she said.

"Normally, I go at a problem head-on, but sometimes a more indirect solution is needed..."

Odette heard footsteps, then turned around. A big man came around the corner, with four other men following. The big man was taller than the others and as thick as an oak. He had a bald head and a thick mustache covering some of his pockmarked skin, which was the color and texture of a well-worn barber's strap. The man reached the patio, then continued walking. The other men stopped.

He walked over to Marcel. Up close, Odette noticed the man's hands. They were massive and gnarled, with white scars running over his knuckles. He looked over at Odette, then gave her a quick, respectful nod.

"Come," he said to Marcel. "We talk."

Odette started to say something, but Marcel shook his head, warning her. She kept quiet as her husband and the big man walked to the front of the villa.

Under her breath, she said, "I hope he knows what he's doing."

CHAPTER 40

epic couldn't sleep.

He stood in his kitchen, wrapped in a robe and holding a stiff drink, hoping it would slow his furious mind. How had John Robie avoided justice again? Lepic was so angry that he couldn't buy himself a second to answer his own question.

He gulped the drink, then kept his chin pointed up and set the glass down with a bang. It had to be luck, he thought. It had to be. No one was that good, especially not John Robie.

He rubbed his eyes. He reminded himself that this was a long game. It might take a year or more to lock up John Robie, but it would happen. Lepic had a portfolio of plots and schemes, and he'd only just begun.

Through the window, he noticed the door to his car was open. He stepped outside, then went to close the door. Sitting on the driver's seat was a small brown bag. It rattled when Lepic picked it up. He opened the bag, then shook the contents into his palm. Out rolled several jewels, the ones he had given to Coco.

And then out rolled a coin, dropping into the middle of the jewels.

An Italian lira.

CHAPTER 41

John's Villa, Saint-Jeannet

Four of Vittoria's brothers barged through the front door, restraining Paul and Armand as if they were common criminals. Once inside, one of the brothers shouted, "They are friends, so they say."

"Easy, now," said John, "they are friends."

With that, the brothers stopped their jostling. They patted Paul and Armand on the shoulders like buddies, straightened their suit jackets, and one brother appeared with a small glass of wine for each of them.

Paul spoke first. "What is going on here?"

"Marcel's men attacked me the other night," said John. "And they'll do it again. So I asked my friends from Italy to stay until it all blows over. Apologies for the confusion."

"They are efficient," said Armand. "I never saw them, never heard them coming." He turned to one of the brothers. "Can I get more wine?"

The brother laughed, then another appeared with a bottle of Chianti. He handed it to Armand, along with a larger glass.

"It's very late," said John. "This isn't a social visit. What's up?"

Paul pointed at John's sitting room, and the three men went in, leaving the brothers in the kitchen.

"We analyzed the pictures you took with the Minox," said Paul.

"And...?"

"And they were valuable," added Armand.

"Good," said John. "That one file, the encrypted one...those pictures helped?"

"Very much so," said Paul. "We're making great progress."

"And the pistol?"

Armand nodded. "Yes, now we know what it is. It's a Tokarev, a standard Russian-military pistol. Their army replaced it with the Makarov a few years ago, so the Tokarev has been recommissioned for other uses. By that, I mean espionage."

"That corroborates Marcel's involvement with the Russians," said John.

"He is working with the Russians," said Paul. "We know that for sure. A little more analysis, and we'll have a good idea what he's doing."

"I'm glad I could help, but you didn't come in the middle of the night for this."

"No, we didn't," said Paul. "There's one more thing..."

Armand jumped in. "You took a picture of a letter and an envelope."

John thought, then said, "Yes, written on the outside of the envelope was the phrase 'Francie's measurements.' I saw that, and I put it back."

"Here's the thing," said Paul. "Those weren't measurements."

"Of course they were," said John.

Paul shook his head. "That was encrypted information, using the same Russian code as the file."

A chill shot through John's body, making his skin crawl. "What do you mean?"

Paul rested a hand on John's shoulder. "I mean that Francie Stevens has been passing information to the Russians."

CHAPTER 42

John stared at the ground, replaying what he'd just heard. Francie passing information to the Russians? Could that be true? John was skeptical, but he forced himself to consider the possibility and imagine why she might do that. Different scenarios came at him like arrows, each repelled with a dismissive shake of his head.

"No," said John. "That can't be."

"I know this is personal for you," said Paul.

"It's not personal. Not anymore. It's over between us. Francie made that clear. She's with someone else now." He searched for the right words. "I...I just can't see it. It doesn't make sense."

John expected Paul to say something, but he just stood there patiently. "Maybe we're not talking about the same thing," said John.

Armand reached into a file and pulled out a grainy photograph of an envelope and a letter. "This is what we're talking about. You took this?"

John looked at the image. "Yes, I took that picture."

"And this letter was inside this envelope?" asked Armand.

"It was…" His voice drifted. "Sorry, but how do you know they're not her measurements?"

"Nothing but numbers," said Paul. "Measurements would have context, defining copy. It might say 'waist' or 'hips.'"

"You're not basing your accusation on that, are you?"

"There's more," said Paul. "Look at how many numbers there are. Way too many. And there's no spacing, no groupings. Just line after line after line, nothing but numbers."

John still wasn't buying it. "How can you be certain?"

"Because of this," said Armand, pointing to the photograph. "See here, on the letter. The encryption key is the first set of numbers in a message like this. It tells the recipient how to decode the rest of the message. And the encryption key on the letter is the same as the one on the file you photographed, which was also in the safe."

"Okay," said John, "but that doesn't mean she gave the envelope to Marcel."

"But she did," said Paul. He pulled press clippings from Armand's folder. "She was photographed handing this exact envelope to Marcel."

John looked at the press clipping. "Something's not right. Francie wouldn't do that."

Paul looked into John's eyes. "You're sure this isn't personal? You're sure it's over between you two?"

"I'm sure."

Paul was measured in his response. "We don't have the full picture, but it's becoming clearer. We know Marcel is working with the Russians, and we know he's collaborating with Hugo. We suspect it involves the French territories or our major trade routes. And we know Marcel keeps a hidden safe in his villa."

"Inside that safe," said Armand, "he keeps documents encrypted with a Russian code."

"And some of those documents were given to Marcel by Francie Stevens," said Paul. "We have evidence of that." He pointed to the press clippings.

John stopped for a moment. "You said 'documents.' Why?"

"There are more than one," said Paul. "According to the newspapers, Francie handed a couple of envelopes to Marcel. At different events."

"Now that I think about it," said John, "there were other envelopes in the safe, all labeled the same. I thought they weren't relevant, so I didn't photograph them."

"We know," said Paul. "That's the issue."

"And the problem," said Armand. "You took a partial photograph of one letter. We can't tell much from that. We'd know what was happening if we could analyze full pictures of all the letters."

John understood. He looked at Paul. "Okay," he said. "Let me think about it."

Paul handed John the Minox camera. "It would help tremendously."

"Help you," said John. "I'm not so sure about Francie."

"We don't know," said Paul. "But one thing we know for sure— Francie Stevens is involved in espionage. And that crime is punishable by death."

CHAPTER 43

John walked Paul and Armand out to their car, then returned to his sitting room and poured himself a tumbler of Armorik whisky. He sat on the hearth, bringing the bottle with him. John threw back a large gulp, then waited for the whisky to calm his mind.

The case Paul and Armand had made against Francie was clear. John couldn't deny that. But at the same time, he couldn't reconcile it with the Francie he knew. Or thought he knew.

His instinct told him that Francie was an unknowing participant. Someone was using her. But who? John took another gulp of whisky. His first guess was Marcel, but that didn't fit. In the newspapers, Francie had been photographed handing the envelopes to Marcel, not getting them from him. That meant someone else was involved. Once again, who?

John raised his cup to his lips but paused halfway. A sense of dread took hold of his mind. What if Francie wasn't being used?

What if she was actively working for Russia? Unlikely, but still possible. She'd changed so much over the last year, and John had to admit, he didn't know her as well as he thought. What if she...?

He stopped. It was too much to comprehend, and too much was unknown. He poured himself another drink and looked at the problem another way. What was fact, and what was speculation? He'd guessed at Francie's guilt or innocence, which was all speculation. But the points were clear. Marcel was involved. That was certain before tonight, and even more so now—after all, Francie had given Marcel encrypted information. Also, Marcel was escalating his attacks against John.

So what to do? Since every scenario involved Marcel, John needed more information about the man. The easiest way to get that information was another late-night visit to Marcel's villa, which Paul and Armand had requested. But that would be very, very risky. Marcel would have his guards on high alert—he'd already been exposed and would increase his security. No doubt about that. John took another big gulp of whisky. He wasn't sure about breaking into Marcel's villa again. Maybe there was another way.

He stood up. Vittoria's brothers were swarming around him like ants, moving in every direction. Through a window, John saw daylight above his vineyard. It was morning already. He was light-headed, but his body was heavy and slow. He couldn't rest, not yet. He had to have a conversation first.

John headed toward the door. Just then, he heard two people arguing.

In walked Vittoria and Luca, shouting at one another.

CHAPTER 44

rancie navigated the hairpin turn, then downshifted as her car began to climb the hill.

The day was warm, and she was ready for it. She wore a sea-green sleeveless dress with white trim around the neckline and sleeves. The body of the dress had a white print, a cross between half-moons and seagull silhouettes. She'd picked a matching sea-green neckerchief and white driving gloves to complete the outfit.

Francie looked over at Alex, who was smiling like a little boy. "What are you so happy about, mister?" she asked.

"It's been a long time since someone planned a surprise for me," he said.

"Well, we're almost there," said Francie. Near the top of the hill, she spotted the little cutout on the side of the road, barely noticeable. She pulled the Delahaye into the cutout, and a small clearing appeared. Francie turned off the car. To her right was a spectacular view, hills and valleys cascading down to a seaside village, sitting right at the edge of a bay. She needed to talk with Alex and wanted everything to be perfect. This was a great start.

Alex looked around. "It's beautiful."

Francie went to the back of the car. "It is." She lifted a basket out of the trunk. "And it's the perfect place for a picnic."

Together, they spread a blanket on the grass, then set the basket between them. Francie reached inside, then came out with a beer bottle. "For you, dear. It goes with this." She pulled out a paper tray with several pieces of chicken. "Would you like a leg or a breast?" Francie paused, then said, "Before last night, I'd have pegged you for a leg man. Now I'm not so sure."

Alex laughed. He leaned over and kissed her, then took a piece of chicken. "This is wonderful. You didn't have to do this. I know how busy you are."

"I'm grateful for all you've done," she said. "If it weren't for you, I wouldn't be a model. I'd be searching for some cause to get behind, but that wouldn't be a career. That's just something to do. But this I love. I can't thank you enough."

He placed his hand on Francie's hand. "I'm happy for you. Is it everything you imagined?"

"Everything and more," she said. "Modeling is so exciting. Being in front of all those people. It's like a performance. But the real surprise is the business side." She turned to face Alex. "Designing is only the beginning. Once introduced, they make the line. That can be large-scale or boutique. And that means taking orders, sourcing fabric, overseeing production, then shipping. So many things."

"There are many sides to the business," he said. "And many interesting people. Like the prince..."

Francie grinned as she brushed aside the comment. "Oh, he was a good sport. But I am meeting interesting people. This week, I met some famous Hollywood types, men and women. I've met members of Parliament, millionaires, an Arabian prince, and"— she lowered her voice to a whisper—"a rival designer, if you can believe it."

"I can. By all accounts, you're a great model. It's only natural that other designers would take notice."

"It's all very flattering, but it feels wrong, talking to other designers. Marcel gave me a chance, and I owe him."

"Yes and no," said Alex. "This is business. Nothing more. If you get another offer, and it's more of what you want, then, by all means, consider it. You can still be loyal to Marcel. Mention it to him and see if he'll offer the same."

"That would work."

"Better yet, if you want to get involved in other areas, tell Marcel. Maybe he'll work with you."

They settled into their picnic, trying different cheeses and jams. After a time, Francie rolled onto her stomach, then propped her head up with her hands.

"So, how was your morning?" asked Alex.

"Nothing special. Karl came around for more tailoring. He spent a lot of time measuring my hips and my derriere, if you must know."

"Were you okay with that?"

"Of course, he's very proper. Except for his 'Marcel' rants. Today he went on about Marcel always telling him to mind his own business, to focus on tailoring."

"And what do you think?"

"Both have their points. But it's Marcel's business." Francie gently flicked a bug off the picnic blanket. "They see things differently. Karl is passionate about details, and Marcel is always thinking big picture. It's only natural for there to be tension."

"Speaking of tension," said Alex, "how are you feeling about John Robie?"

A smile spread across Francie's face. "Quite good," she said. "Oh, he's not bad, all in all. I've clarified my intentions, and he'll be moving on."

He leaned in. "Are you sure you're moving on?"

She nodded. "Yes, dear. I'm moving forward. By the way, and since you brought it up, I hoped we could talk about it."

"About what, exactly?"

"About us. We're getting on so well, don't you think?"

"I do."

"Since we both agree," she said, "what are your thoughts about us...going forward together?"

He waited a moment, then placed a hand on her cheek. "I've wanted to talk about the same thing, Francie. But not this week, not with all you have going on. I thought it best if we waited so there are no distractions."

She caught her breath. "So you're saying..."

"I'm saying let's wait until this week is over. Then we'll have that conversation. I promise. You need to focus on your career."

Francie was anxious. She reached for his hand, more to steady her own than to show affection. "I just need to know," she said. "It's important to me."

"As it is to me. How about this...when the show ends Friday night, the two of us will go somewhere for a couple of days. Maybe

Monte Carlo, maybe Italy. Somewhere romantic. I'll plan it. Let that be my surprise for you. And we'll talk about our future. How does that sound?"

"It sounds wonderful."

"But in the meantime, we'll put the topic aside. This week is about you."

Francie's eyes welled up. She pulled herself upright, then wrapped her arms around him and held tight.

That was all she needed to hear. Things were falling into place. She was sure of it.

CHAPTER 45

John watched Vittoria and Luca argue through his front door, Vittoria raising her voice with each step. From what John could see, Luca was trying to ignore her.

"What's going on?" asked John.

Luca spoke first. "This one"—he motioned toward Vittoria—"tells me to come over, that you need my help. So, of course, I came. I leave work, but if you need me, I'm here. And now I find you don't need me. She does. She wants me to do something for her."

Vittoria interrupted. "Not 'for.' With." She held one hand next to her face, palm open, shaking it. "Is not hard to understand," she shouted. "John needs help, but I can't do it alone." Vittoria turned toward John, then spoke in a normal voice. "I need a simpleton, someone to do what I say. I thought your friend was perfect. Boy, was I wrong. He's a big pain in the—"

"As always, we can work this out," said John. "Let's all calm down. Vittoria, can one of your brothers help?"

She shook her head. "Absolutely not. Too...*testa calda*." She looked around for a phrase John would understand. "Too hot-headed." Vittoria paused, then looked John up and down. "Hey, where you going?"

"To see Francie," he replied. "I need to talk to her."

"That's good," she said. "I'll do some *sorveglianza*, some watching. But I need this idiot."

"Enough," said Luca. "John, whatever she wants, will it help you?" John nodded. "Yes, it will."

"Then I'll do it," said Luca, turning to Vittoria. "But let's be clear. I don't answer to you."

With that, all of Vittoria's brothers burst out laughing. One brother touched Luca's forehead, testing for a fever.

Vittoria grabbed Luca by the wrist and dragged him into the kitchen. "First, you gotta get this crap off your hands. What is this, grease?"

"And motor oil."

"You look like you work in a garage."

"I do work in a garage."

"Not today, you don't." She yanked one of his arms down into the sink, then grabbed a scrub brush.

"Today, you must look like you are on vacation," she said. "Will take a miracle for this, so let's get started." She scrubbed vigorously. "Next, I get you out of those rags."

"These are nice clothes," said Luca.

Vittoria chuckled. "They're not nice. You don't know from nice. But don't worry, I have what we need."

John smiled and shook his head. "Good luck, my friend." He headed outside, then got on the motorcycle and drove away.

CHAPTER 46

WEDNESDAY AFTERNOON

Juan-Les-Pins

epic used his police baton to push aside a long, empty crate, but the object of his search was not underneath. He slammed his club onto the box with surprising power, snapping a side plank. The noise pierced the still air in the alley, causing a handful of cats and dogs to snap to attention.

He surveyed the remaining heaps of trash, then headed toward the most promising one. He held a letter from his superiors in his left hand, opened just moments ago, denying him a promotion he'd sought for several months. Without realizing it, he was crushing the paper into a wrinkled ball. As he passed an open trash can, he threw in the crumpled letter, then wiped his hand on his pants.

There was movement up ahead. Lepic stopped and watched. Large flies buzzed his ears like cocky little fighter pilots, but he remained still. He took a few steps forward, then peered down.

And there he was.

With his baton, Lepic prodded the man. It didn't wake him, so Lepic poked the man hard in his ribs. That worked.

Coco rolled over, then looked up at Lepic through a drunken, sleepy haze. Recognition came slowly, but once he saw it was Lepic, he scattered backward and away from the inspector. Lepic took two steps toward him, then raised his baton.

Coco held up his hands for protection. "I did it," he said. "I placed the jewels."

Lepic lowered the baton. "I know you did. I believe you." He stood up straight and motioned for Coco to sit up. "Unfortunately, John Robie must have seen you, because the jewels were not to be found when I got there."

"But..."

"But you were careless, or maybe you tipped him off."

Coco shook his head. "Why would I do that?"

"So you could fulfill your promise to me and remain loyal to your friend, another crook. You know what they say. 'Loyalty among thieves.'"

"Not this time. He's done nothing for me. That's why I agreed to your offer."

Lepic stood at ease. "That offer assumed success. There was no success. Because you were careless."

"So that's it? I get no help from you?"

Lepic wagged a finger. "I didn't say that. The deal is still on the table. You help me, and I make your problem disappear."

Coco slumped back against the alley wall, relieved. "What do you need me to do?"

"Justice comes in many forms," said Lepic, "and the justice I have in mind requires more drastic measures. You understand?"

Coco nodded.

"Good. I'll tell you what I was thinking. But there's a new requirement. It must happen today."

CHAPTER 47

WEDNESDAY AFTERNOON

Hôtel Belle Rives, Antibes

John parked the motorcycle across the street from Francie's hotel, then observed the flow of guests coming and going. As he watched, he reviewed his plan. He would ask the manager to call Francie's room. Once she came down, John would acknowledge the end of their relationship. Francie would lower her guard, and then John would steer the conversation to gauge her attitude toward the United States. And if she wasn't anti-American, he'd warn her about Marcel.

John put his hand to his heart, feeling a tremble deep inside his chest. He hadn't fully thought this through, and now it was hitting him—he was about to say goodbye to Francie. He would say their relationship was no longer. They would talk, and then it would be over. The finality of that hit John like a cannon shot.

Just then, Francie and Alex exited the hotel. John ducked behind a delivery van, then watched Francie and Alex stroll to her car. Alex got in, Francie kissed him goodbye, then he drove off, smiling and waving. She headed back to the hotel.

John stepped from behind the van. "Francie?"

She stopped walking, then turned around.

"It's not about us," said John. "I know it's over. I just need a minute."

Francie looked around, then pointed toward the side of the hotel, away from the lobby entrance. John headed in that direction, then met with her just around the corner.

"It is over between us," said Francie, "and I appreciate you saying as much. I'm with Alex now."

John watched her intently, paying attention to all details. Her tone was cordial, and his opening statement had worked, judging by her comments.

"He makes you happy," said John.

She relaxed. "He does, and he's thoughtful. Alex is considerate to a fault. I'm sorry to say, that was a challenge for you."

"It was. You told me, but I always tried to explain it away. Now I understand."

John saw Francie hesitate as she thought about his comments. "Well, I'm glad you do," she said. "It'll help when you meet someone special. You will, John. You're a good man."

"But not good enough."

"Not true. You and I had wonderful times. And you have quite a bit to offer. It was just timing."

He lowered his head. "Had I been less stubborn..."

"Water under the bridge," she said. "What's important is we both learned about ourselves, wouldn't you say? And trust me, it will make a difference with the next woman you meet."

John pulled back. Francie's demeanor was not what he'd expected. She was warm, even complimentary. But it was time to segue, and an approach came to him. "Maybe I'll meet someone back in the States," he said. "I've been thinking about returning. It's been a long time."

"I'm surprised to hear that. You suit the Riviera, and the Riviera suits you. But you know best. That wouldn't be for me, though."

"And why is that?"

"To be frank," she said, "our country never embraced me. Not the people, and certainly not the government."

"The government?"

"Absolutely. They're tough on businesses. They have rules for everything. And their hand is always out."

"Ah," said John. "High taxes?"

"Not really," said Francie. "I don't mind paying. I don't. So many need help. But the government has other priorities."

"And that bothers you?"

"It does. Charity starts at home. You've heard that. I believe that's true for taxes, too."

He waited a moment, then asked, "Will you ever return?"

"At some point, I suppose. But not too soon. I adore living abroad."

"Some expats grow to dislike America," he said. "Some even protest the United States. Maybe the time away gives them a different perspective."

"I'm sure it does," said Francie. "But that's not for me. Oh, I carry on, but it's not that bad back home. As Mother would say, I'm just being dramatic."

"I thought you..."

Francie waved it off. "Yes, I complain about it, and I may sound un-American. But I'm not. Far from it."

John was sure of it now. There was no way Francie was working against the United States. He'd given her chances, and she didn't denounce the United States each time. Just the opposite; she'd even called the U.S. 'home.'

Francie checked her watch. "You didn't come here to talk politics. Is there something else?"

"There is," he said. "I'm aware of something that may impact you, and I thought you should know."

"Do tell."

John thought for a moment. He had to be careful with his words. "Marcel Julien, he isn't what he seems. He's involved in illegal activity."

She frowned. "I find that hard to believe."

He expected this response and was ready. "I've got no agenda, Francie. I've nothing to gain by telling you this. I simply want you to be aware."

"And how do you know this? Your criminal friends?"

He shook his head. "Quite the opposite."

Francie paused. He watched her process the information. "Then it must be Paul. He's with the French government now."

"I can't talk specifics," said John. "I just want you to know."

She looked down as she considered the news. "Marcel has been very professional. He does have a big company, and it's international. It takes him all over the world. Maybe he's being 'creative' with new business." She looked up. "If that's what you're referring to, bribery is normal in some countries—expected, even. But none of that involves me. I'm just a model."

"I'm glad to hear that; your employment ends this week?"

"It does." Then a thought came to her. "Did Paul send you here? Does he want something?"

"Not at all. It was my idea. I wanted you to know. I'm not telling you what to do. You're smart enough to figure that out. But Marcel is not who he appears to be, and if you want to move on, that's your decision. There are many opportunities to find a more stable employer with all the designers here. If that's what you want."

"Ah," said Francie. "Now I see. I'm not worried about getting paid, if that's your concern. But I need the experience. So I appreciate the warning, but I'll finish my assignment with Marcel. And I'll keep this confidential, just between you and me."

"Thank you. And please be careful around Marcel. He can be... Hey, why are you smiling?"

"The irony of it all," she said. "Here we are, maybe our last conversation, and John Robie is looking out for me. No hidden agendas, nothing in it for you. Just looking out for me!"

John sighed. "Too little, too late, I know." He looked into her eyes as all his memories of Francie paraded past his mind. A surge of sadness sucked the breath from him, and he put a hand against a wall to steady himself.

Francie reached out and touched his arm.

"Goodbye, John."

CHAPTER 48

John headed back to his villa, taking the motorcycle on a winding rural road.

It was late in the afternoon, and the day was cooling off. There was no wind, but the motorcycle's speed caused John's poplin shirt to billow like a sail. The road was a series of twists and turns, and he leaned in like a pro.

He was in good spirits, but he had no idea why. By all rights, he should have been miserable. After all, he'd just lost the most amazing woman he'd ever known. The conversation with Francie was harder than he'd imagined. But it was necessary. He'd validated her innocence and was ashamed of himself for thinking otherwise. After that, he'd warned Francie without providing details. She'd made assumptions about Marcel, and John hadn't discouraged those assumptions. And it worked. She was now skeptical of Marcel, and she would likely look to move on once the week ended. That was all John wanted.

She'd even been complimentary about his thoughtfulness. That surprised him, and he'd almost lost himself in the moment. But he stayed the course. John shook his head slowly, disappointed in himself for not listening to her. But he'd done the right thing. If he hadn't acknowledged their relationship was over, Francie would have been skeptical of his warning.

John had learned something else, too. She wasn't working against the United States. And since she wasn't knowingly passing information to Marcel, she was being set up by someone. But who? And why Francie? Someone must be using her as a cutout, a person protecting the identity of one or both parties in the exchange of sensitive information. John was familiar with the idea; he'd used cutouts frequently in the Resistance.

But who would be using Francie like that? He knew the person was connected to the Russians, just as Marcel was. But it would take time and effort to identify them. One thing was sure, though. John would break into Marcel's villa again, and he would do it that night. Whatever he found would help Paul and might also exonerate Francie.

John took another turn. Up ahead, he saw a black sedan heading in the opposite direction. The car passed him. Then he heard it brake hard. He looked over his shoulder and saw the car turning around.

It was coming for John. It had to be. There were no missed turns as far as John could see. Nothing was lying on the road. John looked back again, and the black sedan was speeding toward him.

What was this about? John felt his heart leap, then race. Whoever was driving the sedan was after him. He'd been thinking about Francie, but now he had to focus. He turned the throttle and picked up speed.

John looked back, and the car was just a few feet behind him. The car surged forward, and John did the same. The driver was trying to hit him. Just a nudge on the back wheel would send John flying, and a fall could be fatal on these roads. He didn't want that. Or did he? Francie would read about his death and know it happened just after they'd said goodbye; he'd be in her heart forever. John dismissed the thought as quickly as it came; it was adolescent thinking, a luxury he'd never had time for. And it was incredibly selfish. Besides, as long as Marcel was around, Francie would be at risk. And John could help.

Ahead, a hairpin turn appeared. He kept his speed as long as he could. He hit the brakes late before entering the turn, but the black sedan waited longer. John accelerated out of the turn, and the front of the black sedan missed his rear wheel by inches. John looked back to see the car glance off a stone wall, breaking a headlight and smashing a fender. But the driver didn't miss a beat. The car's tires screeched as it came out of the turn like a bullet.

This was serious, and John knew it. He wasn't going to let it end like this; there was too much at stake. He bent over his handlebars to gain speed. On one side, the road hugged a hill, and on the other was a steep drop into a rocky valley. A low stone wall acted as a guardrail, separating the road from the drop-off, but it was no protection. Behind him, the black sedan was gaining ground.

Up ahead, John saw a gradual turn. He entered the bend faster than he wanted and drifted into the center of the road. Coming in the other direction was a two-toned passenger bus. Fighting the motorcycle's momentum, he muscled it back onto the correct side of the road. The motorcycle wiggled under him, but John steadied it as the bus flew past.

Behind him, the black sedan had slowed considerably as it and the bus had to maneuver around one another at a tight section of road. This gave John time. He gunned the engine and sped up the hill while the black sedan inched its way around the bus.

At the top of the hill was a wide, circular clearing at the exact spot where the road turned. The clearing must have been put there for safety, to allow for wide turns and turnarounds. John had an idea. He pulled up next to the stone wall, then stopped. He aimed his front wheel toward the next section of the road, then put the motorcycle in first gear. He kept his hand on the clutch, and with his other hand, he engaged the throttle. The engine was revving, but the motorcycle wasn't moving, and it wouldn't until John released the clutch.

Then he started pumping his foot down as if trying to jump-start the engine. The black sedan came hurtling up the hillside and into view. The driver of the car aimed right at him and accelerated. The car came at him fast. John timed it, and at the last moment, he released the clutch. The motorcycle leaped forward with a lightning-quick pounce. The front of the car clipped the back of the bike, causing it to spin like a top. It went down in a heap, as did John.

But the car had gone too far. The driver hit the brakes, but not before the front of the vehicle broke through the stone wall and reached the very edge of the cliff. Both tires held for a moment, then dropped over the edge, and the car's chassis hit the ground with a bang. Momentum pulled the vehicle forward in fits and spurts, and it began sliding over the edge.

John saw the driver frantically trying to open his door. The man got it open, but not in time. The car dropped over the cliff. The driver was half out of the vehicle when the open door blasted into a boulder, slamming itself back onto the man. The driver's body fell from the car and landed on a ridge. The vehicle dropped straight down into the valley. At the bottom, it smashed into another boulder, causing it to flip over, scattering pieces everywhere.

John waited a moment. There was no fire, no noise—just silence.

John felt the tension release from his body just as an awkward laugh escaped his mouth. He was relieved, but was it because he'd won? Was there another reason? What did it matter? He'd survived. John's legs wobbled, but he braced himself.

Then he looked down. Splayed across a rock ridge was the driver's body, blood fanning out under the man's head like a halo. John took a dirt pathway down the side of the cliff. He stopped and stood over the dead man when he got to the ridge. The man's face was disfigured from the fall, but still, he looked familiar.

Then it hit him. John had seen the man a few times since the weekend.

It was Marcel Julien's chauffeur.

John made his way back to the clearing. The motorcycle's rear wheel was bent, and the engine was leaking oil and gas.

He saw a small building down the road—a store of some sort—and ran toward it. As he got closer, he saw a pay phone out front and a bus stop to the side.

A thought came to John, and he stopped in the middle of the

road. The dead chauffeur wasn't seeking John out. He had no idea John would be on that road. The man passed John, realized who he was, then turned around to chase him.

The man was headed somewhere else. And John knew where.

The man was on his way to Francie's hotel.

On his way to Francie.

Marcel's veiled threat shot into his mind, as big as a billboard. Had John misread the situation? Would Marcel forego a benefit to his own business and harm Francie just to send a message to John? He looked left in the direction of Francie's hotel, then right toward Cannes, where the fashion show would take place. Which way should he go?

John stopped. He was uncertain and felt butterflies in his stomach. Why was he doubting himself? This wasn't like him; he'd always been confident and decisive. Why was he acting this way?

What should he do?

CHAPTER 49

Outside the tent, the fashion show was in full swing, but this time the audience was on the beach, not up on the boardwalk, creating an atmosphere of one big beach party. Francie could hear the unmistakable sound of a ukulele threading itself through every song played by the Hawaiian band. Waiters roamed through the crowds, serving beach cocktails in coconut shells. And in the air, Francie detected a smoky, nutty aroma, which another model said was *Embryolisse Lait-Concentré*, the lotion that had taken over the Riviera.

Inside the tent, Francie was fixating on her image in the mirror. The swimsuit was tiny; there was no denying that. But the bikini fit perfectly. So why was she feeling anxious? She looked over at Karl. His eyes were on hers, not the bikini.

"I know what you are thinking," said Karl. "In five minutes, you will walk in front of hundreds of people, some with cameras, wearing nothing but your underwear."

"Exactly right," said Francie. "It's unnerving."

"So think differently. Imagine this bikini is the first of its kind. Until now, women wore nothing on the beach. They had nothing. But today, you show up. And this design you wear, no one has ever seen this. It brings women some modesty. You bring them modesty." Karl paused for effect. "You see what I did? Is much better to think this way."

Francie posed again, from a different angle. "I guess," she said. "But you've seen the other models. They're stunning."

"And you're not? Listen to me, Miss Francie. Here's what I have learned about women after many years of dressing and undressing them. Regarding their bodies, women always focus on what they don't have. Never on what they have."

Francie stopped posing. Karl had her attention.

"You have much to feel good about. Every part of you is beautiful. And if I can be frank, you should think about your character, your personality, the same way you think about your legs, or your—"

"You're right," said Francie. "That's very insightful, Karl."

He grinned and blinked hard. Then he glanced over his shoulder before saying, "Besides, they're all here to see you, not his swimsuit. Even so, it looks great."

She looked down. The bikini Marcel had designed was white with red polka dots. The dots weren't dense, and they weren't sparse, either—a perfect balance. The bottom, cut low, was tied off on the left side with a fancy bow. And the strapless top had a matching bow right in the middle. Francie had to admit that it was a simple and brilliant design, a classic take on a trending style.

Francie leaned over and kissed Karl on the cheek. "I should listen to you more," she said. "I feel much better."

Karl held up an index finger. "One more thing, in case you want to cover up." Karl reached into his leather satchel and removed a sheer sarong, white with an elongated faded-red print.

"Oh my! It's perfect. Marcel didn't mention this."

"Because he didn't think of this," said Karl. "I did. Always the same old story with that man. Tailor has a great idea, tells designer. Designer dismisses idea, but tailor persists. Designer finally agrees but changes tailor's design." He shook his head. "This is the circle of idiocy playing out right in front of you."

Francie laughed. Behind Karl, she saw Alex appear, coconut cocktail in hand. With a nod, he said, "Cheers, my love."

She melted at hearing Alex's words. The tension in her body drained away, and she threw her arm over his shoulder, then hugged him tightly.

"Did you bring me one?" asked Karl.

Alex chuckled. "My apologies. I didn't."

"Reason I ask," said Karl, pointing behind them, "is now I need one. Here comes the Dictator of Designers, the Master of Misery, the Torturer of Tailors."

Francie turned to see Marcel enter the tent. He stopped at the entrance and stared at Karl.

"You again," said Marcel. "Are we going to argue?"

"We are not, because I am leaving. This tent is too small. It cannot hold all of us and all your bluster." Karl turned to Francie. "As they say on Broadway, break a leg. But don't, please don't."

She patted Karl on the back as he headed for the exit.

"When you're done," said Alex, "I'll be waiting for you right here." He excused himself.

Marcel sized Francie up. He was smiling. "Are you ready?"

She caught a glimpse of herself in the mirror. She began to speak, then hesitated a moment before saying, "I am. I certainly am."

He pursed his lips. "Are you sure, Francie? You seem a little off. Just a little."

"I'm fine. I get flustered in a bathing suit. At first, anyway, but I'm fine now."

"Good," said Marcel. "For a minute, I thought you ran into your old friend, the thief. He's enough to throw anyone off. Have you seen him, by the way?"

That's curious, Francie thought. Why would Marcel ask if she'd seen John? She caught herself, smiled wide, then said, "I haven't, and I won't be. This week is a new chapter, and I love it."

"A new chapter for us both," he said. "Okay, now listen. I'll introduce you, as always. But no coaching from me. You are a natural, and your happiness is contagious. So enjoy yourself. Agreed?"

"Agreed," said Francie.

Marcel headed toward the podium. He stopped, then patiently stood to the side while another designer concluded her speech.

In the background, Francie heard the band play "Hawaiian War Chant." She still had a couple of minutes. She exited the back of her tent, then jogged down to the water, where soft little waves were pulsing onto the beach.

She had one more trick up her sleeve.

CHAPTER 50

John stared at a reflection of himself in the glass of the bus doors. Dirt stains on his clothes and skin, scrapes on his elbows and hands, and a tear in his pants. He dusted himself off, then used a little saliva to remove a stain on his cheek.

Up ahead, he saw a crowd on the beach. It had to be the fashion show, and that's where Francie would be. He spoke to the driver, and the bus stopped two blocks away from the crowd.

He got off and surveyed the immediate area. None of Marcel's men were staked out to grab him. Not this far back, anyway. John walked onto the boardwalk and stayed two hundred yards away from the fashion show on the beach. He climbed the base of a streetlamp and could see the show from that vantage point. He did a quick sweep around but didn't see Francie.

His heart throbbed. Where was she? Had she made it to the show? John calmed himself, then looked again. In a cluster of tents on the beach, John spotted some models in bathing suits.

Then he saw her. She was with an older man who was hunched over and walking with a bit of a waddle. The man had dark, heavy clothing and big, round glasses that made him look like an owl. He was fussing with Francie's swimsuit, making adjustments here and there, and Francie was smiling the whole time.

Then it hit him. John had seen the man before, at Marcel's cocktail party, and it was clear Francie liked him.

John was relieved. She had made it to the show and was in good spirits. Maybe Marcel's chauffeur was just picking her up for the show, nothing more.

Francie's boyfriend, Alex, appeared between tents, heading toward her. John watched the two of them talking, then Francie hugged him. It was a long hug, and John saw Francie whisper into his ear. John's stomach dropped, but he was grateful she had a friend by her side.

Then Marcel appeared. He joined the conversation, and the older man, the Owl, went the other way. Marcel and Francie talked; from what John could see, it was a friendly and respectful chat. Very good, he thought. Marcel treating her well was another good sign.

Marcel said parting words to Francie, then walked toward the main stage. On the way, he stopped to talk to a man John didn't recognize. The man had short hair and a boxy suit jacket. After a moment, the man with the jacket looked into the crowd, then waved his hand to signal someone.

John looked around. Another man with short hair and a similar jacket was up on the boardwalk. That man signaled back, then turned and watched the street. John looked around the crowd and spotted two other men dressed the same, and both had their backs to the beach. All of them on the edge of the show. And all of them were looking in different directions.

One of the men straightened his jacket, and John noticed it right away, the familiar bulge of a handgun in a shoulder holster. He looked around and saw the same protrusion on the other men.

He thought for a moment. These men were not local police, yet they all wore similar suits, and all were armed. Who were they? And what were they looking for?

The answer came to John as a shiver rolled over his skin.

Him. They were looking for him.

CHAPTER 51

A sea breeze swept over Odette, its gentle puffs fluffing her hair. She enjoyed that feeling, like an angel massaging her scalp. She looked out over the water. Sailboats and powerboats floated off the coast, and there wasn't a cloud in the sky—another perfect day on the Riviera.

Her husband was speaking at the podium. This was their best week ever, thanks to Francie Stevens. Odette hoped Marcel understood Francie's true value. She was the best they'd ever had. She was a natural, a unique, radiant beauty who was unafraid to take chances. And her social instincts were uncanny. The other night, at the Juliens' party, Francie threw herself into the crowd without knowing a single guest. She could talk and connect with anyone, always making them feel special. Others saw the beauty, but Odette knew better. What set Francie apart was her personality. Without a doubt, Francie had what it takes to succeed.

She plucked a shrimp and pineapple *en brochette* from a passing waiter, then sipped her coconut cocktail. Even though Francie had impressed her, Marcel had impressed her even more. He'd taken charge of the whole week. He was decisive, he foresaw problems, and he'd come up with his own solutions. Odette had been his singular confidante in the past, but this week, he assumed responsibility for everything. Almost as if he didn't need her counsel anymore. She thought about that for a moment. No, she decided, Marcel would always need her. Nothing to worry about there.

At that moment, the crowd erupted in applause. She looked around, and there was Francie, emerging from the sea, wearing the bikini Marcel had designed. The crowd loved it. Francie shook her head like a wet dog, then threw a sarong over her shoulder. Odette beamed. This was what she'd seen in Francie. Spontaneity, enthusiasm, and a knack for doing the exact right thing.

Odette looked back at her husband, who was at the podium. Marcel was searching the crowd, and when his eyes found Odette, he smiled and raised his eyebrows. Then he shook his head in disbelief.

Francie was exceptional, and Marcel knew it, too.

CHAPTER 52

He couldn't look away. From his perch on the lamppost, John watched Francie work the crowd. They loved her. After a few minutes, she completed her walk and returned to her tent. The crowd was enthralled, and they cheered long after she'd finished.

Except for one man. John looked back to the podium, and Marcel Julien was staring right at him. Marcel started waving at one of his guards, trying to get his attention, but the man didn't see him.

John dropped from the lamppost, then quickly walked in the opposite direction of the fashion show. As he crossed the street, out of the corner of his eye, he spotted a man peel himself from the crowd, then fall in behind him. The man's timing was too coincidental and his pace too deliberate. John was being followed, and he cursed himself. He should have left once he knew Francie was safe, but he'd waited too long. He kept his pace, but realized he'd been clenching and unclenching his hands. John didn't have time to be angry with himself; this was dangerous, and he needed to calm down to be effective. He relaxed his hands and did his best to slow his mind.

John didn't turn around. Better to lure the man away from the crowd before engaging. He kept his pace and direction, directly inland and away from the beach. It was late afternoon, and the sun's angle caused the buildings to cast steep shadows onto the sidewalk. Shadows made it harder to gauge distance.

He walked for a couple of blocks, then turned down a side street. He walked two more blocks, then turned again. The man was still following. Parked cars lined the curb, and in the reflection of windshields, John saw the distance between himself and the man. So far, unchanged. He kept going. One more block, then John slowed down. He noticed the man following had done the same. John crossed an intersection, walked faster, and the man again matched him.

Up ahead, he saw a newsstand. He stopped and bought a newspaper. While waiting for change, John turned a bit to get a better look, but the man moved out of John's peripheral vision. He was still there, but John couldn't get a good look.

He looked ahead and across the street, and from what he could see, no collaborators were standing by and no vans idling on the road. This wasn't an abduction—just an attack.

He kept going, and the man kept following. John drifted closer to the cars' windshields, improving his visibility backward. After a few strides, he saw the man closing the distance. He was getting ready to attack.

It was coming, all because John had been careless. Again his anger started to percolate. He grunted, then pushed the thought aside. He had to get ready. John rolled his newspaper into a tight club.

John continued. He spotted a bright-red sports car parked a few feet away. He slowed as if to admire the car but got a good look at its windshield.

That's when John saw him. The man was coming fast. A couple of yards away, the man reached into his pocket and pulled something out. John stopped abruptly. He planted a foot, pushed off hard, and quickly closed the remaining space, surprising the man, who swung at John with whatever he was holding. John extended his newspaper club to block the attack. It worked. John threw an elbow at his attacker without missing a beat, catching him on the side of his head.

The man went down on one knee. John could see he had a club in his hand, and his hat was pulled down low, making it hard to see his face. John cocked his arm with the newspaper club, then swung.

With great speed and down on one knee, the man spun like a top, whipping his extended leg around. It caught John behind his knees and knocked him to the ground. The man raised his club and swung at John's head. John thrust out a straight arm and ducked to parry the blow. It deflected most of the strike, but the club still made contact with John's shoulder.

John winced in pain. He grabbed the man's wrist, the one holding the club, and pulled the man toward him. The man tumbled forward, and John threw a short, powerful punch, catching the man in the back of his head.

The man dropped his club. John saw the French version of a blackjack, a *casse tête*. He'd seen one for the first time years ago in the Resistance.

John rolled the man over and ripped off his hat, but he already knew.

Coco was staring up at him with a mix of fury and fright.

John punched Coco in the face, knocking his head into the concrete. He saw Coco's eyes roll back; he was stunned, but it would only last a few seconds. Quickly, he pat-searched Coco for another weapon but found none. He grabbed Coco's neck with one hand and the club with the other.

John was seething. "Give me one reason not to kill you."

"I had no choice," gurgled Coco. "I asked you for help, but you did nothing. And my time is up."

"So you decided to kill me?"

"No, it wasn't my idea."

"Whose, then?"

Coco was silent for a moment, then said, "The inspector."

"Lepic?"

Coco nodded. "He hates you. And if I did this, he'd get rid of my debts." He was defiant. "I didn't want this, but what choice did I have? Don't you see? I needed your help, and you turned your back on me." Coco's eyes watered. "I would never turn on a friend, but you stopped being my friend. And I needed you."

John was rattled. For the first time, he saw Coco's desperation. He let him go, then got to his feet. Coco was right; John shouldn't have ignored him. Seeing him so distraught triggered something, and John felt awful. He reached down to give Coco a hand.

At that moment, a rusty car pulled up. John looked over and saw that Luca was behind the wheel.

"What gives?" asked Luca. "On the phone, you told me to pick you up by the beach, not here. What's going on?"

"Change of plans," said John as he rubbed his shoulder. It hurt, but his sense of loyalty hurt more.

Luca looked past John. "Coco, is that you?"

"It's me."

"Are you two fighting?" asked Luca.

"Not really," said John. "Not anymore." He was quiet for a moment, thinking. Then he turned to Coco and said, "I'll help you. I have an idea."

Coco was taken aback. "Are you sure? You're not just saying this to—"

"I'm sure," said John. "Who do you owe? And how much?"

Coco told him. John nodded and said, "I'll take care of it."

"You will?" asked Coco.

"I will. Don't worry."

Coco's demeanor changed. His features softened, and he grabbed John's hand. "Thank you. I—"

"I should have listened the other night," said John. "I'm sorry. I didn't know how bad it was for you."

Coco's affection poured from him like an open spigot. He wrapped his arms around John. "Ahhh," he said, "you're a good friend. That's why I came to you. We have...what is it called?" He stumbled for a word, then said, "We have fraternity! All of us, like the old days, right, Luca?"

Luca smiled. "That's right. Like the old days."

Coco placed his hands on John's shoulders. "That inspector, he's coming for you. He won't stop."

"I know. He wants vengeance for something I didn't do. But

that's my problem, and I'll figure it out." He turned to Luca. "Can Coco stay at your garage? He has to lay low for a day."

"Sure," said Luca. "No problem. Coco, we'll drop you off on the way."

"On the way to where?" asked John.

"We need to talk," said Luca. "You and I are going swimming."

CHAPTER 53

Night had come, making it harder to see. John squinted. In the distance, he could barely see Marcel's yacht, mooring just off the marina, same spot as before.

He made his way to the stern of the heavy, wooden boat where Luca was operating the outboard motor. John had to watch his step; scattered about were buckets, nets, hooks, and other fishing equipment. The dark color of the boat blended with the moonlit water, making it hard to differentiate between the two. John put his hand on the gunwale to steady himself, then sat next to Luca.

"Up ahead," said John. "It's coming into view."

Luca pointed toward the beach. "That's where Vittoria and I sat. You would have laughed; she had me dressed like a tourist. She was playful and smiling; what an actress. Anyway, we could see the yacht and the marina over there." Luca pointed to a different spot on the coastline.

"That's where you saw the big, bald guy?"

Luca nodded. "Yes, at the marina. He got on that little dingy, and they ferried him to the yacht." He let out a deep breath. "John, I'm telling you, he was big. If a bull turned into a man, it would look like this guy."

"He was carrying the briefcase?"

"He was. He and three other guys got on the yacht, and all came back."

"But the briefcase stayed on the yacht?"

"Yes," said Luca. "The briefcase stayed."

"Nice work," said John.

"Whatever is in the briefcase is important. Why else have a monster like that deliver it, and why keep it on a yacht?"

"They want to make sure it's protected."

"Protected?" chuckled Luca. "They don't know you at all, do they?" He eased off the throttle. "Stop here?"

"Perfect," said John. "Not too close, not too far."

Luca grabbed a cinder block tied to the end of a rope, then eased it overboard. He let the line run through his hands. He loosely wrapped the other end to a cleat on the bow when it stopped.

John stripped down to his boxers. He kept his eyes on the yacht and saw two guards. One was pacing the perimeter of the vessel, and one was standing guard at the stern where visitors would board. Both guards were armed.

He focused on the pacing guard to get a sense of timing. Then John slipped over the side into the water. "Like last time," he said. "You see something, or the guard changes pace, give a loud finger whistle. Just one; I'll hear it."

He swam toward the anchor line using silent breaststrokes. He kept his eyes just above the water, and every few yards, he rose up enough to take a breath. Once at the anchor line, he hid behind the thick chain and watched for the pacing guard. From what John had seen, the man lapped the yacht every three minutes.

After a while, the guard reached the bow of the yacht, then turned to march back down the other side. John would be extra cautious this time; granted, he had some information on what Marcel and Hugo were planning, but it was more than that. He felt a strong obligation to Paul, especially after losing Francie and nearly losing his relationship with Coco. John wouldn't fail, not this time. He recalled that Francie used to taunt him about loyalty among thieves, but it was really loyalty among friends. He still considered her a friend, even if they were done.

John grabbed two chain links, then slowly pulled himself out of the water. He didn't want any splashing, nothing to draw attention, so he hung there for a minute. Then he climbed the chain fast. At the top, he transitioned his grip to the side of the yacht, then stopped.

He didn't have time to get onto the deck. The guard would be approaching any minute, so John hung from the side of the yacht, thinking. His fingertips, which curled up onto the deck, were visible from above. He pulled himself up, then stole a glance. A few yards away was a blind spot on the deck, a section with no light shining down. John lowered himself, then headed to the blind spot, sliding his hands one at a time. Up top, he heard progressively louder footsteps. The guard was returning. John arched his back, pushing his torso closer to the side of the yacht. The footsteps drew nearer. John didn't move. His hands started to cramp, then the pain seeped into his forearms. Training was one thing, but this was another level. He held his breath, and the guard passed right by.

He waited a moment, then flipped one leg up and onto the deck. He got the rest of his body up, then barrel-rolled over to the cabin wall and froze. There were no sounds other than the rhythmic footsteps of the pacing guard on the opposite side of the yacht. He got to his feet.

Some water had dripped from his body and pooled onto the deck. He crouched down, then used his hands to swish the water over the side. Ten feet away was the door to the cabin. John pressed close to the wall. He moved toward the door, opened it, and darted inside.

Time to find the briefcase.

No lights were on, but the moon provided enough illumination to see. As always, he scouted out an exit and a hiding spot. For both, there were several options. And the windows encircling the cabin gave him a clear view of the two guards. He located the guard walking the perimeter of the yacht, then closed his eyes and listened as the guard continued. After a moment, John opened his eyes, and the guard had completed a quarter lap. It was enough for him to calibrate his internal metronome; he would know that guard's location at all times.

John searched the salon and found nothing, then moved on to the staterooms with no luck. Returning to the salon, he noticed a small room at the front with a locked door. He checked for a key on the doorframe but found it in a nearby potted plant.

It was a meeting room, a well-appointed and private parlor. Starting from the top down, John searched the storage compartments, and in the second one, he found it. He took the briefcase down and placed it on the floor. It was heavier than he'd expected. John checked the latches. They weren't locked, so he opened them.

Staring up at him were visages of King Farouk, the former ruler of Egypt.

The briefcase was loaded with Egyptian currency.

Something clicked for him, a piece of the puzzle falling into place. John nodded to himself; the late-night visit to the yacht had been worth it. At that moment, the guard's footsteps stopped. John looked up, and through a rear cabin window, he noticed the pacing guard and the stern guard were switching places.

The new pacing guard started his first lap around the yacht's perimeter, and John returned to work. He checked the rest of the briefcase but found only money. A staggering amount of money.

The new guard moved much slower than the first but kept a consistent pace. John loaded the currency back into the briefcase, and for a brief moment, he considered stealing some. The thought jarred him, and he didn't know why. It wasn't unusual for him to think that, but taking this money put him off for some reason.

Just then, the footsteps stopped. By John's calculation, the guard would be outside the salon door.

And in the distance, he heard Luca whistle.

John moved back into the salon. Through a window, he could see the guard bend over and touch something, then tap a fingertip to his tongue. The man tilted his head as if confused, then looked over the side of the yacht, searching the immediate area.

After a moment, the guard turned and touched the outside wall of the cabin—and again tapped a finger to his tongue. He moved toward the cabin door, touching and tapping every few steps.

John could feel his blood surging through his veins. He was in his boxers and soaking wet, making him feel smaller than he was. But still...it was happening. The guard had spotted water on the deck—salt water—and knew it didn't belong. He had traced John's path, and now he was standing just outside. John saw him ready his rifle, then reach for the door.

John rushed to the door and shoved it open. The guard jumped backward. He grabbed the barrel of the man's gun and jerked him into the cabin. For a moment, they stood there, both tugging on the rifle suspended between them. John felt his feet slip, and for an instant he wished he'd been wearing shoes.

Right then, the guard shouted a single word. John steadied himself, then shot a glance out the window and saw the second guard was not at his post.

That meant he was coming.

In a flash, John swept the man's feet out from under him. The guard fell to the ground, then John threw a fast, short punch to the jaw. That did it. The guard was out cold.

One down.

John rushed to the door. Just before he got there, it was yanked open. In the doorway stood the other guard, with his rifle in position to fire. John was two feet away. He pushed the barrel up. The guard squeezed the trigger, and a short barrage of bullets striped the ceiling. The familiar smell of burnt gunpowder hung in the air, immediately transporting John back to the war and reminding him that he was fighting for his life. He felt a sudden increase in strength and shoved the guard against the wall. Both men were now outside. "Not today," he grunted, the words pushing out like gravel.

He headbutted the guard, catching the man across the bridge of his nose as a second stream of bullets was fired into the night sky. He threw another headbutt, striking the guard on his cheekbone. The man slumped against the doorframe, then dropped his rifle.

Two down.

He stood there for a moment, his arms hanging thick and heavy. Where had that surge of power come from? Was it his survival instincts, or was he angry because of... Right then, John heard another whistle from Luca. It jarred him to attention, and he looked around. At the marina, he saw two armed men scrambling into an inflatable Zodiac with an outboard engine.

John didn't have much time. He looked back and saw Luca speeding toward him. He sprinted in Luca's direction, then dove over the railing. He struck the water, then swam as fast as he could.

Luca swung the boat sideways, right in front of John, but didn't kill the engine. He reached down, grabbed John's hand, then pulled him into the boat with one mighty yank. John collapsed onto a bench.

"Go!" said John. "They're coming." He looked around, but Luca wasn't operating the motor. He was standing in the middle of the boat, stripped down to his boxers.

"We can't outrun them," Luca said. "They're too fast. We have to fight."

"They have guns."

"And I have these." Luca held a hook in each hand, both a foot long with a thick wooden handle.

John was confused. "What...?"

"What you need to do is listen. Take the boat straight back. Aim for that buoy, and stay on the line." With that, Luca slid over the side of the boat and into the water. "Okay, go!"

John shouted in protest, but Luca was already underwater. He should be taking the risks, not Luca. But it was too late, and the guards were coming. He scrambled to the motor, then turned the throttle. He noticed his one hand was shaking; he was losing control of the situation, and he despised that feeling.

The Zodiac was coming right at John, and it was coming fast. He aimed for the buoy, then gunned the motor.

Again, he looked over his shoulder. The Zodiac with the two guards was getting closer. One of the guards aimed a rifle at John, but the bow of the Zodiac was bouncing off the water, making a shot difficult. The guard steadied himself, waiting for the boat to smack down onto the water. Just before it did, the man fired. John ducked, and the bullet whizzed by.

His breathing was fast and heavy, and he was squeezing the throttle: all signs of alarm, and John knew it. He was angry with himself for not anticipating this, and for not stopping Luca. Still, he had to calm himself down; the situation was dire, and he needed to be sharp. He looked back again and saw the guard taking aim. The bow of the Zodiac hit a wake, rose up, then started back down. Just then, Luca emerged, his arms spread wide, a hook in each hand. Luca whipped the hooks into the front of the Zodiac. The nose of the Zodiac dipped hard, and the boat flipped, sending both guards flying.

John turned his boat around. He could see the two guards treading water near the hobbled Zodiac. But no sign of Luca.

The guards swam toward one another. One guard shouted to the other, but John didn't recognize the language. Then the man stopped. He was treading water in a tight circle, looking all around. Something jolted the man, pulling him sideways. He let loose a terrifying scream, then, in the blink of an eye, was yanked underwater. It happened so fast that the guard's arms seemed to shoot straight up.

And then it was quiet. The other guard started panicking. He kept looking around, scanning the water, muttering to himself. And just like that, the second guard was pulled under. It was so quick that he didn't have a chance to yell. John inched the boat forward. He could see two funnels of bubbles breaking the surface. Then the water went still.

There was no noise, not a sound. John leaned over the side and looked around, but still no sign of Luca.

Just then, Luca emerged from the water, right under John. He reached up, and John pulled him in.

"You okay?" asked John.

"A little cold," said Luca, his eyes searching their boat. "We forgot towels, didn't we?"

John sat there, staring.

"We need to go," said Luca. "Shots were fired, remember?"

"Right." John made his way to the motor.

"Besides," said Luca, "you still have a busy night."

CHAPTER 54

O dette pulled the curtain back, then looked down onto the driveway. Whatever had happened was bad, but she hoped not too bad.

Marcel was in a serious discussion with some crewmen from their yacht, and that big, bald man was standing to the side, listening with a ferocity Odette had never seen before.

Whatever they were saying had angered Marcel. He pointed at one of the crew members and raised his voice. Then the big, bald man stepped in with authority. He pushed Marcel aside and grabbed the crewman by the neck. With one arm, he lifted the crewman off the ground, then slammed him against a wall.

Odette turned away and let the curtain fall back into place. She got into bed and turned to face the door.

A few minutes later, Marcel came into the bedroom. Odette saw him rip off his jacket, then hurl it into a corner. With both hands on his head, he began pacing the room.

After a moment, she said, "Is everything okay?"

He kept pacing. "No, everything is not okay. But it hasn't cost us. Not this time."

"Good. This week is critical, and Miss Stevens—"

"—has been wonderful, I know," said Marcel. "But she's been attracting attention all week. And not the kind I want."

"I don't like the sound of that," said Odette as she sat up. "Whatever you're planning, we can't lose her."

Marcel stopped pacing. "Of course. But it occurs to me that the problem is also the solution."

"How so?"

"Leave that to me," said Marcel. He sat on the bed next to her. "I appreciate you wanting to help. But I know what I'm doing."

Odette reached out and placed her hand on Marcel's. "I know you do."

"I'll take care of it," he said. "This ends now."

CHAPTER 55

John stood still in the darkness, straining to listen. Someone was coming down the stairs, and John wanted to be sure it was him. He wiped the sweat from his upper lip, then listened again. He needed this to work.

The next few steps sounded heavy. It was him, thought John. Time to move.

He went into the kitchen, as quiet as a shadow. He placed his bag on the table, then took a seat.

The heavy footsteps reached the bottom of the stairs, then turned toward John. A man entered the room, wearing a navy-blue robe with a paisley print and fine leather slippers. He flipped on a light and went to an overhead cabinet. He pulled out a glass, then headed to the refrigerator. The man removed a milk bottle, filled his glass halfway, and turned in John's direction.

That's when the man saw John. He jumped back, nearly spilling his milk. The man gasped, then put his hand over his heart. "What the...?"

John held a finger to his lips, asking for quiet.

"John," the man whispered, "what are you doing in my kitchen?"

"I need a favor."

"How did you get past my men?"

John smiled and shrugged his shoulders. "That's never a problem for me. But seriously, I don't want them to know I was here. And I had to see you tonight."

"You're always welcome," said Roland, "but don't do this next time. You scared me half to death." He grabbed a plate of cookies from the counter, then sat opposite John. He pushed the glass of milk between them, then the plate. "Sablé biscuits. Try one."

John helped himself to one of the traditional French shortbread cookies, then took a bite.

Roland shook his head. "No, no, no. Not like that. Like this." He dunked a cookie into the milk, then took a bite. "Now you."

John did the same. "These are excellent."

"My wife," said Roland. "She makes them for me every week. I sneak down at night, as you saw."

"Well, please pass along my compliments."

Roland and John took turns dipping cookies in the milk. After a few minutes, Roland said, "What's in the bag?"

"It has to do with my favor," said John. "A good friend of mine, Coco. You know him?"

With a mouthful of cookie, Roland nodded.

"He owes you a great deal of money, and I'm here to pay off his debt. If you'll allow me." He pushed the bag toward Roland. "It's more than he owes you, a lot more, but I'm asking a lot from you to accept this gesture."

Roland unzipped the bag, then looked inside. "This is a lot. Is this your money from your accounts?"

"The money found its way to me a few days ago, so, yes, it's mine. But I didn't have to cash in any investments. It's clean, not from your competitor, and the police aren't looking for it. There's also a handgun in there, an old Mauser. Thought you might find a use for it."

Roland pushed back from the table, then shook his head. "I don't know about this."

John jumped right in. "I know it goes against your principles, one man paying the debt of another, but I'm asking you as a friend."

Roland thought for a moment. "You're a good friend."

"A very good friend," said John. "You remember that time in the restaurant when those gunmen came for you?"

"Who could forget?" said Roland. "The maître d', the waiters—they still talk about what you did. You saved my life."

"And that other time, with the Corsicans. Remember?"

Roland softened. "Yes, I remember." He was quiet for a moment, then said, "Okay, I hear you. And I accept your very generous offer on behalf of your friend Coco."

John got to his feet. "One more thing. Can you please ask your men to block Coco, to never again take his bets?"

"That, I can do," said Roland. "But very quietly, you understand."

John nodded. "I understand, and I've got to go. One more stop tonight. It was great to see you, and I can't thank you enough."

Roland got up, then hugged John. "Don't be a stranger. But next time, use the front door."

John smiled. "I will. But now I have to sneak out the back."

"Of course," said Roland. "Hey, how about golf next week? If you can steal the time." He waited a moment, then said, "Get it?"

John laughed. He rested a hand on Roland's shoulder. "I get it, and I'd love to play."

"Great. See you next week."

"You can bet on it."

Roland laughed. "Very clever, John. We'll call it a draw."

CHAPTER 56

John swung his legs forward, then let go of the tree branch. His momentum carried him over the railing, and he landed on the second-story balcony without a sound.

He ducked into a dark corner and stood as still as possible. The moonlight was strong, and Marcel had increased security, making it riskier than last time. John was taking every precaution. Looking down to the ground, he saw two guards passing by, close to the villa, and two more guards patrolling in the opposite direction, near the property line.

He moved to the French doors that opened into Marcel's office. Locked. John quickly picked the lock and stepped inside, heading for the wall safe. He moved the painting aside. The lock on the safe was more secure than the one on the door, and it required different tools. John searched his picks, found what he needed, then got started on the safe. After a few minutes, he had it open. Inside, the contents were the same as last time.

Moving quickly, John grabbed the envelopes Francie had given Marcel, removed each letter from its envelope, laid it on the desk, then took a photograph with the Minox camera. He flipped each one over, took another picture, then put them back into the safe.

He heard footsteps in the hallway. He didn't have time to get to the balcony, so he closed the safe, covered it with the painting, then ducked behind the desk. The footsteps stopped just outside Marcel's office. Someone tested the lock, making sure the room was secured, then headed down the stairs.

John went to the door, unlocked it, then opened it a crack. Two guards were at the bottom of the stairs, reviewing logistics. Most likely a shift change. *Not good*, thought John. Guards were more vigilant at the start of shifts.

The guards finished talking. Then the new guard headed up the stairs. John closed and locked the door, then hurried to the balcony and stepped outside.

Behind him, John heard the guard testing the doorknob, then fumbling with keys. He had to get out of sight fast. In his experience, people's eyes gravitated toward the light and away from shadows. A tree had cast a shadow across the balcony just five feet away. John went to that spot, then hopped over the railing. He held on to the bottom rail and let his body dangle.

Above him, he heard the guard step out onto the balcony. A moment later, the guard stepped back inside the office and locked the doors.

Now John looked around. No guards. He pulled himself back up to the balcony, then headed for the tree he'd climbed on his way up.

He got into the tree, then waited for two guards to pass. John's muscles ached, but he felt good. He'd done what Paul and Armand wanted. John had gotten all he could from Hugo and now Marcel, the only two men definitely involved.

That wasn't exactly true. There was another man. Marcel's chauffeur was involved, until he'd gone over the cliff. John could learn something by searching his premises. Based on his surveillance, there were staff quarters in the basement. But chauffeurs often had different arrangements.

John looked toward the front of Marcel's villa. A couple of cars were parked in the driveway, and the garage had three big bay doors. But John saw a regular house door on one end, and next to that, some windows with curtains. He narrowed his vision and saw a thin slice of light coming from inside.

Maybe a chauffeur's apartment?

It was certainly worth a look.

He'd come down the tree slowly to avoid sudden moves, and wrapped himself around a lower, horizontal branch. Two guards passed, then another two farther away.

John waited, then dropped to the ground. He kept himself crouched so he was the same height as the shrubs. He looked around, then darted to another shrub, farther from the house but closer to the garage. He stayed low and listened. So far, he was undetected.

A minute later, two guards passed between him and the villa. Both looked tired. John figured he had about ten seconds before the other two guards appeared.

That wasn't a lot of time. John had to be quick but keep his movements soft, a difficult balance under the best of circumstances.

His nerves crackled, a potent mix of anxiety and excitement. He stayed low, then advanced along a shadow until he reached a thick tree just off the garage. He paused, and around the corner came the other two guards. When they passed by, John went to the garage window.

He stood to the side so his shadow wasn't visible from inside. John looked closely. There was something behind the curtain blocking views into the garage. After a moment, he knew what it was—a utility blanket. Someone had draped it over the window from the inside.

He moved to the other window with the slice of light shining through, but the guards were due to make a pass. He hid behind a tree, then moved around the trunk so he was always out of sight to the guards.

His foot hit something. He stopped moving and looked over at the guards; they hadn't heard a thing and continued their lap. John bent over to see what he'd hit. It was a conduit pipe for wires, about a half inch across, right at the tree's base, and coming out of the pipe was a wire. It was stapled tight to the trunk and ran straight up the tree. John looked, but he couldn't see where the wire went.

He stepped back, then looked up from another angle. Near the top of the tree was an antenna the shape and size of a rib cage, well hidden among the branches. John looked back to the ground, then traced the conduit pipe back to the garage. He moved closer to the building, and there it was, poking out of the ground, with the same wire running into the garage.

The other guards were due any moment. John crouched down, leveling himself with the shrubs. Like clockwork, the guards appeared around a corner. They chatted as they walked past and were soon out of sight.

Quickly, John moved to the other window. It also had a utility blanket, but this one left a small gap uncovered. That was the light he'd seen. He looked inside.

To his surprise, a man sat on a stool, hunched over a worktable. He was wearing headphones while writing on a pad. A radio was next to the pad, just like the ones John had seen in the Resistance. And attached to the radio was a Morse code transmitter.

It all made sense now. Marcel was trafficking encrypted information and needed a base to send and receive. Here it was!

The man inside was writing, not tapping the transmitter—meaning he was receiving a message. John looked closer. It wasn't Marcel; he wasn't as broad across the shoulders. But John couldn't see his face.

The man pushed away from the table and removed his headphones. He tore a piece of paper from the pad and tucked it into his pocket.

He was leaving! John hid behind a shrub just as the man walked out of the garage. He pulled the door shut behind him, checking to ensure he'd locked it. He was older, with rounded shoulders and a shuffle in his walk. He wore an oversized wool jacket that he'd folded up at the cuffs. The man took a few steps, then looked around, giving John a glimpse of his face.

He'd seen the man before—but where? John thought for a moment, then it hit him. It was earlier that day, on the beach.

The big glasses were the giveaway. They made the older man's eyes look huge.

Like an owl's.

The old man walked toward a car parked at the top of the drive-way. He passed two guards, and they exchanged nods of famil-iarity, but no one said a word. The old man drove away, and the guards continued their march.

John went back to the garage door. He took out his lockpicks, and after some jiggling, he got the door open. The old man had left the light on, and John took in the small room, which was empty except for the light, a table, a radio, the transmitter, and a pad. John walked up to the table. He didn't recognize the radio, so he took out the Minox camera and got a picture.

Then he looked down at the pad. A blank page stared up at him. There was no writing, but there were clear indentations from a previous page. John ripped it off, rolled it up, and put it in his pocket.

He opened the door, then looked around. No guards. He set the lock, stepped outside, and pulled the door shut. There was a series of bushes on the grounds. John zigzagged from one to the next, timing each move to the passing of the guards. He reached the fence around the property's perimeter and started to climb over.

He heard a noise, then looked back. A car pulled into the driveway, and a huge, bald man stepped out. The guy was massive, with a thick mustache and a savage stare. There was no doubt he was the man Luca had seen. He strode like a giant bull toward the villa, looking as if he could swat away cars and trees if they were in his way. Both sets of guards went right to the guy, and after a brief discussion, the big man went inside. Then the guards resumed their rounds.

John exhaled, unaware that he had been holding his breath.

The colossus hadn't spotted him, and John didn't feel like giving him another chance.

He moved fast.

He had to see Paul and Armand.

CHAPTER 57

P aul led John down a long hallway to the library. He could
see Paul's magnificent *jardin à la française*, a classic French
garden, through a window. It was stunning in the morning
light—geometric patterns inside linear boundaries, all created
with plants, bushes, and shrubs.

John was exhausted. He'd left Marcel's and come straight over.
He needed Paul to arrest Marcel, to put him behind bars. John
had compiled a lot of evidence in the last few hours and was eager
to share.

"Another attempt, you said?"

"Yes," replied John. "This time, it was Marcel's chauffeur. He
tried to run me off a cliff."

"Where is he now?"

"At the bottom of that cliff. But more on that later; I've got a
lot to tell you."

"And we have updates for you," said Paul. "Let's go in here." He opened the door to the library. Inside, Armand was sitting at a table, surrounded by files.

"You need to arrest Marcel," said John.

Paul held out both hands. "Let's review what we have before we commit, okay?"

"Okay," said John. "Why don't you start."

Paul walked over and stood next to Armand. "Regarding Hugo's business interests, of which there are many, we found no connections to Marcel and no connections to the fashion industry. The only significant change was with Hugo's family. His brother acquired a shipping company in Caracas, Venezuela. The company ships mainly to French ports. Not southern ports like Marseille, but those in the north—Calais and Le Havre, the main supply centers for Paris."

"That company has grown significantly this past year," added Armand.

Paul moved right along. "And, personally, Hugo is having a secret affair with an Algerian woman."

"But not just any woman," said Armand. "This one, she's an international revolutionary. In fact, she was the leader of the Egyptian Revolution of '52. Remember? Anti-imperialists overthrew Egypt's monarchy, then gained control of the country."

John nodded. "I remember. They kicked out the Brits."

"Yes and no," said Paul. "The Brits still hold territory around the Suez Canal. But their hold is tenuous."

"Here's where it gets interesting," said Armand. "Hugo is scheduled to go to Egypt Friday evening. He's going to Port Said, the city at the entrance to the canal."

"It's coming together," said John. He felt a sensation rip through his body, a deep sense of exhilaration. He pushed his hands into his pockets to keep them still. He could see what was going to happen. He didn't know why, but that would come. "There's an enormous amount of money on Marcel's yacht. I've seen it. And all of it Egyptian pounds."

"I'm not following," said Paul.

"I'll explain," said John. "Remember the man who fell from the roof?"

Paul nodded.

"He was delivering a large sum of money to Marcel, who, in turn, was supposed to give it to Hugo. That money came from Russia. It disappeared the night that man died. But the Russians replaced the money yesterday. Right now, it's sitting on Marcel's yacht. Egyptian currency, and a lot of it."

Paul was piecing it together. "So Marcel is keeping a fortune in Egyptian currency on his yacht to give to Hugo. And Hugo is going to Egypt tomorrow."

"That's right. Oh, before I forget, here's the Minox." John handed the camera to Armand. "I paid a friendly visit to Marcel's last night and photographed the envelopes Francie gave him. It's all there."

"Thank you," said Paul. "I appreciate what you've done."

Armand got up from the table, taking the Minox with him. "I'll get to work on this."

"Before you go," said John, "I have a favor to ask. I spoke with Francie. I didn't tell her anything, but someone is setting her up. She's being used. I don't know who; I don't know why. So whatever you find, can we talk before you do anything? To her, I mean."

Paul and Armand exchanged glances. "You have our word,"

said Paul. "No matter what we uncover, we'll talk." He paused, then said, "I thought it was over between you two."

"It is."

"Then why do this for her?"

John thought for a moment, then said, "Basic fairness, I guess. She deserves that."

Paul smiled. "Well, that's something in and of itself."

"Looking out for a former friend," said John. "Nothing more, nothing less." Then he took a seat. "I'm sorry, but I'm exhausted. I need to rest."

"No problem," said Paul. "Would you like a guest room upstairs? There's a reading room with a big couch down the hall. Whatever you prefer."

"The couch sounds great," said John. He followed Paul out of the room, then stopped. "I almost forgot. Marcel is operating a clandestine radio station out of his garage, complete with hidden antennae, blankets covering windows, all that. While there, an older man who works for Marcel, a designer or maybe a tailor, received a message. He wrote it all down on a pad. After he left, I took the page underneath."

John took the paper from his jacket pocket and handed it to Armand. "You can see the indentations. All numbers."

Armand was excited. "This just happened?"

"A couple of hours ago."

"This is valuable, my friend." Armand waved the paper like a small flag. "This is fresh intelligence. Let me start with this."

"And let me take you to that couch," said Paul. He patted John on the back, then led him away. "Is there anything you need?"

"One thing," said John. "Lepic is determined to get me, one

way or another. I have an idea concerning the good inspector, but it must come from you."

"What's your idea?"

CHAPTER 58

John pulled himself from a deep, deep slumber. As he got closer to the surface, he felt a hand on his upper arm, rocking him gently.

He opened his eyes. Paul was sitting on the couch next to him. Armand was standing behind Paul.

"How long have I been asleep?" asked John.

"Everyone asks that when they wake up," said Armand. "Why?"

Paul ignored him. "You've been out a long time. We were going to wake you for lunch..."

"...but we thought you needed the rest," said Armand.

John sat up, groggy and sore. Armand handed him a coffee in a mug that looked as big as a bucket. "What did you learn?" said John.

"We've decrypted everything," said Paul. "Including that file from Marcel's safe, the one you photographed the other night."

"That took forever," said Armand.

"And here's what we know," said Paul. "Are you ready?"

John sipped his coffee. "I'm ready."

"Marcel is working with the Russians to spur revolutions in our territories," said Paul, "and to disrupt major trade routes. This particular operation concerns the Suez Canal."

Armand spoke next. "It's part of their longer-term strategy. The more disruption the Russians cause—in the territories and with our trade routes—the more France destabilizes."

"To combat this," said Paul, "France must throw people and money at the problem. Whether it's keeping the territories stable or fighting to keep the Suez Canal open, it's a lot of resources."

"Resources the government could use elsewhere," said Armand, "to improve conditions or to grow the economy. Instead, we spend to maintain."

John drank more coffee as he took it all in.

"It's part of their plan to cripple the West," said Paul. "To slow us down."

"Choking off the Suez Canal does exactly that," said Armand. "It slows us down."

"And when we slow down, Russia catches up," said Paul. "That's their plan."

John nodded. "And this plot we've stumbled upon...the Russians want to shut down the Suez Canal?"

"Indirectly," said Paul. "Russia gives money to Marcel and Hugo. And they fund revolutionaries who seize the canal."

John thought for a moment. "That could be devastating."

"Without a doubt," said Armand. "The geopolitical implications are enormous. The Suez Canal is the shortest route from Europe to Asia. And vice versa."

"Imagine if shipping costs tripled, or worse," said Paul. "Inflation would rip through our economy like a flash fire."

"And the oil," said Armand. "That's the bigger problem. Right now, half the traffic through the canal is oil. Two-thirds of Europe's oil flows through the canal from the Middle East."

John rose to his feet. "That's it," he said. "It's about oil."

"What's about oil?" asked Armand.

"Hugo's role is clear," said John. "He and his mistress go to Egypt tomorrow with a briefcase full of money. Then they fund revolutionaries, who seize the canal."

"I see where you're going," said Paul. "If revolutionaries take control of the canal, they may or may not let oil through. If they allow oil through, we have no idea the price. Or the quantity."

"And if they don't allow oil through..."

"Then we have no oil," said Armand. "Either way, we have no control. Maybe we have oil. Maybe we don't. Maybe the cost is reasonable. Maybe it's not. Uncertainty is all we have."

"And markets can't stand uncertainty," said Paul. "Our entire economy would collapse."

Armand chimed in. "Couldn't it be transported over land?"

"It could," said Paul, "but think about the logistics, how many questionable countries it would pass through. And it would cost more. Much more."

"That's right," said John. "It has to come by ship. And if we can't get oil from the Middle East... Are you following?"

"Keep going," said Armand.

"If we're cut off from the Middle East," said John, "who ships us oil?"

"South America," said Paul. "They're the second-largest producer."

"Where in South America?" asked John.

John watched it fall into place for Paul. Armand was a step behind, and when it hit him, he covered his mouth.

"Oh my," said Armand. "It would ship from Caracas."

"That's right," said John. "We know Hugo's family owns a shipping company in Caracas, and they ship to France's northern ports."

"Let's play it out," said Paul. "The canal gets seized, the revolutionaries cut our oil supply, then Hugo and his brother step in and save the day."

"So Hugo would control the flow of oil to France..." said Armand.

"Not just France," said Paul. "All of Europe."

They all paused as they considered the ramifications. Then Armand spoke. "What would Marcel gain from this?" he asked.

"Everything Hugo gains, Marcel gains," said John. "Assuming they're partners." He turned to Paul. "You have enough to arrest them, right?"

"Yes and no," said Paul. "For their plan to disrupt the Suez Canal, we can arrest them right now. But we haven't told you about Francie."

"Her family is in the oil business," said John. "But I can't imagine she's caught up in this."

"You're right," said Paul. "She's not caught up in this. But Marcel is running another operation."

"Concerning what?" said John.

Paul began to speak, then stopped. He collected himself, then said, "Something that could shift the balance of power to the Russians."

"Francie's involved in this?"

Paul nodded. "The envelopes she's been passing to Marcel are solely concerned with this second operation," he said.

"Again, what are we talking about?" said John.

Paul and Armand exchanged looks. After a moment, Paul said, "Go ahead, tell him."

Armand stepped closer to John, then lowered his voice.

"What do you know about the hydrogen bomb?"

CHAPTER 59

John was annoyed. He wanted to know what they'd learned about Francie but couldn't get a straight answer. He was about to protest, but Paul and Armand looked very serious, so he went along.

"What do I know about it?" said John. "Probably what everyone knows. The hydrogen bomb is more powerful than the atom bomb."

"That doesn't begin to describe it," said Paul. "It's over a thousand times more powerful."

"So you have context," said Armand, "I'll share some facts. In miles, not kilometers, okay?"

John agreed.

"As a test," said Armand, "a hydrogen bomb was detonated by the United States on one of the Marshall Islands. The fireball from that one bomb was three miles wide. The fireball! The mushroom cloud was twenty-five miles high and a hundred miles wide. That is unimaginable."

John was surprised. "I had no idea."

"And the island where the test was performed," said Armand.
"Completely gone. The explosion evaporated that island. It left
a hole in the ocean floor a mile wide." Armand was winding up,
getting more demonstrative by the moment. "The blast blew out
windows a thousand miles away. Imagine a bomb goes off in New
York, and it shatters windows in Florida. It boggles the mind."

"Right now," said Paul, "the United States is the only nation
with a hydrogen bomb. But Russia is desperately trying to make
its own. One thing is holding them back."

"What's that?" asked John.

"Tritium," said Paul. "It's a by-product of a nuclear reaction. A
nation would need a nuclear reactor to create its own tritium supply. Russia, as we know, has reactors."

"But that's not enough," added Armand. "A nuclear reaction
creates tritium, but it must be collected. And that's the problem,
you see. Tritium is unstable, and some brilliant science is needed
to make it stable."

"And that science," said Paul, "is holding Russia back."

John got up from the couch. "So the United States figured out
how to stabilize tritium so they could make a hydrogen bomb?"

"That's right," said Paul. "The United States built a reactor just
for that purpose. Then they figured it out."

"I'm following," said John. "But I can't see how this involves
Francie."

Paul rested a hand on John's shoulder. "Everything in the envelopes Francie gave Marcel was about stabilizing tritium."

John rubbed his eyes. The implications were almost too painful to
contemplate. Paul and Armand weren't talking about traditional

treason. They were discussing arming the enemy with the most devastating weapon ever conceived. If Francie were involved, her life would be over. Worst case, she'd face the death penalty. The best case would be prison with no hope of parole. Francie would never move forward with Alex or with anyone. She'd never have her own family, and her career would be finished.

John felt nauseated. He put his hand on his stomach and swallowed. Francie didn't deserve that. No one did. Surely Paul knew Francie was caught up in this, that someone was using her to pass secrets. Paul had to see the brutal unfairness of her situation.

"Francie isn't a scientist," said John. "It stands to reason she's been manipulated."

Paul was solemn. He held John's stare. After a moment, he said, "You're right. She's being framed."

John snapped to attention. "What do you mean?" he asked. "How do you know?"

"That sheet of paper from Marcel's garage," said Armand. "From the radio pad. I deciphered it."

"Tell me!"

Armand pulled some notes from his jacket pocket, then began reading. "FRIDAY NIGHT, OUR AGENT TO PUT FS ON FLIGHT TO COPENHAGEN. STOP."

"Our agent is clearly Marcel Julien," said John.

"And FS is Francie Stevens," added Paul.

Armand continued, "FLIGHT DIVERTED EN ROUTE. STOP."

"To where?" asked John.

Armand stopped reading. He looked at John. "To St. Petersburg," he said. "To Russia. The message said that's where her recruitment will be finalized."

"They're not recruiting her," said John. "They're going to blackmail her."

"Right, again," said Armand. "They expect she'll resist. And because of that, the Russians want men following MS, in case leverage is needed."

"MS is Maude Stevens," said John. "Francie's mother."

Paul had been staring out a window. "A classic Russian tactic," he said. "They have Francie passing secrets. She has no idea they're classified, but still, she's breaking the law. Then they approach her, telling her no one has to know. With one stipulation—she keeps working for them, spying for them. If she resists, they threaten someone close to her. Her mother, maybe her boyfriend."

John was angry, and it took considerable effort to keep his emotions in check. He wasn't surprised Marcel was attacking him. After all, John had taken that money. But Francie's situation was different. She'd done nothing. Yet she was being forced into two terrible choices. Whether she agreed or not, she was throwing her life away. To them, Francie was disposable. And to John, that was appalling.

John focused his intensity on Paul. "You heard Armand. You know Francie's innocent. You can't charge her. We have to do something. We..."

"...need to let this play out," said Paul. "We do this the right way. I wish Francie weren't involved. But she is, and..." Paul stopped. He was running scenarios in his mind. Then he pointed at John. "I know what you're thinking. Don't do anything to derail this investigation."

"I'll stay out of your way, when it comes to guilty parties."

Paul shook his finger. "That's not good enough. If you try to help her, you endanger everything. We can't have that. I'm sorry, John." Paul collected himself, then said, "It's best if you stay out of this. At least until tomorrow night."

John brushed past Armand and walked right up to Paul. "I want to be clear. Whatever you do with Hugo, with Marcel, I'll stay out of your way. I won't compromise your investigation. But I'm not going to hide at home while Marcel and his thugs put Francie on a plane to Copenhagen."

"Don't you see?" said Paul. "Marcel knows you'll try to help her. He'll be waiting for you."

"I know," said John. "And I'm counting on it." With that, he put down his coffee mug and left the room. John checked his watch. There wasn't much time. He had less than a day to warn Francie in a way that didn't impact Paul's investigation.

But how?

CHAPTER 60

Vieux-Port de Cannes, Cannes

From the back seat, Odette leaned forward. She could barely hear Marcel over the thick purring of the Riva Tritone runabout, the glistening mahogany boat Marcel used for quick runs to the yacht. Marcel was at the wheel, and next to him was a broad man with a flattop crew cut, a man Odette had never met. They were murmuring. Odette tried to listen.

She caught snippets of conversation. "Tomorrow night is... more men... how many..." She didn't like this at all. Lately, Marcel dismissed her input, and now he was planning who-knows-what with a stranger. She would have none of it.

Odette interjected herself into their conversation. "Whatever you are discussing," she said to Marcel, "I'd like to be included. I can help."

Marcel looked back at her. "It's already decided. We're just going over details."

"I'm good with details," said Odette. "This—"

"—this discussion is over," interrupted Marcel. "No more. I know what I'm doing."

Odette sat back. Ignoring her, excluding her, and now dismissing her as a child—enough was enough.

Marcel had better have this under control, she thought.

If he didn't, they stood to lose everything.

CHAPTER 61

epic followed Paul through the entrance of his venerable villa. He'd never seen a home this monumental. Every step revealed a famous painting, a magnificent bronze, or an architectural detail that astounded the mind. Lepic knew the man was royalty, but he had no idea he was this well off.

When he'd answered his phone earlier that evening and discovered Paul Du Pre on the other end, Lepic's legs nearly gave out. Single-handedly, he could rectify Lepic's situation. The man was that powerful. Caution was required, however. Lepic wouldn't raise the issue. Not today, at least. One had to earn trust and respect.

Paul steered Lepic into a study. "Here," he said. "Nice and private."

Lepic entered the study, biting his lip. He would do whatever was asked, without question. He would never turn down a request from a man like Paul Du Pre.

"Have a seat," said Paul. "Coffee, tea, something stronger?"

Lepic sat opposite Paul. "Nothing for me, but generous of you to offer, Monsieur Du Pre."

"Call me Paul. That's what my friends call me."

"Paul it is," said Lepic, with an extra dose of enthusiasm. "How may I be of service?"

"I have a favor to ask; not what you might expect."

"Anything," said Lepic. To himself, he thought, *Please, not a favor for John Robie. Do not ask this of me.*

"Your reputation in law enforcement was beyond reproach," said Paul. "That is, before last year when unfortunate events conspired to hold you back."

Lepic was dumbfounded. Paul Du Pre, or rather "Paul," admitted that last summer's investigation of John Robie had derailed Lepic's career. His frank acknowledgment was priceless. Lepic struggled to say something but couldn't. He simply nodded as if to say, "please proceed."

Paul continued, "Since that happened, it's been a concern of ours..."

Again, Lepic was stunned. He said "ours," implying that others were of like mind.

"...and we would like to see that rectified."

Was he hearing this correctly? Lepic loosened his tie, then tried to push words from his mouth. Finally, he said, "Are you talking about reinstating me?"

Paul smiled. "Much better than that, Inspector. I'm asking you to take action. Action that will be critical to the security of France. Then, at my request, and with my full endorsement, the authorities will have no choice but to reinstate you."

"I don't know what to say. This is beyond words. I shall be indebted to you for the rest of my life."

"Not true," said Paul. "You are owed a debt, and I believe this goes a long way toward paying it."

Lepic rocked in his seat. The excitement was overwhelming him, and he had to focus. "This action you speak of, what are we talking about?"

Lepic saw Paul glance around the study. Paul lowered his voice, then said, "In my new role, a case has come to my attention. Our nation is being victimized by foreign spies, working closely with some of France's leading citizens."

Lepic sat up straight. This had nothing to do with John Robie. Nothing at all. "Betrayal against our homeland? And you need my help?"

"Yes. It reaches the highest levels of government. But it isn't your help I need. It's your partnership."

Lepic hesitated. Something wasn't right, but he didn't want to offend. He chose his words carefully. "I'm very appreciative, but why me?"

"A few reasons. First, the case was discovered here, in your jurisdiction."

To steady himself, Lepic placed both palms flat on his thighs. Then he took a deep breath and said, "Please do not mistake what I'm about to say for lack of gratitude. But is that enough for someone like you to partner with someone like me?"

"It's not," said Paul. "But this is—things are moving fast. Arrests will be made tomorrow, and I have no men on the ground. They won't arrive in time. You, however, have men."

"I do, indeed. Good men."

"But none as good as you," said Paul. "And that is most crucial. I need a true law enforcement professional to help me plan this out."

Lepic closed his eyes, then blessed himself. This was more than he'd hoped for. "I shall do whatever is necessary. I'm honored."

"Wonderful. I'll brief you. Then we'll plan it out. If you have time."

"Of course," said Lepic. "Justice never rests. Not with me."

Paul shook Lepic's hand. "There is one small matter," said Paul. "I'm sure you won't find it objectionable."

Lepic chuckled. "I object to nothing. What you're doing for me is incredible."

"Good," said Paul. "It has to do with my friend, John Robie..."

CHAPTER 62

John buttoned the collarless shirt, then slipped on the vest. He looked at himself in the mirror. It was remarkable—John looked like any one of Vittoria's brothers. Then again, he would need to if...

There was a knock on the door, then Vittoria asked, "Is okay to come in?"

"Yes," said John. "I'm ready."

Vittoria entered with one of her brothers, wearing John's clothes. He wore loafers, crisp linen slacks, and a well-ironed white poplin shirt.

"What you think?" asked Vittoria.

"I think he looks like me," said John. "And I, him."

"Mmmm, yes and no," said Vittoria. She stood between both men, looking at one, then the other. "For the clothes, yes. For the body, no. You have these big muscles." She smacked John's upper arm. "Still, it will work." She stepped back, then focused on her brother. "From far away, he will look like you." Vittoria then concentrated on John. She smoothed some wrinkles, then started to button his vest. "Here is what we know. Marcel has even more men watching us here at your villa. Not too close, but not too far. The good news—they're not planning an attack. They're just watching, making sure you're still here."

"I expected as much. The roads, too?"

Vittoria's brother nodded.

"But there is a blind spot," said Vittoria. "In the corner of your property. We put the motorcycle there. You must drive through a field for a while, then the road. This is okay with you?"

"That's fine," said John. "Good plan."

"Yes, and gets better," said Vittoria. "This one"—she placed her hand on her brother's back—"is going to walk around outside, the way you walk. Anyone watching will think you are still here."

"What does that mean, 'the way you walk'?" asked John.

"You know," she replied. "Shoulders back, chest out, chin in the air." Vittoria impersonated the description she'd just given. "Here I come," she said, marching about the room. "John, the big prize."

"Is that what you think of me?" asked John.

Vittoria let loose a rough laugh. "Not what I think," she said. "Is what you think. But no more baby talk..."

"You mean small talk," said John.

Vittoria ignored him. "You and my other brothers will patrol the grounds. Like a pack. When you get near the motorcycle, you slip away."

"Got it." John headed toward the front door, where three of Vittoria's brothers were waiting for him.

At that moment, two other brothers pushed their way in, holding a captive between them. John looked over, confused.

"Coco?" he asked. "What's going on?"

John took a step in Coco's direction, but Vittoria pushed him aside. She flicked her wrist like a scorpion sting, and a switchblade appeared in her hand. John had no idea where it came from. She marched toward Coco.

"Son of a bitch," shouted Vittoria. "Sneaking again. I'ma gonna..."

"No, no, no," said Coco. "I'm here to help. I want to say..."

"Say it quick," said John. "She doesn't listen to me."

Vittoria stopped, one step away from Coco. "If you lie, I'll know. And it will happen fast. You understand?"

Coco held out his hands, asking for calm. In his gravelly voice, he said, "I want to thank John. I made a phone call this morning, and my debt was erased. I have my life back. What did you do?"

"I did what you asked," said John. "I helped you, and now we're even. You agree?" John searched around for the keys to the motorcycle, then found them on a small foyer table.

"No," said Coco. "We are not even. After what you did for me, I owe you. Forever."

John smiled, then caught himself. He'd seen how distressed Coco was, he'd helped, and now Coco was declaring loyalty for life. John felt a deep sense of achievement, almost pride. "No need for that," he said.

"But there is," said Coco. "You are in trouble." He looked around, pointing at the constant flow of Vittoria's brothers. "I came to thank you, but I find something is not good. And if you have a problem, I have a problem." He shook himself free of Vittoria's brothers, then stood at attention as if he were a soldier. "I will help."

John thought about it. Who knew how many men Marcel had at his disposal? Having one like Coco on his side would help. But it was going to be dangerous.

"I know what you're thinking," said Coco. "There is risk. But I don't care. You know what I can do. Let me help. Please."

John waved away the two brothers standing guard on either side of Coco.

Vittoria stepped forward, then took Coco by the arm. "Okay," she said. "You help. But not like this, not stinking like a sewer." She pulled off his jacket, dropped it on the floor, then kicked it toward the door. She spun him around, then ushered him away.

"First a bath, Signore Coco. Then I give you a shave. I have nice *rasoio affilato*. You know these words?"

Coco shook his head.

"Means sharp razor," she said. "Very sharp."

Coco came to a complete stop. He turned back to John, but Vittoria shoved him into the bathroom.

"What's wrong?" she said to Coco. "You no want a shave?"

"No," he said. "Not from you."

"Today, I take the whiskers," said Vittoria. "Not the head. My promise to you."

John caught a glimpse of Coco in the bathroom, trying to pull away from Vittoria. Then she kicked the door shut.

There wasn't much time left. John adjusted his vest, put on a coppola cap, then headed out the door with the brothers, all dressed alike.

He had to warn Francie.

If he could.

CHAPTER 63

Francie thought it comical. Across the table, Alex and Mother were flipping through newspapers. Both were talking to themselves, not to each other, sharing bits and pieces of the articles they skimmed. Francie reached for Mother's Sidecar cocktail, a yellow-orange drink with cognac, orange liqueur, and lemon juice. She took a thin sip, then hummed her approval. More refreshing than expected! Francie took another sip, then another. The faster the cocktail disappeared, the sooner Mother would leave. And the sooner Francie could press Alex for details about their romantic getaway.

"This reporter likes you more than the fashion." Alex turned the page to show Francie. "He goes on and on about your inspired performance."

"And this reporter doesn't know you at all," said Maude. "Listen to this: 'Francie Stevens, the delightfully pleasant model...'"

A bubbly laugh escaped Alex's throat. He caught himself, then played it off as if he'd been coughing.

"Very funny, Mother," Francie said.

She smiled back, then glanced at Alex. "Some think so."

"All that wit must be tiring," said Francie. "How about a nice nap in your room?"

"I don't want a nap," she protested. "I want another one of these." She held up her nearly empty cocktail, then looked for a waiter.

"And I want a minute alone with Alex," replied Francie. She sighed, then dropped her head onto the table. "But woe is me; it's not to be." Francie lifted her head to peek at her mother. "So neither of us gets what she wants."

Maude peered at Francie over her glasses. "Oh, I'm getting another cocktail."

"Seriously. Alex and I have to talk."

Maude got up, then gathered her things from the table. "To be young and in love."

"Oh, Mother. Hush."

"My dear, you have many fine qualities, but subtlety isn't one of them." Maude called a waiter, then handed him her glass. "Can you send another up to my room?" With that, she excused herself.

Alex waited, then said, "What is it, Francie?"

"You know quite well," she said. "You've been teasing me about a weekend away, and I need to know where we're going."

He laughed. "The trip is my surprise to you. And you want me to tell you the surprise? Doesn't that defeat the purpose?"

"Yes, but it's different for a woman. I must know what to

pack—which outfits, jewelry, shoes. Do I pack shorts, pants, bathing suits, cocktail dresses?"

He placed his hand on Francie's arm. "I'm sorry. I didn't realize. We're going to"—with his fingers, he tapped out a drumroll—"San Remo, Italy! Surprise!"

Francie perked up. "The Italian Riviera," she said. "Oh, this is so exciting! Tell me about it. What do you know?"

"It's a beautiful town, right on the coast. It's not as 'high society' as the French Riviera. It's less formal, I would say. The weather is just like here. There are good restaurants and cozy cafés. And wonderful beaches. I've booked us a nice hotel. Not like this one, but it's in my budget."

Francie reached over and squeezed his hand. "It sounds wonderful, dear."

"Best of all—no reporters. No press. Just us."

"When are we leaving?"

"Right after the show. Assuming we take your car."

"Not to be a bother," said Francie, "but Marcel likes to parade me around like a prized racehorse after each show."

"Not a problem," he said. "We can stay as late as you like. It's only two hours away."

"Perfect. And thank you, Alex. I can't wait!"

He got up from his chair. "I've got a few things before the show tonight. Are you heading up?"

"Not yet," said Francie. "The beach looks so inviting. Maybe I'll doze in the sun."

Alex kissed her goodbye. Francie rose from her seat, then looked out over the Mediterranean, its dark-blue water a stark contrast to the bright-white beaches.

She smiled to herself. The significant parts of her life fell into place, and she felt a pervasive and calming sense of well-being. Life was unfolding just as she'd imagined.

CHAPTER 64

John had to speak with Francie, but her hotel was swarming with Marcel's men. Out front, there were eight, by his count. Two more by the entrance, one in the parking lot, and at least one in the lobby.

The back of the hotel was just as bad. From the next beach over, John could see Francie and Alex having lunch on a terrace overlooking the water. He could also see more of Marcel's men, two seated at a nearby table and one man sitting by himself, drinking coffee. All three had their eyes on Francie.

John began pacing with short, fast steps. He ran his hand through his hair, then took a deep breath and held it. What was he to do? He might get past those men, but then what? He wouldn't be able to speak with her, not with any substance or discretion. A phone call wouldn't do—she might not answer. And a message with the front desk wouldn't work—what would he write without tipping his hand? No, it had to be in person. And right now, that was impossible.

Just then, John saw Alex kiss Francie goodbye. A moment later, Francie got up, then went inside. Marcel's men didn't move, though. That meant more men were inside. *Think*, John told himself. There had to be a way.

He moved closer to the water, then stood behind a palm tree. To his surprise, Francie walked onto the beach. She looked around, then chose a chair under a cluster of palms.

John removed his borrowed cap, then started unbuttoning his vest.

He had an idea.

CHAPTER 65

Francie startled herself awake. She'd fallen asleep in the shade of some palms, a rare treat she thoroughly enjoyed. A heat pulse ran through her, leaving sweat on her cheeks and forehead. She sat up, then dabbed her face with a towel.

Everything was peaceful. Francie checked her wristwatch. She still had time to relax.

Francie took a *Cosmo* magazine from her bag. She flipped through some pages, then looked out over the sea. There was a floating dock off the beach, a platform for the hotel's swimmers. Next to the platform, she saw a man's head, half-submerged. The man saw her, too, and he rose out of the water.

It was John Robie, holding a finger to his lips, asking for her silence. She looked around, then nodded. John motioned for her to swim out.

Francie had no idea what he was doing, but something about his mannerisms made her nervous. They had said their goodbyes, yet here he was, with his puzzling behavior. Francie was confused, and curious. Why hadn't he approached her on the beach? What could he possibly want? She had to find out. John slipped back into the water, then made his way behind the platform. From the beach, she couldn't see him anymore.

She walked down to the water, then waded in. She moved around, gradually dunking herself. Even on a hot day, the water felt cold, a shock best managed in phases. Then she swam out to the platform.

Quietly, she said, "John, is that you?"

From behind the platform, she heard him say, "Yes, but no one can know we're talking. Pretend I'm not here."

Francie climbed the steps of the short ladder, then took a seat on the platform, facing the beach. She lounged back as if taking in the sun. "What's going on? Why can't we be seen talking?"

"Marcel has men stationed all around your hotel," he said. "They're on the terrace, where you were dining." Francie could hear John, but she couldn't see him.

"Where?"

"See where you were having lunch? Look ten yards to the left. You'll see two men in sports jackets. Short hair, like soldiers."

"I see them."

"They were with you the whole time," said John, "I'll bet they're watching you right now."

Francie glanced up at the men, and both were staring down at her.

"Act like you don't see them," he said. "And look to the other side of the terrace. There's another man, by himself. Looks like the others."

All three men were watching Francie. "I see him," she said.

"There's one more on the beach, sitting behind your chair, to your left. He took off his jacket." Francie saw the man. He looked just like the others. Short hair, thick body, wearing short sleeves. He was smoking a cigarette and looking right at her. A chill raced over her skin, and her breathing became short, shallow pulls.

"You're scaring me, John. Why are they watching me?"

"It's not you that they're interested in," he said. "It's me."

"How did they know you'd be...?" Francie stopped. She knew the answer before she finished her question. John was there because she was there. And these men knew John would come to her.

A sense of panic grabbed hold of her. "It's not safe," she said. "John, you need to leave."

"Not yet. I need to tell you something, so act relaxed."

"I'll try." She put her hands together and scooped up some cold water, splashing it onto her face. Then she tilted her head to the sun and smiled.

"Marcel has committed some serious crimes," said John, "and tonight he'll be arrested. It will happen after the fashion show, not before and not during."

"Because of his business practices?"

"I'm not talking about tax evasion or bribery. I can't say much, but it's worse. Marcel is dangerous."

Francie perched herself on the platform's edge. Her arms and legs felt dense and slow, like in a bad dream, but she managed to dangle, then kick her feet in the water. "It's hard to imagine. The man you're describing is very different from the one I know. Marcel values what I've done. He isn't a danger to me."

"He is. He's ruthless. One man killed himself because of Marcel."

"What do you mean?"

"I mean, I was on the roof of the Hotel Carlton with the man. He'd gone over the edge, but I had him by the collar. I could have pulled him back up. Instead, he raised his arms and slid out of his jacket. On purpose. He surprised me. I didn't expect that."

"The papers mentioned something... You were there that night?"

"I was."

"How do you know it was because of Marcel?"

"That man was under investigation. He was delivering something to Marcel. We found out, and we had him cornered. The man was about to be arrested, so there would be no delivery. He knew what Marcel would do to him, so he killed himself."

On the beach, Francie saw the man with the short sleeves get out of his chair. "Hold on," she said to John. Then she dropped into the water, just in front of the platform. Francie floated on her back, aimlessly kicking while staring at the sky. She glanced over, and the man was back in his chair, lighting another cigarette. She paddled back to the platform, then placed a hand on top to hold herself still.

"Maybe I shouldn't go to the show," said Francie, more to herself than to John.

"I agree," he said. "Stay far away."

She was quiet as she thought it through. She believed John. He was right about the men at the hotel. They looked rough, like gangsters. If those men were present when Marcel was arrested, anything might happen. It wouldn't be safe.

On the other hand, it was her last show. She'd done far better than expected, and the press was eager for more. Tonight was to be the perfect denouement to Francie's introduction as a model. If she were absent, there would be questions as to why. Questions about her dependability.

Francie wiped the water from her eyes. It was all so complicated. She couldn't decide. Then a thought came to her.

"Why arrest Marcel after the show?" she asked.

"The authorities know he'll be there, and his movements during the day are unpredictable, but he never misses a show."

"Then I'll be there. I'm his only model tonight. If I back out, he'll suspect something. He won't go."

"What makes you say that?"

"Models arrive before the designers," she said. "Makeup, hair, all that gets done before the show. Then the designers arrive. And Marcel always checks on us before he comes. He calls ahead and wants to know if we need anything. If I'm not there, he'll be suspicious. And he won't show."

John was silent for a moment. Then Francie heard him say, "I know you. I understand what you're doing and wish you wouldn't go. Before you decide, there's something else you need to consider."

Francie looked up and noticed all three men on the terrace were now together. They were standing at the rail, looking up and down the beach. Francie pulled herself back onto the platform.

"And what is that?" she asked.

"Paul picked up a secret communication involving Marcel. He's to put you on a plane to Copenhagen tonight. Right after the show."

She started to speak, then caught herself. "That's impossible. Alex is taking me to Italy tonight."

"Marcel isn't going to let that happen. He's putting you on that plane. Against your will, if he has to."

"It makes no sense. Why would he kidnap me? For ransom? He doesn't need money."

"It's not a kidnapping," said John. "They're going to blackmail you."

"What can he possibly use to blackmail me?" She waited for John to reply, but he said nothing. "I don't gamble, I don't get drunk, and despite what you may think, my virtue is intact. For the most part..."

"We...we don't know what he has on you," John lied. "But we know Marcel is determined to get you on that plane. Then he'll blackmail you."

Francie sat up. She swallowed hard, trying to make sense of everything. Her heartbeat quickened, and her breathing became shallow. What should she do?

"I didn't mean to upset you," said John. "But you're at risk. You can't go to the show tonight."

She was terrified. If she went, she'd need every ounce of caution and composure she had. And if the arrest didn't go as planned, Marcel might still try to abscond with her. But if she didn't go, Marcel would know a trap was being set, and he would run.

Francie was deliberate when she spoke. "I understand," she said, "and I'm going. Please, not another word on that."

He waited a moment, then said, "I'll be there, too. With some friends."

"Don't, John. It won't be safe for you. I can take care of myself."

"I know. Just in case. And, Francie—you can't mention this to anyone. Not a word."

TO CATCH A SPY

"I know."

"Not your mother, not Alex. Not a soul, okay?"

"You have my word." She glanced toward the men again. Two were intensely staring at her. The third one stepped onto the beach. "I better go back. They're nervous."

"I'll wait before I swim away," he said. "And, Francie...be careful."

She slipped back into the water. "You, too."

"One more thing," said John. "There's someone who works for Marcel. An older man with big glasses. He's a designer or a tailor."

"That's Karl," she said. "He doesn't work for Marcel. He doesn't even like him."

"Whatever the case, he's also involved. Don't trust him."

Francie started to swim back to shore. She stopped after a few strokes. Her hands were shaking, and her breath was quivering. What just happened? In one conversation, her whole world changed. She treaded water, thinking. She couldn't tell Mother, and she couldn't tell Alex. Mother was too timid and Alex too protective. Both would want her to pull out for different reasons.

But that wasn't Francie. She'd decided long ago she wouldn't be bullied and would never let a man force her into something. Both principles had served her well.

Francie collected herself, then resumed swimming. With each stroke, she felt her strength of spirit returning.

No one would ever intimidate her or force her hand.

No one.

CHAPTER 66

Rooftop Terrace Overlooking Boulevard de la Croisette,
Cannes

Francie was a nervous wreck. Her modeling session had gone very well, and she'd just met with the press. But she was struggling to maintain her composure.

She wore a black sleeveless cocktail dress, with a cinched waist and a hemline falling just above the knees. She thought it revealed a little too much skin, making her feel exposed. The rooftop setting for the end-of-Fashion-Week celebration didn't help, either. It was a large open-air space, with a waist-high parapet running along the sides. Strings of bulb lights illuminated some spots better than others. All that made Francie even more nervous.

A gust of wind swept over the rooftop, scattering cocktail napkins and flapping dresses. Francie reached down to her side and bunched her skirt into her fist, hoping to keep it down. Near the stairs and elevators, French crooner Charles Aznavour was singing a mellow ballad, his rich tenor voice in perfect harmony with the evening setting.

Francie wanted to leave. She scanned the party crowd, searching for Alex. She hadn't seen him since they'd arrived, but she knew he was there. Where, though?

Across the rooftop, she made eye contact with Marcel. He was talking to someone but staring at Francie the whole time. Francie dreaded having to speak with him again. She'd steeled herself to get through the show. Now that it was over, she felt her resolve slipping away.

From behind her, a tap on the shoulder. Francie turned and found Mother, cocktail in hand.

"You were wonderful," said Mother. "I've teased you all week, but I'm so proud of you."

Francie forced a smile. "Thank you. That means a lot to me." She hugged her. "Have you seen Alex?"

Maude pointed to a far corner of the rooftop. "He was over there, but I haven't seen him in a while. If I do, I'll send him your way." She glanced over Francie's shoulder. "Here's the man of the hour."

Francie turned, hoping to see Alex. Instead, she found Marcel.

"Congratulations on a very successful week," said Maude.

"Thank you, but much of the credit goes to your daughter. She's been an excellent find." Marcel turned his attention to Francie. "I've good news to share. Pierre Sterlé is partnering with me on a new line of Riviera jewelry, and both of us want you to be the exclusive model. He'd like to meet you."

Francie's heart pounded. "I can't," she said. "Alex and I are leaving for the weekend. Right now, in fact." She searched the crowd again. "I don't know where he's run off to."

Marcel looked around. "Hmm, where is the young man? That's odd."

Francie's mother chimed in. "While you two talk shop, I'll say hello to some friends. If you don't mind."

"Not at all," said Marcel. "Enjoy." With a grand gesture, he directed Maude back into the rooftop party. Then he turned to Francie. "While you wait for Alex, I'll get Pierre. It'll only take a minute." He started to walk away.

Francie fumbled her words. "I... I..."

Marcel stopped. He turned around, then looked at Francie. Something about him was different, and it made her even more uncomfortable. Then Francie realized what it was. Marcel wasn't looking at her. He was studying her.

"What's wrong, Miss Stevens? You haven't been yourself all evening. Is something the matter?"

Francie shook her head. "Nothing, really. A tough week is all."

Marcel said nothing. He kept staring at her, reading her. Then he said, "Do not run off; do not leave this spot. Wait here."

Francie couldn't speak. Instead, she bobbed her head. Marcel headed off to find the jeweler. She kept her eyes on Marcel, and he looked back several times as he navigated his way through the crowd.

He knows, thought Francie.

CHAPTER 67

rancie didn't want to leave without Alex, but the tension was getting to her. She was starting to perspire, and her legs were weak and shaky. She felt as if she might collapse at any moment.

Francie had to get out of there, but how? The elevators were out of the question. If Marcel saw her getting in, he would shout over and have someone hold the door. Then she and Marcel would be alone. That wouldn't do. Her hands trembled at the thought. So the stairs were her best bet. The stairs had constant traffic, up and down. Even if Marcel chased after her, the presence of others would be a deterrent. Francie watched Marcel bump and jostle himself through the crowd. *Keep going*, she thought. When he was far enough away, she'd run.

Once again, she looked for Alex, but she didn't see him. He must be downstairs. Francie crossed her arms, then rubbed each upper arm with the opposite hand. The tension around her sizzled like electricity.

Marcel was talking to someone. Then he turned his back to her. That was all she needed.

Francie spun around to head for the stairs.

And she spun right into Karl. He'd been standing behind her. She put a hand to her chest. "Oh, my."

"Miss Stevens," said Karl. "Sorry to frighten you."

"No, no. I was looking for a friend. If you'll excuse me."

Karl held up a hand. "Before you go, I want to congratulate you on a tremendous week."

Francie was shaking. If she didn't calm herself down, her heart would explode. She took a deep breath, held it, then exhaled slowly. "Thank you, Karl. You were very helpful."

"Marcel gave you a great opportunity. Good things will follow."

That's when she noticed it. Karl's cadence of speaking and his overall tone were very different. There was no bumbling speech, no skipped words, no thick accent. Karl sounded like an academic. He had on a well-appointed suit and an aura of confidence about him. He wasn't hunched over, either. He was standing as still and straight as a statue.

An image of a lamb roped to a stake flashed through her mind. Francie shook it away. That would never be her. She wouldn't allow it. She had to balance the situation. To do that, she had to put Karl on the defensive. That thought alone caused her to relax a bit. She was on the right track.

Francie lifted a drink from a passing tray, then took a strong sip. "How do you know Marcel? I never asked."

"We're both in the trade."

"That being...?"

Karl stared into her eyes. "What trade do you think?"

Francie was settling down, but she knew it was tenuous. She'd always been comfortable with repartee, but this was different. There was something underlying this whole exchange, and she couldn't put a finger on it. Then it came to her. Francie felt threatened. She took another big sip, finishing her drink. "How did the two of you meet?"

"We've worked together over the years," said Karl. "How we met, I don't recall. Is that information of consequence to you?"

"Not really. Just curious. I was wondering why you dislike Marcel so much." She looked over Karl's shoulder, hoping to spot Alex.

"We see things differently, that much is true. *Dislike* is a strong word, though. Why the sudden interest in our relationship?"

"Just curious."

Karl nodded slowly. "There's an old saying where I come from." He raised a finger and, with a trace of a smile, said, "If you know too much, you get old very quickly."

Francie looked past him, but still no Alex. "Where is that, by the way? Where are you from?"

Karl stopped smiling. "I don't talk about my past. It's not relevant."

She started to say something, but Karl cut her off. "I know, I know. You are 'just curious.' Why do you keep looking over my shoulder, Miss Stevens? Who is it you are hoping to see?"

Francie shifted her weight from one leg to the other. As she did so, Karl immediately slid to that same side as if he meant to block her way. She backed off and found herself in a corner. This time, she stared at Karl. "Why did you do that?"

"Marcel told you to stay here. I'm just making sure."

"How do you know he said that?" asked Francie. "You weren't here."

"I know how he thinks. Wait a minute or two. Perhaps another drink for you."

In a deep, aggressive voice, Karl commanded a waiter to come over, then took a glass of wine from his tray. The anger and explosiveness of his words shocked Francie.

He handed her the wine. "Calms the nerves. Drink it."

"You're different tonight."

"On the contrary, it is you who are different. I'm sensing concern on your part. I've seen you nervous before, like every model, but I've not seen you concerned. And I'm sensing a strong desire to leave. To run, perhaps?"

"I've had enough," said Francie. "I'm leaving."

Karl stepped in front of her again. "Do that, and someone gets hurt," he growled. "Someone close to you."

CHAPTER 68

John entered the building's long, spacious lobby. Through the bustle of the crowd, he could hear the distinct voice of another friend from the Resistance, Charles Aznavour, performing on the rooftop. *Good sign*, he thought. *The fashion show is over, but the party's still going.*

The lobby was teeming with people. Waiters were rushing every which way, some carrying cases of champagne, others carrying trays of glasses. John adjusted his bow tie, then brushed off his tuxedo jacket. He was nervous but determined. It would happen tonight, and he was ready.

At the far end of the lobby, he saw a greeter standing next to a large easel poster of the fashion show. She was directing several well-dressed individuals to the elevators and stairs. Two of Marcel's men stood to the side, just far enough away to go unnoticed. They weren't talking to one another, just monitoring the lobby. They didn't recognize John, not from that distance. He kept going, getting closer until one did recognize him. The man tapped his associate, who turned and glared at John.

John stopped a passing waiter and asked for directions to the lavatory. The man pointed him to the end of another hall. John headed that way. Marcel's two men fell in behind, keeping a short distance.

The hall had shops on each side, all closed for the night. And there were a couple of waiters milling about. John caught reflections of Marcel's two men in the darkened shop windows. One kept looking over his shoulder, making sure no one was following. The other was patting his jacket, looking for something.

As they approached the lavatory door, John sensed the men moving closer. They were just a few feet behind him. As he pushed open the door, the two men rushed him. John expected it and moved quickly into the lavatory, then turned to face them.

One was grinning as he pulled something from his jacket pocket. Just then, a waiter came through the door. Marcel's two men turned to see. One brushed the waiter away, telling him to leave. The waiter had a surprised look on his face and started to back out. Then, in a flash, a *casse tête* appeared in the waiter's hand. He launched himself at Marcel's men, swinging his club and striking with a speed and ferocity that surprised John.

It was short work. One man fell toward John, and the other fell backward toward the waiter. He caught one man in his arms, and the waiter caught the other.

"Impressive," said John. "Just like the old days."

Coco smiled. "Into the stalls before anyone comes."

They dragged the two men into the farthest lavatory stalls, then shut the doors.

Coco ran tap water over his club, then wiped it dry before putting it in his pocket. "He has men everywhere. Not in the lobby, but ten or more upstairs. Very dangerous."

"Francie needs to see me," said John. "I'm going up."

"I know. Wherever you go, I have your back. No one gets past me."

"Thank you, my friend."

Coco stepped away from the sink, then pointed at the door. "Let's join the party."

CHAPTER 69

John stepped into the elevator and pressed the button for the rooftop.

Francie was his priority. He had to make sure she was safe. Then he would check on his friends before turning his attention to Marcel.

The elevator doors opened, and John stepped right into the rooftop party. He looked to his left and saw Coco enter from the stairway, breathing heavily. He'd run up the stairs to arrive at the same time as John.

Coco took a tray of discarded glasses from a waiter's stand, then held them at shoulder height. John stepped into the streaming partygoers and saw Coco follow, staying a few steps back.

The crowd was larger than he'd expected. He raised onto his toes but still couldn't see Francie. He moved to a different vantage point, and once again, nothing.

John saw Luca tending bar. Luca gave him a thumbs-up and motioned toward the elevators. John turned to find Paul and Armand joining the party.

There was a commotion behind John, then the sound of broken glass. He turned. Coco was balancing his tray and stepping aside, letting a man in a suit fall to the floor. Two waiters rushed over. Coco said something about "too much to drink." John leaned over a little and saw Coco had his *casse tête* flush against the bottom of his tray.

John went over to Luca's bar. "Was that man…?"

"Yes, he was," said Luca. "But Coco got him. Quick, too. I was looking, and I almost missed it. Can I get you something?"

"Have you seen…"

Behind him, he heard a woman's voice. "I would like something."

John stepped away from the bar, and a stunning brunette in an equally gorgeous dress took his place. "An Italian wine, if you have it. Who can drink this French *pipi*?"

"Vittoria," whispered John, "is that you?"

She turned and smiled. "For sure it is me. What do you think?" She did half a pirouette.

Luca shook his head. "Don't say it, John. Don't say it."

John was looking her up and down. "Beautiful."

"There, you said it," whispered Luca. "She was impossible before. Now…who knows?"

She hushed Luca. "Thank you," she said to John. "The American girl, your friend, the model. She looks good, too." Vittoria held out her hands, palms up. "Her hair maybe is not so good. Shoes, the same. Not so good. But her dress is okay."

"Francie looks great," mumbled Luca. "I don't know what this one is talking about."

"Before you ask," said Vittoria, "she's over there." She pointed to a corner of the rooftop.

John darted his head from side to side to get different views. Across the way, Francie was engaged in a tense conversation with Karl, who had her trapped in a corner. Not good. John excused himself, then headed in Francie's direction.

About twenty feet in front of John, the enormously wide man from the alley fight stepped from the crowd. He glared at John, then shook his head no.

John stopped. The man wasn't tall, but his shoulders looked twice as wide as John's. "I remember you. Saturday night, was it?" He feigned forgetfulness. "You had a friend with you. He won't be joining us. In case you haven't heard, he's dead. And you're next."

The wide man started moving in his direction. John's stomach dropped. He shook out his hands and arms, getting ready. The guy was wide and angry, a bad combination. It was starting...

Just then, Luca stepped between them, carrying two crates of glasses. "The other way," he whispered to John. Luca kept going, then bumped into Vittoria. Luca fumbled the crates, then dropped them both. And Vittoria spilled her Italian wine, some of it on the wide man. She put a hand on his arm and apologized. Then she began cursing at Luca as if she didn't know him.

Between the crates and the two of them, they formed a barrier between John and the wide guy.

He moved away and slipped into the crowd. He had to get to Francie. He pushed and twisted through the mass of people. The crowd parted as he made his way across the rooftop, creating a short gap.

Through that gap, John saw Marcel on the other side of the rooftop.

And Marcel saw him.

CHAPTER 70

Francie was dizzy. The revelers were a blur of colors and shapes, and the festive sounds blended into a single hum. She placed a hand on the parapet.

What did Karl mean when he said someone might get hurt? Someone close to her? She looked across the crowd, hoping to see Alex. Nothing. She looked again, this time for Mother. And there she was, happily chatting with some friends at the party's edge.

But something was off, and Francie didn't know what it was. She looked again. Mother was fine, the same as always. But there were several men around her. Some had their backs turned, and some were facing her.

Then she knew. All the men were by themselves. None were in conversations with anyone. They were just standing there, almost forming a circle around Mother. None of them had drinks in their hands. And their suits were all the same. Same color, same boxy jackets.

Those were Marcel's men. Earlier in the day, John had pointed them out to her. One of the men caught Francie looking, and the man wouldn't stop staring back. Then slowly, very slowly, he licked his lips.

Francie gasped. She tried to lunge past Karl, but he stuck out a hand, blocking her. Karl whistled. Immediately, another man was behind Francie, pulling on her shoulders. The man was strong. Francie looked back—he was one of them. Short hair, bad suit.

"Be quiet," said the man in heavily accented English. "And stop moving. What a tragedy if your mother went over the side."

And then a rush of hope welled up in her chest. Over by the elevators, she caught a glimpse of Alex. Francie sighed out loud. Alex was there; nothing had happened to him. Francie waved and was about to yell when the man behind her uttered a single word. "Don't."

Alex had seen her. He moved to get a better look and squinted his eyes. He mouthed the words, "You okay?"

Francie shook her head so slightly, Karl and the other man didn't even notice. She watched Alex put down his drink, then move toward her with purpose.

CHAPTER 71

epic led his men, all wearing black suits, off the elevator.

"Fan out," Lepic said. "You know what to do." His men split into packs, then headed off in different directions.

Lepic spotted Paul up ahead, searching through the crowd for someone. Paul's associate, Armand, was right next to him. Lepic approached.

Armand spoke first. "How did it go?"

Lepic glanced around. There were too many people to speak freely. "It's done," he said quietly. "Hugo is in custody. We raided his hotel room just after this show started. We found the evidence, including that bag of Egyptian currency."

Paul placed a hand on Lepic's back. "Good work, Inspector. How about the other...place?"

"Even better. Before we raided Marcel's villa, I had a man cut the phone wires. That way, the staff couldn't warn him."

"And?"

"And we found everything, just as you said. The wall safe, the radio room, and much more. My men are questioning the staff now. Some have information; some don't. We'll detain them all until we're done here. Where is he, by the way?"

Armand pointed. "There."

Lepic found Marcel at the center of the party, in the middle of a serious conversation with several men. Marcel said something to the men around him, and they dispersed.

"It's almost over," said Paul. "The reporters have gone; the waiters are cleaning up. Just a few more minutes."

"In that case," said Lepic, "I need a word with someone."

CHAPTER 72

Odette stood by herself at the edge of the party, where she'd been all evening. She finished her drink. The effects of the liquor had caught up to her, and she put her glass down. She didn't need any more; it would only make her angrier.

Her husband was in the middle of the rooftop, in deep discussion with some very conspicuous men who were obviously not in the fashion industry—not how they dressed. Odette shook her head. What had happened to Marcel's discretion? And what was he up to? She'd picked up bits and pieces but didn't know for sure. One thing she did know was that arrogance makes one an imbecile. And Marcel was arrogant.

On the other side of the roof, she noticed John Robie looking sharp in a perfectly fitted tuxedo. That was another thing she knew—John's presence was terrible news. Her husband despised John Robie, and if Marcel noticed him, there would be trouble. And now the crowd was thinning, making it more likely Marcel would spot him. In her heart, she felt a twinge of emotion. Compassion, maybe? Or sadness? Whatever it was, John should have stayed away.

And then, to her great surprise, Inspector Lepic strode right past her. Instinctively, Odette turned away. Lepic looked very serious, which told her the inspector wasn't there as an invitee. He was here for another reason. But what?

Odette looked at her husband, John Robie, then Inspector Lepic. None of those men were enjoying themselves. All looked tense and determined. This was bad. Something was going to happen, and she didn't want any part of it.

Odette grabbed her handbag and headed for the stairs.

CHAPTER 73

epic sidestepped people left and right. Some party; the remaining folks were laughing, dancing, and drinking, having a wonderful time.

He squeezed through a tight group of older men with cigars and drinks. He pivoted to avoid a waiter, then ended up right in front of a beautiful brunette in a stunning dress. The woman smiled at him.

"Pardon me," said Lepic. Then he pulled back. "Do I know you? You look very familiar. Have we met?"

The woman leaned toward him. "Trust me," she whispered. "If we met, if we really met, you'd remember."

"The accent," he said. "You're Italian."

The woman flashed a devilish smile. "I am many things," she said. "None of them good for your health." She curtseyed, then walked away, grinning the whole time.

She's an odd one, he thought as he continued through the crowd, finally approaching the man he'd sought.

"There you are," said Lepic. "We meet again."

"Good evening, Inspector," said John Robie. "I heard a rumor you were partnering with Paul." John kept looking over the crowd, watching every angle.

"Not a rumor, but you knew that. Paul said it was your idea."

John shot a glance at Lepic, then turned back to the crowd. "I'm just glad you're here."

Lepic pivoted. He was standing shoulder to shoulder with John, both of them surveying the crowd. After a moment, he said, "This doesn't make us friends."

"I know," said John. "But it puts us on the same side."

Lepic lifted up to see over the crowd. "Ah, Marcel is over there." He looked around the party. Everything was winding down. "I think it's time."

"Be careful," said John. "His people are all around."

Lepic tugged on his cuffs. "I figured as much. Truth be told, this doesn't frighten me. I fought organized crime in Marseille for ten years." He chuckled. "*Mon dieu*, those people."

"Still, watch out for yourself."

Lepic patted John on the shoulder. "You do the same."

He slipped behind John, then headed toward Marcel. A waiter carrying an empty tray bumped into Lepic. The waiter kept going, but Lepic reached out and grabbed his arm, spinning the man around.

The inspector looked at the man. "I know you," he said. "You look different, but...did we...?" It was right on the tip of his tongue, but he couldn't summon the answer, much less the question. "Never mind."

With that, Lepic let go of the waiter and headed off.

CHAPTER 74

Francie pushed past Karl and the other man, then threw herself into Alex's arms.

"You're okay," she said into his ear. "I didn't know..."

"Of course I'm okay."

"Where were you?"

Alex whispered, "I got a message from the embassy. But I'm here now."

Francie was shaking. She squeezed him even more. "Let's leave. Right now."

"What happened? Did these men do something?"

Francie didn't answer. She kept her arm around Alex as she gently pushed him toward the elevators. Alex stopped, held Francie at arm's length, then peered into her eyes.

"What's going on?" he asked. "Tell me what happened."

"Nothing," she said. "We need to leave. Now."

They started to move again. The man next to Karl stuck out a hand to halt them.

Alex pointed at the man's face. "Back off."

"Marcel wants to speak with her," said Karl. "He was very insistent."

"He had all night," said Alex. "Tell him to call."

Alex wrapped his arm tightly around Francie's shoulders. He planted a hand on Karl's chest, then pushed him back.

"I've got you," he said to Francie. She felt strength returning to her legs, and she kept up with him as he led her to the elevators.

Then Francie stopped. "Mother," she said. "We have to get Mother."

"I will," he said. He guided her to a spot against a wall near the rooftop lavatories. "Wait here. I'll get her."

Alex started to walk away, then Francie pulled him back. She took his face in her hands, then kissed him. "Do hurry, dear. We'll get Mother back to her hotel, then you and I can go to San Remo. I want to get as far away—"

"About that," said Alex. "Slight change of plans. The embassy needs me. Just one day. Then you and I are off to Italy."

Francie fell forward into his chest. "I don't want to be alone. Not now."

"You won't be. I was hoping you would come."

Francie's whole body shook as the tension released like air from a balloon. "Of course. The car is downstairs; our suitcases are in the trunk. We'll see Mother gets back to her hotel, then drive—"

"We can't drive," interrupted Alex. "It's too far. We have to fly. But I have a plane waiting."

"Where are we going?"

"Copenhagen," said Alex. "We're going to Copenhagen."

CHAPTER 75

John kept his eyes on Francie. Whatever had just happened upset her. Thankfully, her boyfriend had gotten her away from the tailor. But she was still rattled. John kept watching. Alex said something to her, then headed back to the party. Francie put a hand to her stomach, then bent over.

She needed help. John started walking toward her.

Then the big, bald man John had seen at Marcel's villa stepped out of the crowd. John stopped. The man was halfway between him and Francie. He spread his legs, then crossed his arms as if daring John to try and get past him. Everything about the guy was oversized. Whereas the wide guy from the alley was heavy, this man was different. There wasn't an ounce of fat on him, and he was a half foot taller than John. And he looked strong—like he could juggle wrecking balls without breaking a sweat.

The big man just stood there, seething. Luca had been right about him—he was exactly like a bull. The man's quick, powerful breaths were heaving him into a frenzy. His nostrils were flaring. With a hand the size of an anvil, the man reached up, then ran his thumb across his own throat.

John loosened his collar. He could feel the sweat on the back of his neck. He'd been dreading this moment since he first saw the bald guy, and now it was here. He kept nodding, telling himself how much was at stake. Then he squared his shoulders and took a deep breath.

"Let's get this out of the way," he said. Just then, Vittoria stepped in front of him.

"Not like this," she said, "and not now. I'll go to her."

CHAPTER 76

Francie was swaying, so she leaned back against the wall. Questions overwhelmed her, and she struggled to focus even for a moment. But she had to. She didn't have much time.

She recalled her conversation with John, who said Marcel would put her on a plane to Copenhagen. And yet it was Alex who mentioned it. So what did that mean? Either Alex was involved with Marcel, which she couldn't fathom, or Marcel was using Alex, which made more sense.

Alex and Mother were approaching. Mother stopped a few steps away to say goodbye to her friends.

Alex came over, then rested a hand on Francie's shoulder. "I told her you weren't feeling well. She'll be right over. We'll get her a cab back. Then we'll leave."

Francie's throat was as dry as the beach. Her voice cracked when she spoke. "Is Marcel coming with us?" she asked.

"No," said Alex. "This is embassy business. It's got nothing to do with him. Why would you think that?"

"He didn't put you up to this?"

"How could he?" He laughed nervously, then said, "What are you getting at?"

Francie was nauseated. She looked away, then swallowed slowly. "If it's okay with you, I'll return to the hotel with Mother. You'll only be gone a day. Then we'll go to Italy."

"Nonsense," he said. "Copenhagen is beautiful. You'll love it."

Francie, head bowed, said, "You'll be busy. I don't want to see it without you."

"Just a morning meeting, then I'm free for the day."

"I don't feel so well. Maybe some rest..."

Alex's demeanor changed. No more soothing speech, no more concern. "Enough!" he said. "You had a long week, that's all. It's nerves. You'll be fine once we get out of here."

A beautiful brunette walked past Francie on her way to the lavatory. The woman stopped, then reached down near Francie's ankle.

"You dropped your earring," said the brunette. "Here, let me..." The woman picked it up, then moved in close to put it back on.

Francie reached up and touched the side of her head. Her earring was still in place. It hadn't fallen out.

"I'm a friend of John's," whispered the brunette. "Meet me in the ladies' room."

Francie hadn't expected that, but it gave her a quick bolt of energy. She pointed to the ladies' room, then told Alex she'd be right back.

Tentatively, Francie pushed open the door. The brunette

grabbed Francie by the wrist, then pulled her inside before locking the door.

"I don't know what's happening," said Francie. "But they won't let me leave. It's like John said—"

"We know," interrupted a woman. "This is why we talk. Not much time. You need to, ah...*comporre* yourself. Pull yourself together. Right now." She reached out and grabbed Francie's hand and squeezed.

Francie closed her eyes, then pushed back her shoulders. She took a deep breath.

"I'm Vittoria," said the brunette. "I help you. Is going to get crazy out there. You must be ready."

Then it hit her. Mother was still at the party. She wasn't safe. "Oh no," she said. "My mother..." She shot for the door, but Vittoria grabbed her and held her back with surprising strength.

"Your mother is safest one out there," said Vittoria. "John made sure. Anyone tries to hurt her..." Vittoria raised her eyebrows and said, "...will not be good for them."

Francie backed off. "She's safe?"

"Very," said Vittoria. "Now, back to you. You need weapon."

"For what?"

"For protection, of course. Will be fighting, and we"—she waved a finger back and forth between herself and Francie—"rely on no one. We take care of our business."

"I understand," said Francie.

Vittoria smiled. "They think we're soft," she said. "Idiots, these men. All men, really." Her voice became assertive. "So we use this stupidity against them. Okay?"

"Okay."

"Surprise them. Trust me, is the best revenge." Vittoria pulled up her dress and then raised a foot onto the sink basin. "Which you like better, gun or knife?"

Vittoria's lack of modesty surprised Francie, and she looked away. But Vittoria snapped her fingers, then patted Francie on the cheek.

"No time for that," said Vittoria. "Choose."

Francie saw a small gun strapped to one of Vittoria's thighs and two knives strapped to the other. "I've never fired a gun."

"Then you like knife better." She pulled one from her stocking. "Always on the outside of the leg. Never inside. Is easier to grab." She hoisted the front of Francie's dress. "Hold this up," she said, handing Francie a handful of her dress. Then she secured the knife strap to Francie's thigh.

"To use, hold handle tight, very tight. And you stick. Then you do it again. And you keep going." She mimed the action for Francie. "But you must hold tight."

There was a loud banging on the door. From outside, a voice yelled, "Francie, hurry up."

Alex's voice startled Francie. Vittoria patted the air with both hands, telling her to be calm.

"I'm coming," yelled Francie. Together, she and Vittoria headed for the door.

"Go to boyfriend," said Vittoria. "He look out for you."

Francie stopped. She turned Vittoria around to face her, then whispered, "No, he won't. I need you to tell John something."

CHAPTER 77

T he big bull of a man had stood his ground. From that position, he had flagged the attention of other men, and those other men were closing ranks on John. Two were approaching from John's left, one from his right. They were moving slowly, cautiously.

Across the party, John saw Lepic approach Marcel. But Marcel noticed Lepic and directed some men to head off the inspector. Then Marcel waved to get someone's attention. John looked in that direction but couldn't be sure who he'd signaled.

Over by the lavatories, John saw Alex walking toward Marcel. Or toward Maude; it was hard to tell.

Paul and Armand, who had kept to themselves, were now positioned next to Lepic. Marcel's men were standing in their way, and Marcel himself was retreating.

At that moment, Francie and Vittoria emerged from the lavatory. Francie looked around the crowd, searching for someone.

Vittoria caught John's eye, tilted her head toward Francie, then waved John over. Something was wrong with Francie, and Alex wasn't at her side.

Over the crowd's noise, John heard Lepic shout, "Monsieur Julien, I need to speak with you." John turned away from the big man, then headed straight for Francie. He could hear more shouting and jostling as Lepic got closer to Marcel.

Then a shot was fired.

People screamed and ran in every direction. John heard glass shattering. People pushed over high-top tables and knocked others off their feet. Marcel's men, who were closing in on John, were fighting with men in black suits.

He kept going. Across the way, Francie stood stone-still, her eyes locked onto John's. He pushed people out of his way, sidestepped a couple of brawling men, then stepped over a fallen table.

He was less than ten feet from Francie. A man reached out and yanked Francie's arm, pulling her off the wall. The man stepped behind Francie, wrapped an arm around her torso, then pulled out a gun. He pointed it at John.

It was Karl. Dressed differently, but the same man.

"Stay back," he said. "She's with us."

John slowed down, but he kept moving toward Francie and Karl. Matching his pace, Karl dragged Francie back toward one of the parapets. All around, the frenzy on the rooftop continued.

"I know who you are, John Robie. Come any closer, and I'll shoot her."

John shot a glance at Francie. Karl had a firm grip on her, and he was dragging her backward, but she wasn't afraid. She looked calm and serious, and she kept her eyes on John.

"Let her go," said John, "and I won't kill you. You have my word."

"The word of a thief is worthless; you've been nothing but trouble." He raised the gun.

Just then, Francie nodded at John. She shot her arms straight into the air and began sliding out of Karl's grasp. It happened fast, and it caught Karl off guard. With both hands, the man struggled to maintain his hold on her, but she slipped to the floor.

John launched himself at Karl. Two quick steps, then he dove at the man, fist cocked. Karl ducked his head. His punch landed on Karl's shoulder, sending him back against the parapet wall. Karl lost his footing and stumbled backward, knocking over a trash can and spilling garbage around them. John shot forward again, and with both hands, he grabbed Karl's wrist, the one with the gun.

Karl was lying on the ground, and John was straddling his chest. John banged Karl's gun hand against the parapet. Karl tried to rake his fingers across John's eyes with his other hand. John turned his face away from the clawing hand. Karl then began slapping the floor. Or was he trying to grab something? He kept banging Karl's hand against the stones of the parapet. The gun dropped, and the slapping stopped.

Karl had found a wine bottle with his free hand, and he swung. John didn't see it until the last second. He tried to dodge the blow, but the bottle clubbed him just above his ear.

He rolled onto his side. Someone fired back-to-back shots from the center of the party, causing even more panic. In front of him, John saw Karl on his stomach, crawling toward the gun. He got to his feet and grabbed Karl by the belt of his pants, stopping his progress. Karl flipped onto his back and threw a leg up and over, breaking John's grip on his belt. Then Karl started pumping his feet like pistons, and his heel caught John on the cheekbone. John dropped to his knees.

Karl scrambled to his feet, then bent over to pick up the gun. He didn't get a good grip on it. The weapon slipped and fell, but he caught it before it hit the ground. Then he turned toward John.

John hopped to his feet, and from a crouch, he shot his body at Karl, shoulder first. He hit Karl right on the hip. Karl bounced off the parapet, and the gun came loose. He pawed at the weapon with both hands, causing it to pinwheel into the air.

The gun landed on the parapet wall, then skidded toward the edge. Karl lunged for it. In his nervousness, he hit it with his hand, knocking it over the side of the building. Karl's weight followed the gun, and he tried to stop himself. He stretched out his arms to grab hold of something, but his feet slipped out from under him.

Karl was suspended in space for a moment, looking straight at John, his face twisted in fear. He landed on the parapet in an awkward sitting position, but his center of gravity was too high. He clawed at the wall but couldn't get a grip.

Karl let loose a high-pitched scream as he fell from the rooftop.

John spun around, looking for Francie. Alex had an arm around her, and he was directing her down the stairs. And at the center of the rooftop, Marcel and a handful of his men were in the middle of a wild brawl with Lepic, Paul, and Armand.

Francie was safe, thought John. She wasn't with Marcel. Paul and Armand, however, looked like they needed some help.

Vittoria sprung out from the crowd, right in front of him, her hair loose and hanging in front of her eyes.

"Francie's safe," said John. "She just left."

"By herself?"

"With her boyfriend."

Vittoria grabbed hold of his arm. "Francie's not safe," she yelled. "The boyfriend is no good. He's the one, John. He will put her on the plane."

CHAPTER 78

Francie felt a hand dig deep into her hair, then jerk her head back. She almost lost her footing. Alex yanked her upright, then aimed her toward the stairs.

"You're coming with me," he said. "Now!" Alex pushed her forward. She reached back, trying to break his grip on her hair. It was no use. She caught a glimpse of Mother, standing in the middle of a circle of waiters, all lean, dark-haired young men. The waiters were holding knives, protecting their perimeter. At their feet were four men in boxy suits, like those who had been watching Francie at the hotel. All were lying face down, none of them moving.

Another man in a bad suit stepped from the crowd. He was holding a pistol, and he aimed it at Mother. To his side, another waiter appeared, seemingly from thin air. He was carrying what looked like a sawed-off shotgun. The waiter fired; the sound was deafening. The shotgun blast hit the man with the pistol, blowing him off his feet and over the parapet wall.

Alex shoved Francie into the stairwell. She grabbed hold of the handrail. "No," she shouted. "Mother is still... Let go of me!"

Alex spun her around so they were face-to-face on the stairs. He thrust his jaw forward; his eyes were wild. Francie saw him pull back an open hand to slap her.

And then, as if someone flipped a switch, her world went dark.

CHAPTER 79

John wanted to follow Francie down the stairs but couldn't get close. The remainder of the crowd had stormed that area, and there was no getting through.

He ran to one side of the parapet wall, then looked down. He didn't see Alex and Francie, and he didn't see her car.

He then ran to another side. Again, he didn't see them or Francie's car.

Luca was a few feet away. He had the wide man from the alley in a choke hold. The man was losing consciousness but still struggling. Then the wide man stopped moving. Luca let go, and John helped him to his feet.

John searched for his other friends. He saw Coco, crouched like a lion, with bodies scattered around. He was safe.

Paul and Lepic had control of Marcel, with each of them holding one of Marcel's arms. They were safe.

Maude was safe, surrounded by Vittoria's brothers.

And Vittoria was safe. She and one of her brothers were heading toward John, stepping over bodies on their way. The brother was holding his lupara, and smoke was coming from the barrel of the sawed-off shotgun.

All safe so far. But where was Armand?

One of Marcel's men rushed forward, a gun in his hand. He was shouting as he aimed at John.

The man fired. At the same time, someone knocked John to the floor. Then a shotgun blast roared across the rooftop, and John saw the man with the gun get blown off his feet. His body flew ten feet before it slammed into a table. Both the dead man and the table tumbled off the rooftop.

Armand was lying on top of John. "Are you okay?" he asked.

John sat up, then looked at his arms and his body. "I think so. But you're not." He could see a bullet wound on Armand's back, up near his shoulder.

Vittoria rushed over with a knife in her hand. With three lightning-quick strokes, she cut a large section of fabric from one of Marcel's fallen men, balled it up, and pressed it against Armand's wound.

Armand stirred, but the pain stopped him. "No, no, no," he said. "I have a family."

"You will be fine," said Vittoria. "Many times, I see this *ferita*, this wound. Is going to be okay." Then she looked up at John. "You need to go."

He looked down at Armand, who nodded his consent, then said, "Go."

John shot a glance toward the elevator and stairs. The big bull of a man had Marcel by his jacket collar and dragged him through the crowd, tossing people aside like they were weightless. John saw Paul and Lepic lying near each other, where they had been standing just a few seconds ago. Paul got to his feet, then rushed after Marcel. The big bull grabbed someone with one hand, then flung the guy at Paul, who went down in a heap. The big man shoved Marcel into the elevator, threw some people out, and the doors closed.

Vittoria pointed at Luca. "You, too," she said. "Go with John."

John and Luca took off. They ran to the far parapet wall. About a block away, John saw Alex throw Francie into the passenger seat of her car. She was unconscious. Then he got behind the wheel and sped away.

John shuddered as Francie and her car disappeared from sight. He pressed both hands to the sides of his head, uncertain of what would happen to her. Uncertain of his next move.

"You know where he is going?" asked Luca.

"That old airstrip. He'll want privacy."

Luca was calculating something. "We can catch them."

John felt a jolt of hope rip through his mind. He turned to Luca, then they sprinted to the stairs.

CHAPTER 80

F rancie awoke, but she didn't open her eyes. And she didn't move.
A memory flash of a rooftop riot was a reminder she was in danger, although she couldn't remember what kind, exactly. And she had no idea where she was. Francie had to piece it together; she had to get her bearings.

Francie knew she was in the passenger seat of a car, and it was speeding down a road, although she had no idea which one. It was late in the evening, and the side of her face was numb.

Then big parts of the day came back to her. The warning from John, the fashion show, the chaos... She cracked open one eye, then peered sideways. Alex was driving and paying no attention to her. And it was her car, her Delahaye, with the steering wheel on the right side of the vehicle, the passenger seat on the left.

That's when it all came back to her. Alex had taken her against her will and was going to blackmail her. Details were coming back in no particular order, making her sick.

Francie cringed. Knowing Alex had faked his feelings to manipulate her was a humiliating truth. And she'd fallen for it, every step of the way. She had allowed herself to dream of a perfect life with him. And a dream, it was. She was nothing more than a prop to Alex, which infuriated her.

How had she not seen this coming? Surely there were signs. Had she ignored them? She grimaced when she thought about how intimate they'd been, what she'd given to this man. What had been most valuable to her meant nothing to him. All the things he'd said, all those tender moments—none of it was true. Francie was furious. How could he do this to her? Anger rushed through her veins, seizing hold of her thoughts.

She opened her eyes, then pushed herself up out of a slouch. Alex shot her a look but didn't say anything. With the top down, the car was barreling along a country road etched into the side of a hill. On Alex's side of the road was a wall made of big stones and boulders, and on Francie's side was a valley. She looked down; the drop-off was steep.

Her anger kept advancing, and it overtook her like a tide. With her left hand, Francie reached for her door handle. Her wrist jarred to a stop, and it hurt. She looked, and her left hand was handcuffed, one end to her wrist, the other fastened to a metal structure at the bottom of her seat. She didn't care. She reached for the door handle with her right hand, then pulled on the lever. The passenger door opened, and Francie could see straight down into the valley.

A long way to fall.

Alex shouted at her, then pulled on her shoulder, pinning her back into her seat. He purposely swerved the car, causing the passenger door to slam shut.

"You could have killed yourself."

"Not what I wanted," she mumbled. "This is." She reached over with her free hand and tugged on the steering wheel.

"What the...!" shouted Alex. Francie felt her side of the car drop lower as the wheels began edging off the road. Alex slapped her hand off the wheel, then muscled the car back onto the road. It took a moment for Alex to straighten the tires. Francie shifted in her seat and caught a glimpse of a single headlight following the car.

She grabbed for the steering wheel again. Alex clubbed her hand away, reached back, and let loose a punch.

The last thing Francie saw before losing consciousness was Alex's meaty fist against the dark of the night, thundering toward her like a freight train.

CHAPTER 81

John held tight as he and Luca tilted into a very sharp turn.

Luca had been right. His motorcycle was much faster than a car. It had taken a few minutes, but they had almost caught up to Francie and Alex. He could see them up ahead, and it looked like they were fighting each other. He saw their car swerve, then get back under control.

"Almost there," said John. He didn't have a plan, but he did have a goal—helping Francie avoid being abducted, and that meant stopping Alex. Luca had grabbed one of the luparas from Vittoria's brothers and tucked it into his belt, but John couldn't fire it at the car. Not safely. He thought about different options, but none seemed feasible. Then an idea came to him. "Get close," he said to Luca. "I'm going to try something."

"I know what you're doing, and I can get even with the rear tires."

"That'll work," said John.

"I'll draw him toward the stone wall, then I'll shoot outside to give you more room."

Luca's motorcycle was gaining on the car. As they got closer, John could see Alex looking back over his shoulder, steering the vehicle to one side and then the other to block the motorcycle. Francie was in the passenger seat, her head bobbing left and right. *She's unconscious*, thought John.

Luca lowered his head, then gunned the throttle, aiming it between the car and the stone wall of the hillside. Alex swerved over to pin them against the wall. Luca tapped on the brakes, and the motorcycle skidded but stayed upright. It worked. The bike dropped back, and the car kept going. The side of the car scraped along the stone wall, leaving a trail of shooting sparks like a Roman candle.

Quickly, Luca shot forward, coming up next to the passenger's side door.

John put his hands on Luca's shoulders, then pulled himself up into a crouch, his feet planted where he had just been sitting.

"Now!" said Luca. John felt the bike lean toward the car. Luca was compensating for what was coming.

John propelled himself off the motorcycle and toward the car, his body horizontal, his arms spread-eagle in the air. He landed face down on the trunk. With his hands, he hooked on to the rim of the car body, behind the back seat. Off to the side, he saw Luca on his motorcycle, dropping back behind the car.

Alex spun around and made eye contact with John. He made a fist and hammered down at John's hand. John saw it coming and pulled one hand back just in time. Alex's heavy fist thumped off the back of the car.

John was hanging on with one hand. Alex must have realized this because he sped up, causing John to slide down the back of the car. He stretched out his free hand but couldn't reach the rim of the car body. Then Alex swerved sharply, causing John to roll across the back of the car. Alex veered in the other direction, and John rolled back the other way. He couldn't control his movements; his weight was working against him.

Alex repeated the moves, causing John to roll from one side to the other, then back again. Alex changed up the side-to-side pattern. He swerved toward the wall but was too aggressive. The side of the car hit the wall, and the car slowed down. But the contact was violent, and John lost his grip. He slid off the back of the car and landed hard on the road. John tucked his arms around his head and barrel-rolled forward. He stopped rolling in time to see the car, with Alex and Francie, shoot through a turn, then speed away.

Luca pulled up next to him and stopped the motorcycle. "You okay?" he asked.

John did a quick inventory of his body. No broken bones, but scrapes and bruises everywhere. "I think so."

"Get on," said Luca. "We can't catch them, but we can meet them at the airport."

"How?" asked John, as he threw a leg over the back of the motorcycle.

"They have to stay on the road. We don't."

With that, Luca took off. After a few hundred yards, he turned into a field.

"Hang on, John. It's going to get rough."

John looked at his elbow. The tuxedo had been ripped away,

and he was bleeding. Off in the distance, John saw the headlights of Francie's car. Luca saw them, too.

"Don't worry," said Luca. "We'll make it. Hold on."

CHAPTER 82

Francie came to, and she noticed the car wasn't moving. It was parked.

Her head throbbed like a deep, dull drum. She blinked and noticed a bright light speeding toward her in the distance. It had to be him. *John's coming.*

Francie slumped back into her seat but kept her eye on the approaching headlight. The light was getting closer. She kept watching it. As it approached, the light turned into two rays. So, not a motorcycle, but a car. It screeched to a halt, fifty feet away. The passenger door opened.

And out stepped Marcel. Then a huge, bald man emerged from behind the wheel, and a shorter man got out from the back seat. Francie bit her lip. She hoped it would be John, but that wasn't the case. She still had time, though. She'd think of something.

Marcel looked right at Francie, then shouted, "Get her on board now, before anyone sees."

Alex appeared right next to her, and Francie was startled. He must have been silently standing there the whole time. He pulled open her door, then went to work unlocking her handcuff.

That's when she saw the airplane behind him. It had two propellers, a half dozen windows on the side, and a stair ramp leading up to an open door.

Alex grabbed Francie's arm, then pulled her from the car. She fought, but he was strong. He dragged her out and onto the tarmac. Francie got her feet under her. Then, with her free hand, she grabbed one of Alex's fingers and bent it back until it snapped.

Alex groaned from the pain. He released Francie's arm, and with his good hand, he grabbed hold of her by her hair. He bent her over, then pushed her toward the plane.

Her pounding head and pulled hair caused her to yell out. Then Francie grabbed Alex's wrist with both hands and held on tight as she tried to relieve the pressure.

They reached the stair ramp. She looked up and saw the open door.

"No," said Francie. "I'm not."

Alex yanked her upright, then shoved her up the first step.

"Get on," he said. "Move!"

CHAPTER 83

John was on one knee, ensuring the tall grass beyond the edge of the tarmac covered him. He could see a path of moving grass as Luca crawled away, getting himself in position to flank Marcel and his crew.

Francie was on the side of the plane with the stair ramp, and John was on the other side. He checked the windows to make sure no one was watching, then ran toward the plane in a tight crouch. He stopped behind one of the plane's tires. No one had seen him. And not ten feet away, Alex was shoving Francie up the stairs.

John didn't have a specific plan. Often, in the Resistance and as a cat burglar, he'd had to improvise once he'd sized up a situation. That was different, though. He felt a lump in his throat the size of a baseball, and for the first time in his life, his knees were shaking. Everything about Francie was at stake, so whatever he did, there was no room for error.

He thought through his options—Marcel and the other two

men with him were armed. So a confrontation wouldn't work. But an unexpected disruption might, especially if Luca was in place for support. But how? There wasn't much to work with.

Just then, a car burst onto the airstrip. It turned toward the plane, its tires shrieking as it fought to right itself. Marcel and the others turned to look.

They were distracted, and it was all John needed.

That's when he heard the scream.

CHAPTER 84

She wasn't going to let this happen. There was no way Alex was getting her on that plane.

Francie heard tires skidding. She looked up and saw another car at the far end of the runway, speeding toward them.

She was halfway up the stair ramp. There was a handrail running up one side, and Francie grabbed it. Alex was behind her, still clutching a fistful of her hair. He pushed her forward to break her grip on the rail. It didn't work, so he shoved again, this time with more ferocity.

She fell to her knees, then rolled to one side. Her dress was up, exposing her to Marcel and the others. She let go of the handrail, then tugged on her dress to cover up.

The approaching car slammed on its brakes. It came to a stop. Then its doors flew open. Francie saw Paul Du Pre and Inspector Lepic scramble out. Both men shielded themselves behind their car as they drew guns.

Francie was lying on the stairs, with Alex one step behind. He pulled on her hair to get her to her feet. She heard a muffled clang as the knife Vittoria had strapped to her thigh made contact with the stairs.

Francie had forgotten about the knife. She hiked up her dress on that side, then pulled it out. She held it tight, just as Vittoria instructed, then rolled onto her back. She was lying on the stairs, and Alex was standing above her.

She swung the knife in a short arch, catching Alex behind his knee. He screamed, let go of Francie, then reached for his leg. She stabbed again, this time piercing Alex's hand. She pulled back quickly, then stabbed a third time.

And that strike did it. The knife lodged itself in the bones of Alex's knee. He wailed, even louder than before, and kept on screaming. She tried pulling it out, but the knife was stuck. So Francie twisted the handle. Alex bent over and flailed at Francie's hands, then lost his balance. He fell over the side of the ramp and landed on the tarmac, the knife still wedged into his knee.

She got to her feet. Alex wasn't moving. Marcel and the others looked back and saw Alex lying there motionless. Then they turned their attention back to Paul and the inspector. They weren't watching her; she had a chance to get away. She took off down the stairs.

From behind her, inside the plane, Francie heard someone cock a gun. Then a familiar voice yelled, "Don't move."

CHAPTER 85

John saw Francie head down the stairs, then stop.

Over at Marcel's car, he saw the big bull of a man rummaging through the trunk. Marcel and the shorter man were standing to the side. They all looked when Alex screamed. Then they turned back to Paul and Lepic as if they weren't concerned about Francie escaping.

Whatever their reason, Marcel and his men were distracted. That was the diversion John needed. He ran to Francie. Just then, the shorter man glanced back. He spotted John. The man shouted something, then aimed his pistol at John. He fired, and the bullet careened off the stairs. Marcel yelled, "Kill him!" The shorter man aimed again. There was a loud noise, like an explosion, and it made John's heart leap in his chest. The shorter man was blown off his feet in the blink of an eye. His body flew sideways, then landed on the tarmac. The man was dead.

Luca stepped out from the tall grass. He was holding the

double-barrel lupara. There was a trail of smoke several feet long, suspended in the air just in front of the lupara.

Marcel was growling with anger, and he raised his pistol at Luca. Without missing a step, Luca fired again. The blow hit Marcel square in the chest. He flew backward, hitting the side of his car. Marcel dropped face-first onto the tarmac, leaving a yard-long dent in the door panel. John saw an exit wound the size of a cannonball on Marcel's back.

Luca cracked open the lupara. He tilted it to drop the two spent shells, then started to reload. He didn't see the big bull of a man rush up behind him until the last moment. Luca turned, and the big man slapped the lupara to the ground. He grabbed the front of Luca's shirt with one hand, then punched with the other.

John saw Luca's legs go slack. His friend was out cold. The big man held Luca upright with one hand, keeping him suspended half a foot off the ground. He grabbed Luca's shirt with both hands, then spun like a discus thrower, heaving Luca into the side of the car. Luca's unconscious body hit hard, then fell to the ground next to Marcel.

Francie was standing on the stair ramp. She hadn't moved at all, and John didn't know why. He ran to the bottom of the stair ramp, then turned toward Francie.

But the big man got there at the same time, and he grabbed John's shoulder from behind. John spun around, throwing an elbow at the big man's head. It hit him right in the middle of his face. Blood poured from the big man's nose like a faucet. He blinked, let go of John, then reached down to his hip.

The man pulled out a pistol. John kicked the gun, knocking it from the man's grip. The gun landed on the ground, right at the base of the stair ramp.

The big man rushed forward. John backpedaled as he threw punches, but the man swatted them away. He grabbed one of John's arms, then threw a short punch. It traveled less than a foot, catching John on the side of his face.

John saw a flash of darkness. All feeling ceased, and silence surrounded him. It lasted a second, then everything returned. John was hurt. He couldn't afford to take another punch like that. He had to protect himself; he had to buy some time. He ducked under the man's arms and pushed forward, then wrapped both arms around the big man's torso, pulling tight until the side of his head was flush against the man's chest. He was clutching and clawing at John but couldn't get leverage. John held on and wondered why Paul and the inspector weren't rushing to help.

Just then, a machine gun ripped a burst of bullets through the still night air. The big man stopped pawing at John and looked up at the plane. John followed the man's eyes.

At the top of the stair ramp, the barrel of a machine gun was sticking out from the open plane door.

And holding the gun was Odette Julien.

CHAPTER 86

J ohn saw Odette glance down at him and the big man. She
nodded, and the man stopped fighting. He pushed John
away.

"We have a situation here," said Odette. "But I have an advantage,
wouldn't you say? I've got this..." She tilted the machine gun's barrel
up, then quickly brought it down and aimed it at Francie. Then she
looked at Paul and the inspector. "You might shoot me, but I'll kill
Miss Stevens before I die. You don't want that, so lower your guns."

Paul and Lepic hesitated, then lowered their weapons.

"This can go well for everyone," she said, "or we can fight it out.
Your choice."

John looked around. The big man was three feet away. Alex was
out cold and lying on the ground next to the stairs. Francie was
halfway up the ramp, and Odette was standing in the airplane's
open doorway, machine gun in hand. The dented car was about
fifty feet away, with Marcel's body lying alongside. Luca was right

next to Marcel, moving ever so slightly. And fifty feet past Luca were Paul and Lepic. John made eye contact with Paul, then gave him a deferential nod.

"Go ahead," Paul said to Odette. "What do you propose?"

"You arrested Hugo Rousseau earlier today, and you were about to arrest my husband for crimes against the state." She waved the barrel of her gun over Marcel's body. "You prevented a conspiracy to sabotage trade routes, a plot organized by French nationals— Hugo and my husband."

"True," said Paul. "And the plot to obtain tritium."

Odette nodded wistfully. "That source is compromised. She looked down at Alex, unconscious at the bottom of the stairs. "So, yes, you prevented that, too. In both cases, you have your conspirators, one in custody and one dead. All the evidence points to those two men, correct? And this one here." She pointed toward Alex.

Paul nodded.

"Hold on," said John. "It was you all along. You orchestrated the whole thing. Marcel and Hugo—they worked for you."

Odette smiled. "Now you're speculating. Besides, you could never prove that."

Over by the car, John saw Luca prop himself into a seated position, then rub his head with both hands. Luca looked around, got to his feet, then picked up the lupara.

Luca held up one hand like a traffic cop. "I'm no threat," he said. Then, in a quick second, he popped two new shells into the lupara and snapped it shut. Luca looked up at Odette, the lupara hanging at his side. "Go on. I'll catch up."

"We're done," said Odette. "You have what you need; no one gets shot, and I leave. Do we have an agreement?"

John looked over to Paul and Lepic. Both men looked at each other, then Paul nodded.

"Good," she said. Using the machine gun's barrel, she motioned Francie to go down the stair ramp.

John went to Francie, but she held up a finger, asking John to wait. Francie looked up the stairs. "Why me?" she asked Odette.

"There's only one reason for anyone," said Odette, "and the reason never changes. You had what was needed—you had access."

"To what?"

Odette was surprised by the question. "To anyone," she said. "To everyone. After this week, every person in power will open their door to you. You can get into any home, any office, and we would have trained you to obtain information. That's priceless, you know. You would have been effective. Very effective."

"She's of no interest to you now," said John. He reached for Francie's hand.

"That's true," said Odette. "It was Marcel's idea, anyway."

"What do you mean?" asked John.

"Marcel wanted her; I never did." Then Odette looked at John. "I wanted you."

John didn't understand. He looked up at Odette, confused.

"We're the same," explained Odette. "She would have been effective, but you would have been perfect."

John glared at Odette. "We're not the same. We're nothing alike."

"Oh, but we are. We have morals that are—what's the word?— flexible. Yes, that's it. We tell ourselves what we need to hear. We justify our actions. In that sense, we are exactly alike. Where we differ is the reason. I take to further an ideology. Not you, though. You take for yourself."

John started to protest, but Francie cut him off.

"That's not true at all," said Francie. "You don't know John. You don't understand him."

Odette shrugged. "We'll see." Then she waved the big bull of a man up the stairs.

The big man paused, then looked at Odette as if awaiting instructions. She nodded, but it was very subtle. John almost missed it. The man raised both hands, turned in a circle, then slowly picked up his pistol, the one John had kicked from his hands. Then he headed up the stairs, again very slowly. He stopped near the top, then looked down at Alex, who was starting to stir. The big man aimed at Alex and fired. Alex's chest jerked up off the ground, then collapsed.

Francie gasped. She turned away, then sheltered herself in John's arms.

"He wasn't part of our agreement," said Odette. "But you knew that."

The big man stepped into the plane. Odette started to close the plane door, then stopped. "I did as I promised," she said. "Miss Stevens isn't hurt. None of you were killed. I expect you to honor your part of the agreement and let us leave." She looked at John. "Honor among thieves, is that the phrase?"

"If you ever come back to my country," shouted Lepic, "I'll kill you. That is my promise."

"I'll never be back," she said, "Certainly not to France." Then she looked down at John. "Till we meet again."

With that, Odette slammed shut the plane door.

And she left.

EPILOGUE

Cannes-Mougins Country Club, Mougins

Lepic walked into the lobby, and he saw the manager of the club waiting for him.

"Inspector," said the manager, "thank you for coming." He led Lepic down the hallway.

"Congratulations," said the manager. "You're all over the news, catching those spies."

"Thank you," said Lepic, "but the credit goes to our Intelligence folks. We should all sleep better knowing they are on watch."

The manager directed Lepic into a spacious office. They took seats on opposite sides of a magnificent desk.

"I'm only here because you asked me to come," said Lepic. "You could have mailed the rejection letter. It would have saved me the trip."

"I couldn't do that because there is no rejection letter."

"What do you mean?"

"As of today, you are officially a full member of the club. You can avail yourself of all its privileges." The manager reached over and shook his hand. "We have some paperwork, but would you like a tour first?"

Lepic hesitated. "I...I...I never thought this would happen. I'm honored, and to be honest, I'm surprised. I didn't bring any money. I don't have checks. Had I known..."

The manager leaned over the desk, then said quietly, "It's all taken care of."

"What is taken care of?"

"Everything. The initiation fee, the monthly dues...it's all been paid. And not just for this year, but for as long as you stay with us."

Lepic was floored. "Are you waiving fees for me?"

"We cannot waive fees for anyone," said the manager. "Our charter prohibits that. Another member sponsored you."

"Was it Paul Du Pre?"

The manager smiled. "Yes, it was. And the board approved your application earlier this week."

"Paul sponsored me, then paid my fees?"

"Not exactly," said the manager. "Let's just say you have two very grateful friends."

Lepic's eyes teared up. He pulled a handkerchief, then turned away while he dabbed his face. "Was it...?"

"The other member wishes to remain anonymous," interrupted the manager.

"Was it John?" asked Lepic. "John Robie?"

The manager smiled evasively. "Again, I cannot say. But Mr. Robie is a good friend to have. He's very popular here. Before I forget, he was wondering if you would golf with him next week?"

"Of course," said Lepic. "Every day, I'm available." He stumbled for the right words, then said, "Please forgive me. I am at a loss here. I can't believe they did this for me."

Both men got to their feet. The manager came around the desk, then patted Lepic on the back. "Your friends were grateful. The whole of France is grateful. You're a national hero."

Lepic straightened himself out, then adjusted his suit. "To be honest," whispered the inspector, "the true hero was John Robie. The public knows him as a burglar, but let me tell you something— John Robie is one of a kind. What he did for the Resistance is legendary, but what he did for this investigation is astounding. He was able to..."

Luca's Garage, Saint Paul de Vence

"That's it over there," said John. He pointed to an old stone structure attached to an even older barn. There was a sign above the open barn doors that read "Réparation," followed by a cartoonish drawing of an automobile.

He grabbed a case of wine from the trunk of Francie's car, and they headed in. The barn was bigger than it looked. Vehicles in various stages of repair were slotted into stalls intended for horses. Halfway into the barn, Francie stopped walking.

"Are you okay?" he asked.

"I'm nervous," she said, "and I don't know what Paul will say. I broke the law. I handed those envelopes to Marcel. That's critical evidence. Paul and Armand are building their case on it, and they haven't said a word to either of us."

"We'll ask about it," said John.

"Is that you, my friend?" said a voice from the barn loft.

John looked up and found Coco standing at the loft rail, with a very organized living space behind him. "Is that your new place?"

"It is," said Coco, "and I like it very much. Luca lives on that side." He pointed to a similar living space at the other end of the barn. To Francie, he said, "We fixed your car, right where you are standing. How do you like it?"

"Looks brand new," she said. "Are you coming to lunch?"

"I'll be down. I caught the fish he's cooking."

John whispered to Francie, "With all the time on his hands, he took up fishing."

"I'll bet it's the best fish you ever tasted," said Coco.

John laughed. "No more betting. But I can't wait to try it."

The back doors of the barn were open wide. John and Francie walked out into the yard. It was a postcard day, thought John. Sunshine, wisps of clouds, low humidity, and the lightest of breezes. On one side of the property, he saw Luca cooking on a makeshift grate set over a cobbled-together firepit, with Armand at his side, acting as Luca's instructor. Paul and Vittoria were laughing beside a wooden table pushed against a stone wall. A ledge on the wall served as a bench, and a collection of unmatched chairs provided seating on the other side.

"How is everyone?" asked John as he put the case of wine on the table.

Greetings and kisses flew around, and Paul began pouring the wine. Vittoria kissed John and Francie on both cheeks, then whispered, "I make no promises for the food. When I got here, your friend was boiling meat. Can you imagine? There is one way to cook meat, one way only—with fire. Never in water! Pff."

"I can hear you," said Luca. "Irish people boil meat all the time. English, too."

Vittoria rolled her eyes. "Good idea," she yelled. "Those countries are known for bad weather, not good cuisine." She shook her head, incredulous. "If I didn't stop him, we would have pies of meat for lunch. It bothers me even to say that." She yelled to Luca, "Next time, I no help you. I keep my mouth shut."

"Doubtful," replied Luca.

"Anyway, I straightened him out," said Vittoria. "Should be fine. Come, take seat."

Paul handed a glass of wine to Francie, then one to John.

"How is Danielle?" asked John.

"Home in two days," said Paul. "I can't wait to see her. A lot happened while my wife was away."

In unison, everyone clinked their glasses together like a toast.

Luca, Armand, and Coco joined them, each carrying a large plate. "Beef and two types of fish, thanks to Coco," said Luca. "All of it cooked to perfection over an open flame." He gave a nod of appreciation to Vittoria. "And bowls of vegetables and fruit, up and down the table. *Bon appétit.*"

They dove in with enthusiasm. At one point, John sat back and listened to three conversations occurring simultaneously—Armand's wound, a debate about cheese, and how Vittoria's brothers had gone sailing with Francie's mother. Incredibly, everyone at the table was involved in all three conversations.

The lunch took effect, the conversations slowed, and sleepiness settled in. Coco grabbed an apple from a bowl, then dropped himself into a hammock. Luca and Vittoria left the table and began playing a game of boules, which Vittoria proudly explained was similar to bocce but not as good. That left John, Francie, Paul, and Armand.

"We have information about the tritium plot," said Paul. "I know we all had questions. Now we have some answers."

The table quieted, and all eyes turned to Paul.

He directed his comments to Francie. "As we all know, you passed envelopes with classified information to Marcel Julien. He then passed that information along to the Russians. And because you were involved, he was going to blackmail you into working for the Russians. That was their plan." Paul paused, making sure everyone was following. "All of that, we already knew. What we didn't know was this—where was the information coming from?"

"And now you know?" asked Francie.

"We do," said Armand. "The only country to stabilize tritium is the United States, and they do this at one facility."

"Where?" asked John.

"Near a town called Aiken," said Armand, "in the state of South Carolina."

"Alex was from the Carolinas," said Francie, "but he hadn't been there in years."

"That's correct," said Paul. "His family owned land along a major river..."

"The Savannah River," said Armand.

"More than a hundred miles of riverfront property, and they had big plans for that land."

"But they lost it," said Francie.

"Not exactly," said Paul. "They didn't lose it. The United States government seized it. The result was the same, though. His family was left with nothing, and they were angry about it. They fought the seizure with every penny they had. His family went bankrupt, on top of losing their land."

"Why was it seized?" asked Francie.

"The United States needed land to build a huge complex, one to refine materials for their nuclear arsenal," said Armand. "For many reasons, that land in South Carolina was perfect."

"So, how does that tie back to Alex?" asked Francie.

"Russia has been targeting that facility since it opened, trying to trick, trap, or bribe vulnerable workers for information," said Paul. "Turns out, Alex's brother was one of those employees. He was an engineer at that plant."

"Let me guess," said John. "He worked on tritium."

"Exactly right, and he's under arrest now."

"After the government took their land," said Armand, "they felt a great injustice was done to them. So they had no loyalty to their government. And when they got the chance, they repaid the injustice..."

"...by selling secrets to the Russians," said Paul.

Everyone was quiet as the information sank in. Then John said, "Any updates on Odette Julien?"

"We now know she's a very high-ranking officer in Russian Intelligence," said Paul, "responsible for disrupting French trade routes and destabilizing our territories."

"And stealing nuclear secrets," added Armand.

"She failed this time," said Paul, "but she'll try again. We don't know where she is, and we know nothing about Karl."

"Doesn't matter now," said Armand.

"Something has been on my mind," said Francie. "I was hoping we could talk about it. Those envelopes I passed to Marcel—the ones that incriminate me. I assume you had to hand everything over to your colleagues."

"That information is vital to the investigation," Paul said.

Francie looked down, then sighed. "I know, and I'm prepared to face the consequences. What happens to me now?"

"What do you mean?" asked Armand.

"My name was on the envelopes," replied Francie. "And I gave them to Marcel. Everyone knows. There were pictures in the papers."

"That's the funny thing," said Paul. "The vital information was inside the envelopes—all those coded numbers. The envelopes themselves had nothing useful for the investigation. Just your name. I know because I had two of them in my possession."

"And I had the other two," said Armand.

"Somehow, those envelopes were lost on my way to headquarters," said Paul. "They were in my briefcase, nice and secure."

Armand looked surprised. "The same thing happened to me. Both envelopes I had are gone."

Paul continued, "Armand and I were sitting in the den last night and we saw a piece of one in the fireplace. Strange, right?"

"It's safe to say they're gone forever," concluded Armand.

Francie hopped out of her chair, then ran to Paul and Armand. She threw her arms around them, but she didn't say a word.

Paul and Armand got up from the table. "Shall we go?" asked Paul. Armand nodded, then pointed to his shoulder. "I still can't drive."

John caught Armand's eye. "Don't worry about Friday. I'll pick up your wife at the train station, then I'll drive her to Paul's."

"Wonderful," said Armand. "She'll be so surprised. The famous John Robie. She still doesn't believe we're friends."

"We're more than that," said John.

With that, Paul and Armand left the lunch.

"Let's walk a little," said Francie.

Francie looped her arm through John's, and they strolled away from the barn. The yard was more extensive than Francie first thought, with long stretches of grass sprinkled with clusters of wildflowers.

The past month had been the most emotionally exhausting period of Francie's life. The incredible start to her career, her initial confrontation with John, the brutal reality of her relationship with Alex, and that tense night where everything came to a head left her feeling empty, as if she had nothing more to give. The situation with Alex was more complicated than she'd realized at the time, and she was just now understanding that paradox of emotions. To further complicate things, John seemed like a completely different person. They'd spent a lot of time together, and lately, she wondered about John's feelings for her. She glanced at him and saw him smiling, just as he had been all afternoon.

"Why so happy?" she asked.

"Couldn't say for sure," he replied, "but I feel calm and settled. For the first time in my life, really." John pointed at a weather-beaten bench in a clearing of wildflowers. "Why don't we."

They each took a seat, side by side.

"You've got a couple of days before you leave," he said, "and I was wondering if you need me to do anything? Aside from taking you to the airport."

"Nothing I can think of."

"Well, if anything comes to mind, you know how to reach me."

Francie was quiet for a moment. "I hope you understand. After what happened, I thought a trip home would help. Some perspective to sort through everything."

"Of course I understand," said John. "It makes sense. I don't want you to worry. If you forget something or need something, just let me know."

Francie placed her hand on John's. "Thank you," she said. "There is something."

"Whatever you need. What can I do?"

"It's nothing you can do," she said. "I wanted your thoughts on something."

"Ask away."

Francie hesitated, then said, "What would you think if I stayed for a while? If I didn't go home?"

John smiled. He shifted on the bench to face her.

"You're smiling again," said Francie.

"I am," said John. "And I can't stop. That's what I think."

IF YOU ENJOYED
TO CATCH A SPY BY MARK ONEILL,
READ ON FOR AN EXCERPT FROM ITS INSPIRATION—
TO CATCH A THIEF BY DAVID DODGE

FIRST PUBLISHED IN 1951 AND REISSUED BY POISONED PEN PRESS
AND LIBRARY OF CONGRESS ON APRIL 1, 2025, AS A SELECTION IN THE
LIBRARY OF CONGRESS CRIME CLASSICS SERIES.

DIRECTOR ALFRED HITCHCOCK TURNED DODGE'S CAT-AND-MOUSE
PAGE-TURNER INTO A CHARMING AND HIGHLY ACCLAIMED 1955 FILM,
STARRING CARY GRANT AND GRACE KELLY.

THE AGENTS *de police** came for John Robie sooner than he expected them.

It was a hot, still summer evening in August. Crickets sawed at their fiddles in the grass, and a bullfrog who lived in a pool at the bottom of the garden boomed an occasional bass note. John was burning letters in the fireplace when first the crickets, then the bullfrog, stopped their music. His setter, sleeping on the rug, woke suddenly and cocked her ears, but he did not need the dog's help. The crickets were better watchmen.

He had already changed his clothes and was ready to leave the house. He kicked the ashes in the fireplace, crumbling them, before he went into the kitchen. The setter growled, deep in her throat.

Germaine, his cook, was making a ragout, peering nearsightedly into the big iron pot on the stove and muttering to herself. She was too old and deaf to hear the dog until it began to bark. She heard John come in, but the ragout was more important at the moment than he was. She did not look up.

*Police constables; that is, police officers of the lowest rank.

He said, "Germaine."

"M'sieu?" She still peered into the pot.

"I'm going away. Dinner won't be necessary."

She looked up at that, surprised and indignant. He had no time to tell her more. He said, "Au revoir" and ran up the back stairs. The dog growled again, more loudly.

He found his passport and billfold in the dark bedroom, buttoned them into the inside pocket of his jacket, and looked out at the rear garden from behind a window curtain.

It was early evening, not yet full night. A shadow was out of place against the wall at the back of the garden, just inside the gate. He could not be mistaken. He knew every shrub in the garden. Except for the olive trees that were there when he started, he had planted everything himself, down to the endive and the leeks and the fines herbes in the vegetable patch. He had not planted a shadow by the gate.

The dog began to bark. There was still no sound at the front door. He turned to a side window, saw another misplaced shadow and went quickly to another window at the far end of the house. They had it watched from all sides.

The dog was barking steadily by the time the doorbell rang.

He had one path of escape open to him. It was not the easiest, but it would do. It will leave no doubt in their minds, if there is any doubt, he thought. When he heard Germaine's loose slippers slap across the floor as she went to answer the doorbell, still grumbling over the wasted dinner, he stepped out on the little terrasse where he slept on hot nights, climbed the low railing, balanced himself for a moment, and jumped.

The man in the garden below heard feet scrape on the railing of the terrasse. John, in mid-air, saw the white blur of an upturned face, and the dark blotch in it that was the agent's open mouth. The agent was too startled to shout, at first.

John had never made the jump before, even in daylight. But he had looked at it many times, subconsciously measuring the distance, estimating the knee-spring that would be necessary and the swing to follow after he caught the branch of the olive tree. He had it all timed and pre-calculated in his arm and leg muscles. He could not see the branch against the dark background of the tree foliage, but it was there when he reached for it, flat out on his face in the air and stretching. As his feet went down he bent at the hips, kicked hard on the upswing, let go of the branch while he was still rising, arched his back, and went over the top of the high garden wall with inches to spare.

It was a fine jump, one that the agent talked about for a long time afterward, when he was permitted at last to talk. John came down on his toes in the middle of the lane beyond the wall, and was running up the hill through a vineyard toward the shelter of the orchard at the top of the hill before the agent let out his first shout. By the time they came through the garden gate and began to hunt for him, their flashlights bobbing around like little bright balloons in the dusk, he was safe in the orchard.

There were only four men in all, not enough to search the whole countryside. They gave up soon and went back to the house.

He was not afraid of what Germaine might tell them. She knew nothing about m'sieu except that he liked her cooking and would not ordinarily abandon a good ragout. She was an old peasant, half blind, nearly deaf, a fine cook.

He hoped she would stay on at the villa and keep the garden in shape. She liked green things growing around her. With the olives, the garden patch, a few chickens and her way of making a little go a long way, she could live there comfortably forever, if nobody told her to leave. He meant to write her a letter after he was safe from pursuit, tell her that the Villa des Bijoux was hers. M'sieu would not need it any more.

But it was hard to think he would never see the villa again. There were too many things in it he hated to leave behind, too many ties to a good life; the books, the fine guns and fishing rods, the dog he had trained, the garden he had planted, the good wine he had laid down in the cellar, the comfortable chair by the fireplace. It was all finished and done with. He did not have even a photograph of the house.

It's just as well, he thought. From the orchard on the top of the hill he turned his back on the Villa of the Jewels and set off for the coast.

It was full dark by then, but he knew the country well. He knew all of the South of France well, even to the odors. Most of the farmers who were his neighbors cultivated patches of flowers to sell to the perfume factories at Vence* or Grasse.† All Provence was a flower garden during the summer months, and

---

*A small village on the French Riviera. The 1948 *Michelin Guide for Côte d'Azur/Haute-Provence* advises, "In the land of roses, carnations and violets, olive and orange trees, Vence, 10 km. away from the sea between Nice and Antibes, is a charming winter and summer resort" (Clermont-Ferrand, France: Pneu Michelin [Michelin Tire], 1948, 144. Hereinafter the "*Michelin Guide.*" Original is in French; all translations in this book are by the editor). See also map on pages vi–vii.

†A French town, just north of Cannes and the center of the French perfume industry. The 1948 *Michelin Guide* describes it: "Climbing the first slopes of the high limestone plateaus and dominating the fragrant plains from which it derives its fame and richness, Grasse has a seductive and varied charm" (71).

even at night the perfume was strong. It was not safe for him to go through Vence, where he was well known by sight, so he walked around the town by way of the heady, sweet-smelling flower patches, returned to the road on the other side, and kept on in the direction of Cros de Cagnes* and the Route Nationale, where he could catch a bus.

It was a ten-kilometer walk. To be safe, he stepped off the road into the shadows whenever he heard a car coming, and at the bus station he bought a copy of Nice-Matin[†] to hide his face. There was nothing about him in Nice-Matin. It would be still another twenty-four hours before the French papers picked up the Paris Herald Tribune's[‡] lead and spread it across the front page with headlines and photographs. He thought he would be safely out of the public eye before that happened; or on his way to a French prison. One or the other.

There was only a single passenger on the bus when he boarded it. He did not have to hide his face from her. She sat in one of the extreme rear corners, so that he could not take a seat out of her line of sight, but after one quick, incurious glance she paid no attention to him. He would not have given her a second thought except that caution made him observant, and she was clearly out of place on a rattletrap Route Nationale bus. She was dressed for the evening; a long gown, fragile, spike-heeled

---

*Another small village on the coast, heavily developed in the last few decades.

---

†A regional French newspaper, first published in 1944, covering the south of France.

---

‡The newspaper, written for English-language readers, began publication in 1887, as a Paris edition of the *New York Herald* under publisher James Gordon Bennett Jr. In 1924, it was sold to the owners of the *New-York Tribune*, and so it became the Paris *Herald Tribune*. In 1967, having changed owners again, the paper became the *International Herald Tribune*. In 2013, it became the *International New York Times*, but in 2016, the Paris office was closed.

slippers, a fur wrap. He knew enough about furs to guess that the price of her wrap alone would buy an expensive car and pay the salary of a man to drive her wherever she wanted to go. She was one of a type he knew well, had made it his business to know. Girls of her class did not ride buses.

Force of habit made him look at her fingers and ear lobes. Afterward he watched her until a movement of her shoulders opened the wrap far enough to let him see her throat. She wore neither rings, necklace, earrings nor, as far as he could see, jewelry of any kind, not even a wrist watch. It was not in keeping with the wrap, any more than the wrap was in keeping with her presence on the bus. The class he knew always wore some ornament, frequently a great deal.

He wondered if the explanation could be that she had lost her jewelry to a thief. It was incongruous that he might be fleeing from the police on the same bus with one of the women whose losses had set the police on his trail. They would make some kind of a point of it, if they caught him now.

The bus filled gradually. When it reached the end of its run opposite the big pink stucco casino in Cannes, several other passengers were between him and the girl when she got off. He lost sight of her, and did not think of her again. He joined the strollers along the promenade of La Croisette, the boulevard skirting the beach.* It was a lovely night for strolling; warm, with a quarter moon hanging low over the Mediterranean and a faint breeze blowing in from the water to rustle the leaves of the

---

*The *Michelin Guide* picturesquely advises: "This meeting place for sojourners, who come to stroll here mainly from 10 a.m. to noon, owes its fame to its particularly elegant setting: flower gardens with rare species, avenues of palm trees, hotels and shops with luxurious facades. This is where the flower battles are fought" (52).

palms and plane trees along the promenade and make shadows dance on the sidewalk. He kept to the beach side of the promenade, where the lights were dim, and crossed the boulevard only when he was opposite the shabby front of the Hotel Napoleon.[*]

The Napoleon was a poor distant cousin to the newer, more fashionable hotels which faced La Croisette farther up the beach near the casino and the yacht harbor. It was not a popular place even with the people who stayed there. No one was in the musty hotel lobby but the concierge and a porter who doubled as elevator operator.

The faded red carpet had a new patch since his last visit. Bellini's sign near the elevator still advertised the same services in the same three languages. The English part of the sign read:

HENRI BELLINI

Insurance—Sales and Rentals—Tourist Agent
Imports and Exports—Domestic Help
Interpreter—Stenographer
Investments

—

MEZZANINE FLOOR

An arrow pointed up the stairway to the mezzanine.

He nodded to the porter as he walked by the elevator cage. His nerves were strung tight, but he did not hesitate, climbing the stairs. He had complete confidence in Bellini.

---

[*]Possibly a real hotel in Cannes, but now only an apartment there, a five-minute walk from Plage de la Croisette (the beach mentioned).

Bellini was reading the Paris edition of the New York *Herald Tribune* in the cluttered cubbyhole that served him as an office. He had the paper spread open on his desk under the fan of light from an old-fashioned lamp with a green shade. He did not move when he heard the doorknob turn. The door had a spring lock, and could be opened from the outside only with a key, but he always left the key in the outside lock, except when he had confidential business to transact in the room, so that his callers could let themselves in. He did not like to walk to the door unnecessarily.

John brought the key with him when he entered. He put it on the corner of Bellini's desk.

Bellini took off his spectacles and peered at him under the lamp shade, smiling his oily smile of welcome.

"I was wondering when I would hear from you," he said, chuckling. "Have you seen this very interesting article in the newspaper?"

He tapped his stubby finger on the paper. He read, wrote and spoke seven languages. John spoke French and English almost equally well, but he and Bellini used English with each other because it was John's native language. One tongue was the same as another to Bellini.

John said, "I've read it."

Bellini chuckled again.

He had not changed in the months since John had seen him. He always looked the same; small, round, oily and happy. A German soldier had broken his shoulder with a rifle butt during the Occupation.* The bones had not been set properly,

---

*In 1940, Germany invaded France and administered the country from May 1940 to December 1944. This period was known as the "Occupation." Nominally the Vichy government (the État français, or "French State"), named after the town of Vichy that was its headquarters, was in charge, though the real rulers were the Nazis.

so the shoulder stayed hunched up around his ear in a permanent half-shrug, and one arm was shorter than the other. He wore heavy horn-rimmed glasses that made him look like an owl. In the summertime he dressed in cotton trousers, a loose shirt and slippers, and oozed perspiration. In the wintertime he wore all the clothes he could put on, toasted his feet on an electric heater wedged under his desk, and oozed perspiration just the same. He never stopped smiling, and no one could say anything remotely humorous in his presence without earning an appreciative titter or gurgle or bubble of laughter. His manners were excellent, even too good; he had the smooth graciousness of a professional confidence man. He had never been known to break his word. In addition to his legitimate business activities, he was an importer of smuggled goods, a black-market operator and a dealer in stolen property. He was careful to carry on these activities through intermediaries, and since he commanded the absolute loyalty of everyone who worked for him, he had never been arrested nor had his reputation as an honest businessman challenged publicly. He was John Robie's best friend.

"You will ignore the implications, no doubt?" he said, peering at John under the lamp shade. He was still speaking of the newspaper article.

"The implications are too difficult to ignore," John said. "I'm leaving the country."

"The police?"

"They came for me tonight."

"And you?"

"Off the terrasse and over the wall."

"Like old times." Bellini giggled. "I would like to have seen the flics'* faces. They never took you but once, did they?"

"No. I don't think they will take me again, if you can fix this for me."

He took the passport from his pocket. Bellini looked briefly at the passport, then up at him again, still beaming.

"What do you want done to it?"

"Change the number and name, set my birthday back ten years, and alter the date on the entry stamp so it won't be more than three months old when I leave. I'll dye my hair, pad myself around the middle, and have a new photograph taken. The only pictures they have of me are newspaper prints, and those date back to before the war. They won't have any reason to look twice at a middle-aged tourist. Once I'm out of the country, I'm safe."

"You are not afraid of extradition?"

"I don't think they will bother. I'm not that important. When they learn that I've left the country, and the thief keeps operating, they'll see their mistake."

"Will the thief keep operating after you leave, John?"

"There'll be no reason for him to stop."

Bellini chuckled again. He blinked behind the spectacles, looking wise and owlish.

John said, "Did you think that Le Chat had come back?"

Bellini lifted his good shoulder to the level of his crippled shoulder, then let it drop again.

"It's been a long time since I saw you last. A man might change his mind."

"It isn't Le Chat."

---

*The police, the cops.

Bellini nodded, satisfied. "I was waiting to hear you say it yourself. Now, what can you do about this story in the newspaper?"

"What I told you. Run. It doesn't leave me any other choice."

IF YOU'D LIKE TO READ THE REST OF
TO CATCH A THIEF,
RECENTLY RE-RELEASED BY POISONED PEN PRESS,
AN IMPRINT OF SOURCEBOOKS,
AND LIBRARY OF CONGRESS CRIME CLASSICS
(ISBN: 9781464225345),
ORDER YOUR COPY AT SOURCEBOOKS.COM.

AUTHOR'S NOTE

I have been obsessed with *To Catch a Thief* since I was a teenager, when I'd found an old copy of David Dodge's 1952 novel and read it in two days. The hero, John Robie, was a circus acrobat turned jewel thief, a man who'd also fought for the French Resistance. As portrayed by Cary Grant in the 1955 Hitchcock film, he had easy grace and charisma to spare. He was independently wealthy, living on the French Riviera, and had Francie Stevens (Grace Kelly) as a partner.

Seriously, who wouldn't want to be John Robie? I ordered a lockpicking guide from a pulp magazine and made burglar tools in shop class. I tried breaking into our home hundreds of times; none worked. Then I read that pull-ups were a great exercise for climbing (a vital skill for a cat burglar), so I did them every day, working my way up to twenty at a time.

As the years went by, it hit me—why not write a sequel? I had no experience writing a novel, but I had a tremendous amount of passion for the story. So I spent a year learning how to write, then I got in touch with the estate of David Dodge. After seeing the first few chapters, they granted me permission. How grateful I was!

And here we are, with the continuing adventures of notorious cat burglar John Robie and adventurous socialite Francie Stevens.

Then there's me, an author whose dream came true. Trust me, I'm nothing like John Robie. But I get to "be" him every day, and it's better than I imagined. I hope you enjoy reading this story as much as I've enjoyed writing it.

By the way, I still practice lockpicking. And I do pull-ups every day.

ACKNOWLEDGMENTS

Acknowledging all the folks who helped me is a monumental task. There are more than listed below, but I have a limit on how long this can take. So, my sincere thanks to all of you!

My wife, Victoria—who bears no resemblance to the character Vittoria, even though they are both Italian, muscular, and incredibly strong-willed—was my first supporter. She's also a very honest critic, so when she liked the first draft, I knew I had something. My son, John, and daughter, Alicia, were unbelievably helpful. John and his wife, Danielle, built my website, and he coaches me through newsletter creation every month.

Then there's Alicia, my first editor, who also advised me through several sensitivities—I'll always remember her guidance: "No damsels in distress; men don't save women." She and her husband, Chris, have been incredibly supportive.

Nancy and Neil Bader were unbelievably helpful. Nancy, a talented editor, improved the first draft, and Neil has always been interested and encouraging.

My brother Mike is an avid reader, and he loved the early draft. He's also in the entertainment business and continues to give me great advice.

The rest of my family has been wonderful, too. Walt, Donna, and Paul have promoted this book more than I have, and my mother, Judy, has been a strong advocate. She's supported my dream since I was a teenager.

Two other people were key supporters. Mike Post, the legendary composer, read the first few chapters and actually called to tell me how special it was. He then gave me great advice, which I follow to this day. And Mark Pedowitz, the entertainment giant, did the same. He called with strong encouragement. Imagine people like that reaching out to someone like me.

Early in the process, I met Randal Brandt, the publishing consultant who put me in touch with the original author's estate— Kendal and John Lukrich. All of them have been incredible supporters.

None of this would have happened without the hard work of my agent, Kerry D'Agostino, at Curtis Brown, Ltd. Her guidance has been brilliant, overshadowed only by her patience with me.

And, of course, my editor, Diane DiBiase, and the entire team at Sourcebooks/Poisoned Pen. I've learned so much from them. Having Sourcebooks take me on has been amazing. Words can't describe my gratitude.

But most of all, I'm grateful to David Dodge, the author of *To Catch a Thief*. He wrote a story that captured my heart. David passed away in 1974; I never met him, but his talent touches me every day.

ABOUT THE AUTHOR

© Alicia Seeley

Mark ONeill is the author of *To Catch a Spy*, the official sequel to *To Catch a Thief*. This is his first novel.

Mark lives in Bluffton, South Carolina, with his wife, Victoria, where he spends his days writing new adventures for John Robie and Francie Stevens.

You can follow Mark's writing journey on X or Instagram, both at @johnrobieisback and at tocatchathief.com.